No One Blames San Antonio for the Civil War

By Eric Dreyer Smith

Cover Design by Melody Simmons

"Don't forget to pay the cannibals to eat you last..." {Old Texas Saying}

"It ain't home unless someone sends the bus fare to bring you back..." {Overheard at a VIA bus stop in San Antonio, Texas}

CHAPTER 1

Fun in the Sun

He cruised the road with the A/C blasting at two-thirds strength while the windows were cracked open as to combat the April heat. As he passed business after business he continued to fumble with the radio dial while song after song annoyed him, he must have switched the dial eight times before finally shutting it off – the reverberations of the radio noise still echoed violently in his head:

"Dice que en el amor lo major está en el sur, que tiene magia y ritmo, que

Sabe a vino y ron," blared the rado violently before he changed it for the first time.

Then,

"despistarsu atención cántale una canción," before it was changed again.

"Y desgarrándome algo en mi vida cambió," again a change.

"Porque tu sabes que te quiero Y todo lo que dije no es verdad," another song, another changing of the channel.

"No obstante, la iglesia de Cristo está impactando las comunidades y haciendo brillar la luz para exponer las obras malas de los hombres y darles la esperanzadel perdón de sus pecados. Dios le concedaa la iglesiabrillar de tal manera que el aborto sea expuesto en toda su maldad y los hombres y mujeres vengan en arrepentimiento al pie de la cruz," the pastor's words held his attention slightly longer, then came another change of the radio dial – again more music:

"Sola, sola, en el olvido sola, sola con su espíritu sola, sola con su amor el marsola en el muelle de San Blas," and finally,

"Que respira nena Y es que tienes todo en esta vida pa´gozar," before the radio was shut off.

He had wanted to find a particular business on this road. Having driven the street several times the location still eluded him. He'd have to pull over and look it up in the yellow pages. He spotted a convenience store a short distance ahead to his right. He adeptly positioned his car to the far right lane and made a quick turn into the store lot. The spot in front of the payphone was free so he sped up ahead of possible rivals and took it before undoing the seatbelt and bounding out of the car, this with vigor that looked out of place. He could see three phone books of various sizes stacked in the metal cubby below the phone. With two long strides he was at them, thumbing through each, but the three books: Seccion Amarilla, Mi Pueblo and La Vista would offer no insight. It was that fucking language barrier again. The man got back in the car, pressed the reverse pedal somewhat excessively and got back on the road.

He decided he was hungry and that eating something would comfort his mood. Shortly ahead, again on his right, he saw a destination that should take care of this need. It was the Taqueria called El Boco #36. There were hundreds of Taquerias in town and if the odds held up it would be tasty enough food at reasonable prices. Trying to drive more carefully he lead his vehicle into El Boco #36's parking lot and took the first space available even though it was toward the back of the lot. This action was perhaps closer to his natural temperament if he had not been for the last few years viciously engaged in a war of culture. Parking gently he went inside sitting at the first open table by a window away.

"Hola – como esta?" asked the waitress.

Adam Carter pointed toward the menu.

"Caffe?"

"Ah no - Agua," said Carter.

"Si un momento," replied Rosella Sanchez as she took the order and walked away.

The restaurant was just northwest of the central part of the city. The main road outside, Fredericksburg, had once been fashionable earlier in the history of this metropolis: San Antonio, Texas. Businesses still lined the wide street. They were a cat-work of jumbled purple and yellow spray painted auto repair garages, Chinese buffets, immigration lawyers operating out of Speedy Tax Refund huts, Army and Marine recruiting stations, Taquerias, cell phone stalls and slick car audio shops. Yet just behind this sales zone were ancient neighborhoods of ivied brick and stone houses each built, not from a cookie-cutter, but rather by impassioned masons whose design spoke of a lost golden age when pride and care reigned in these parts. Carter's hand reached to stroke his copy of Don Quixote that he always carried with him. Why had these people not paid attention to their moral grandfather Cervantes?

Though Carter disdained it, the current Fredericksburg Avenue was one of his sales territories. He had bumped into a guy at a bar the other night who he thought might want to do business. Miguel said he ran a parts store next to the Hunan Palace on this road. Carter didn't see it. His calculation was that Miguel might buy an advertisement from him on the perception that Carter, who seemed to fit in at the Lion & Rose Pub, might be a conduit for cash flow to Miguel's store. It was obvious that Miguel was stretching his social range by occupying a stool at the trendy Lion & Rose further north in the city. Carter had learned that sometimes, small business owners, liked to buy ads from people they thought were maybe better than them. He wanted to capitalize on the brief window of shame that he had opened while drinking Stolli's together at the pub. Miguel had probably just discovered Stolli's that month. From experience Carter estimated this "shamed to buy window" had about a two-day shelf life. It was a similar principal as his sales to Hunan Palace. The Chinese Buffet would always buy an ad within a week of being featured on KENS-5 "In the Kitchen" television news expose for having rats and roaches found by the food inspector. Roaches had a one-week "ad buy" window, while rats generally maintained a three week window. Carter had visited four shops on that road before he had stopped to eat. He had wanted to look up Miguel's phone number, but the yellow pages had all been in Spanish. The waitress didn't speak a lick of English either. Carter knew a few words in Spanish like the ones for water, bathroom, love, friend, big, good, very good and President. It wasn't enough to really understand or say anything important. Unless maybe one wanted to say, "Love to see the big, very good President go to the bathroom good." No, it was useless. That was the way Carter felt about himself in this city. Years before, if he had been driving down the once glamorous Fredericksburg Avenue, still with it's renovations; ceramic tiled bus stops and matching retro street signs, while listening to Latin music it would have been a dreamy experience. Now it seemed like foreign occupation.

Carter had had a deep fondness for the Latin culture. Most of his childhood friends had been Mexican-American. When growing up he had been taught to enjoy diversity by his mother. Martin Luther King was a family hero. He had sampled and been educated on the concepts and items of appreciation that other backgrounds had to offer. He had thought of himself as openhearted and loving of all peoples. The last few years had changed that. The intense house-to-house battles of identity politics and territory control in San Antonio had made Carter think of himself as a casualty. If he had to guess the ground war was ultimately lost around 1983; specifically at he raging hormone wars and gang fights that occurred at the old Drive-In Theater on Bitters Road and San Pedro Avenue. Carter had the script of this city's history in his head. It was at the Drive-In that violent teenagers, rednecks and Mexicans, dueled for land supremacy and mating rights. Over the years the rednecks numbers in metro San Antonio dwindled because their gringo fathers no longer won air conditioning, electrical and plumbing contracts. Country and Western dancehalls closed all over town as Affirmative Action and ethnic nepotism awarded contracts to the brown people. Many Anglos families, the ones with big, blue collar balls, moved away and the battle was forfeit by attrition.

The commercial market as well reflected this slow, invisible war of race transition. There was the air war, Carter had changed the radio eight times and each station played similar raucous, high-pitched Spanish crooners. Carter couldn't get away from it. This was supposed to be America. Now San Antonio, Texas was something separate. It wasn't the same town he grew up in thirty-five years ago. Mexicans had taken it over. Literally eight of ten faces were Mexican. He never had hated Mexicans back then as a kid, but being back for just over four years he felt a hatred for these people. He believed they were in fact treating him like "less than" and actively hurting his means of survival. It began when he noticed how effortlessly perceptions reversed themselves with a new, dominant majority. Mexican clerks at the H.E.B grocery store constantly confused him for some other white person, Tex-Mex bank tellers always asked for his ID while scrutinizing his motives and rich Mexican Nationals openly cut in front of him in line at Dillards or Macy's – often physically bumping him without apology. His bosses and landlords were all Mexican. At the newspaper he had been the only white male under fifty years old in an office of nearly two hundred and the boss singled him out to be fired at the beginning of the downturn for no good cause. He got no breaks here. The landlord had threatened eviction when he was late one month by two days. He had been paying on time routinely for two and half years.

Funny to think that thirty-five years ago San Antonio had the most Soviet Intercontinental Ballistic Nuclear Missiles targeting it. It had become such a worthless place. With all its manpower, now 2 million people – the 7th largest city in the United States, it never built on a strong central focus of positive growth. The military presence had shrunk by half. Carter thought how Rosella Sanchez likely knew nothing about how high priority a target San Antonio had been during the Cold War. In a way it was the right place for Carter. He had fallen through the cracks of purpose and social status. At thirty-seven the cracks on Carter's face had increased. He was lined with bitterness.

"Un momentito per favor," said a husky voice to Carter's left.

Carter recognized him. It was Councilman Felderman. He had done a lot for the city back when he was Mayor. Carter's sister, Patrice, had mentioned the city momentarily looked to be experiencing sustainable growth. He didn't know enough of the city's chronology as to join in his sister's praise for the man though having been given only one term he doubted its overall significance. Carter gave a momentary glare at the Councilman. He didn't like anyone who had more power than him and unfortunately for Carter that was quite a lot of people. Felderman didn't notice the glare from the malcontent seated near his table. He was absorbed in an affable conversation with Barry Juarez the main reporter for the metro beat of the San Antonio Light; the city's only newspaper. Barry wrote "Barry's Corner" a weekly scoop, critique, investigative and/or editorial article always on the right lower quarter of page 3. The Light was a Hearst paper. One of the last four from his old media empire that still stood. Carter understood newspapers. His parents had worked for them all his life. He also thought he understood history and karma. All of Hearst's previous empire seemed to be falling. That made sense to Carter. Hearst had built a wicked thing of words based on lies and it was bound to tumble like a house of cards. It could not be true fruit. San Antonians who still remembered the past knew how the Light came into being. It was erected in 1866, the year after the Civil War ended, as a northern watchdog against Confederate sympathizers. The paper still prided itself on exposing corruption. Just last year Barry Juarez had brought down Sheriff Bud Ortega. The sheriff had been skimming money from the budget for personal use. He had gotten away with about one hundred sixty-five

5

thousand dollars before a leak brought the news to Barry Juarez. It took two weeks of front-page articles revealing the details of the evidence before Sheriff Ortega was indicted. It only took three more months before the Sheriff, his wife, his chief lieutenant and his secretary were sentenced. Justice in that case moved swiftly. Still, Carter wasn't fooled. San Antonio had always had a reputation for corruption and the one thing he knew about corruption was that it always went deeper than the public ever found out about. In his version of the end game corruption could only be imagined, never identified.

Tacos. It's always tacos in San Antonio. The rest of the country better get used to the taste of carne guisada, fajitas, bean with cheese and chorizo. There were ten thousand restaurants in San Antonio and surely seven or eight thousand served tacos. It was easy to argue for fair immigration standards when you lived in Michigan ruminated Carter. The future of America though is taco. San Antonio is what all cities and most towns in the United States will be like in thirty-five to sixty years; Mexican food, Mexican juries, Mexican democracy, Mexican vibes, Mexican judges, Mexican cops with tattoos laced completely around their whole arms, Mexican music, more Mexican food, Mexican sensibilities and Pancho Villa taught favorably in every Middle School. "Michiganers" will get a shock when mariachi music plays at 110 decibels from many a neighbor's home until five in the morning each and every night. Mexicans were wonderful people, but they were Mexicans – which meant they were different and that difference, when in the majority, was a threat to what Carter had found himself to be deep down when the veneer was stripped. So went the Gospel of Carter.

Carter ate his tacos in silence. He had noticed his waitress's attractiveness. He offered furtive stares. She had big breasts, a nice ass and a sense of modesty. Her blouse carefully covered her biological assets. Carter wished he could have made a play for her, but trial and error had demonstrated how unappealing he was to Hispanic girls. He wasn't a racist he said to himself. He was minority. He was also in the know. That was the source of his disquiet. He grew up with an expectation of privilege and right before his eyes the world was turning on its head. He acknowledged it was a natural phenomenon.Adam Carter had disappeared from the middle classes and was now a renegade observer. He unfairly blamed the Latin newcomers and younger Mexican-Americans for their vast unawareness of how good white people used to have it in San Antonio before the great shift. In a way the change was so sudden and absolute that they did not know Anglos once ruled here. The new normal was all they knew. They had little idea of white sacrifice, white creation and white feelings. The old time Mexicans were in awe. Having grown up with little power they too saw first hand how sheer numbers decide who stands tall, who speaks, who stays and who goes first. The old timers jumped on to the glory of the new power structure with both feet. Of course they knew of the power white men had in other parts of the nation, but how could they resist watching a young Hispanic clerk or car repairman get over on a struggling Anglo colleague or customer.

Most of Carter's Hispanic peers, the ones he grew up with in his generation, had at least one good white friend. Many had never bothered to learn Spanish. They had sold out completely to the white dream and the only thing they had really prized was a strong education and career. Now this demographic was testing the water of its new powers. Salsa dancing and open, reverse mockery were big now. Carter remembered in high school how Mexicans used to pretend to be silly and simple just to let the white culture have its sway. This was no longer the case. "Mexicaness" was here to stay.

Carter randomly opened Cervantes's Don Quixote of La Mancha:

{A DISCOURSE ON ARMS AND LEARNING}
"... with the fear a solider knows when he is besieged in a fortress, on watch or guard in some redoubt or strongpoint, knowing that his enemies are mining towards the spot where he is, and that he may on no account leave his post, or run away from the danger which threatens him so closely The only thing which he can do is to inform his captain of what is happening, in the hope that he will meet the situation with a counter- mine; and he must stand calmly, though in fear and expectation of suddenly rising to clouds without wings and sinking again to the depths against his will. If this seems a small danger, let us see if it is equaled or surpassed in the head-on collision of two galleys in the midst of the high seas."

How did Cervantes character Don Quixote know so much? This was Carter's exact situation. Maybe some noble other, a far off

Captain – maybe not yet born, would discover meaning and path from Carter's destruction.

The grease from Carter's fingers was satisfying as he licked them clean then used a napkin to wipe the residue from the corner of his mouth. Carter had luck with tacos if not women. He mainly rotated Chinese and Mexican food in his diet. Occasionally he went to Jim's Restaurant for a frontier burger, fries and a chocolate milkshake. He was on the cusp of obesity. The frown that could be seen on his first baby picture had etched itself to his face as if it had been applied with permanent make-up. He had been born to an air of tragedy; the doctor that performed his delivery into the world was murdered in the parking lot on the same day. It was discovered that sixteen years before that doctor had delivered the man who had killed him. The home his parents took him to after birth had housed shackled slaves in the cellar that had freshly arrived to Rhode Island a few hundred years before. Late in the night the moans of their ghosts could still be heard.

Carter didn't sport any tattoos. He possessed a bit of freedom and a lack of money. He saw himself as what most white Americans would become in years ahead. In this way he considered himself an unknown prophet. Prophecy was a funny concept to Carter considering he went to college. Still, it was the classification he would announce himself under if anyone were listening to him these days. He based his analysis of prophecy on what was happening to him and took that out to larger proportions in order to divine the macro trends happening in the greater whole of society. His method included a combination of mystical reasoning that communed truths to him from codes written in license plates, CNN, the pattern of local bird flight, social slights and silent hunches. Oddly it was more accurate than any formula or statistic Carter had learned at University and it remained the only answer for his intense predicament of sheer failures, sociological evolutionary positioning and uncanny epiphanies. He was a lighting rod of the times, a nexus of social schemes and litmus for undeclared justices. Why couldn't he be the Moses of the last great chosen people: the Anglo-Saxon White Protestant Males. It couldn't be disputed that this group had had a large and special place in the history of the last six hundred years. Ever since the Spanish Armada of 1588 there was a divine grace over the actions of the white man, but the Armada was coming back. History would pivot with Carter in San Antonio where he was the single, observable lynchpin to the giant changes right around the corner. As the comedian George Lopez said, "We {Mexicans} were taking over the country when you were doing your Soduko". So continued Carter's mantra.

For some time Carter held his own in this schema. Travel and itinerant work hid the true problem for some time. It was not until he came back to San Antonio five years before that the full effect began to strike. His position, the fulcrum where cultural destiny met the ultra-politics of San Antonio was colliding with a series of tipping points. He had been teetering on the verge of daily destruction for months, but each new day definite plans for surviving kept emerging in his imagination. In short, despite the benefits of early status, some intelligence, education and skill he had no clout. His status was dropping further each day. He could not live with it much longer. Privately he sang for himself as the unsung; the best and first to fall in a war others did not fully realize was happening. He knew others would have their turn later. It was a matter of history.

Carter imagined the history of Whites came in two batches that came to this country: those with some vestment and the utterly poor and disenfranchised folk to work the dirty shops and the land. The second batch was where Carter's people had started back when one of them was in the infantry under George Washington in 1776. None cared about that honor these days, but it ran as a deep pride in Carter's heart. His line's blood had formed this land. When the rest of America figured out what was happening today it would be too late, Carter smirked at the thought. The Anglos would then scatter to the mountains, Europe or the moon. They couldn't see yet. The sunglasses of democracy, industry, elections, equal rights, civil rights, affirmative action, the demands of capital and affordable labor currently blinded them.

Carter glanced up from his meal. The bold mustache seemed to scold him as it looked down at him from the wall. The man in the poster pointed a finger and the words read, "PANCHO VILLA WANTS YOU GRINGO – FOR THE MEXICAN REVOLUTION!" Villa's posters were hung heroically in eighty percent of the taco houses in San Antonio, he was everywhere ready for resurrection, Villa photographed with women, Villa photographed on a horse, Villa with his companeros, Villa in his colonial whites complete with Pith helmet, Villa in the center of a prestigious celebration: Villa, the man who offered one dollar for the head of any Chinese. He blamed them for being sympathetic with the Americanos. Everything old would be new again. It was easy to be politically correct about all this when you were in the comfort zones of the majority like New Jersey or Marin County. Wait until those places become like San Antonio thought Carter as he looked away from Villa's eyes. Yeah, Villa would have his revenge.

It was ironic. Carter had grown up with his parents teaching him to adore tolerance and diversity. He loved the movie Gandhi. It wasn't the same though when you were the poor minority as he was in San Antonio. Everyone ganged up on the poor. Poverty was the hardest job one could have. It eviscerated one's humanity. Thinking of it, money, Carter realized he had better get back to fishing for business. Carter reached in his pocket for a ten-dollar bill then he heard something that made him pause. He had been so stuck in his own angry ruminations it was as if a red halo of disdain encircled him keeping out any sound or light from his immediate environment. Councilman Felderman was telling something important to the reporter, Barry Juarez, - something that seemed secret. Yes, who else, but Carter would have even recognized these two inside this taco joint – El Boco #36 on the lame part of town. It must be where they went to pass on information. That should have gelled for Carter. He had always prided himself on being observant. Anytime one sees a councilman and a reporter alone together something was going on. He tried to listen without being found out:

"Hey did I steer you wrong with the info on Ortega?" insisted Juarez.

"It's not that. The council might get edgy if I try to take on another scandal so soon. They've been touchy on that subject," said Felderman.

"Yeah like they have a vested interest these days? What happened to our old college pledge to always fight the good fight?" pleaded Juarez.

"Yeah I hear you. So you're sure something is going on with the Chief Medical Examiner for the city, Chin, - you're sure..." countered Felderman.

"Just look into some of the cases he classified as suicides – here look at this one," answered Juarez.

Felderman slid a large size manila envelope to Barry Juarez, his old dorm room buddy from Incarnate Word.

Carter made his move. It was the only way he'd see the photo. He had to time it right just as Juarez was looking at it. That was when he left his table and peeked without being noticed. Sure enough it was a morgue shot. A dead dude with what looked like a knife wound in his side. How could anyone call that a suicide?

"Are you done sir?" – it was the waitress, Rosella, talking and she blew his cover.

"Yeah sure thanks – keep the change," said Carter as he handed over the ten spot and left the El Boco #36.

Maybe with the big tip Rosella would remember him fondly next time. He'd try to buy her if he had had enough money. Carter looked over his shoulder from outside the taco house. The councilman and reporter did not seem worried that he had noticed anything important. That was a relief. He did not need that kind of heat.

It was intense information; a councilman and reporter, old friends, fighting some kind of conspiracy - the good fight - and a city medical examiner calling murders as suicides. It verified further what Carter thought of this junk town with its nasty lies.

In the parking lot the dents in Carter's 2001 Honda reflected the angles of his psyche. Overall the Honda held up well over the years. It only needed regular maintenance except for the time the teenager without insurance slammed into Carter while he was parked. Inside the Honda Carter spun the radio dial to the far right. ACDC's song "Dirty Deeds Done Dirt Cheap" popped up. The old rock song fed Carter's hostilities as he accelerated out of the parking lot. It was too perfect. The universe knew what was going on. Don Quixote knew what was going on. Felderman and Juarez were beginning to know. Yet none of these people came to Carter's defense. None supported him. He had no allies. It sounded like psychological trouble even to him.

There were a lot of cars on Fredericksburg Avenue; too many – they were buzzing back and forth like yellow jackets... Carter made his move into the thoroughfare. Downtown was stationed at one end of Fredericksburg and Loop 410 at the other. The intersection to I-10, which went out to the The Rim, La Cantera, The University of Texas at San Antonio, and the Hill Country, was close by. 410 lead to the better enclaves of the North Central and Northwest parts of town depending on whether you took a right or left from Fredericksburg. The whites always moved north. Anything to get away from the encroaching "Southside Ghettos" that in the white's minds carried with them the promise of, "people many did not want to deal with, a culture gap, a growing language barrier, lowered housing values, worsened schools, at least one murder a day, now sometimes two or three including drive bys and the occasional random car jacking. In American speak – Ethnic minorities."

The real whites, the ones with money, moved north out I-10 and past outer Loop 1604 into the central Texas hills. It was pretty lush up there. White boomtowns like Boerne were doing well. The hills were replete with multi-million dollar homes. The I- 10 corridor lined itself with the bright red and yellow colors of Italian Ducati motorcycle dealerships, boutique Bicycle stores and Outdoorsman Outlets the size of villages that were full of massive stuffed animals ranging upon manmade fiber hills complete with vegetation. These were the people that knew what a vacation was while the rest of society was working six or seven days a week year round – year after year just to get by. It was said that that acreage held more millionaires per square foot than anywhere else in the nation.

Carter had squeezed his aging Honda in between traffic by feigning a quick right then circling back into the buffer lane before merging into full traffic heading north.

Carter peered to the sides of Fredericksburg Avenue scanning for possible business targets he could sell too. He passed the Goodwill, a Super China Buffet, a Pocket cell phone dealer, a three bit hotel with pink awnings that once hoped to capture some of the Mexican national shoppers, a large Mexican National clothing chain store that sold to the poor and then as he came upon a strip of the road full of auto garages he felt a force, a sonic pressure, slightly pressing him from over his left shoulder. In his left side mirror he saw purple as a second later he made out the blare of Tejano music at full amplification. The low rider car blasted past Carter as he slowed. One did not see many of these in San Antonio like could be expected in Los Angeles. It warranted a stare. The Mexican behind the wheel fit the stereotype of what a person with assumptions would expect to see behind the wheel of a low rider. The driver had a rough look, a red bandana, sunglasses and lots of stubble. Carter thought he had the grin of someone who was high on marijuana. This overall look was not exactly common in San Antonio. The thought came to Carter's mind that this cat likely had a gun with him. Danger could be that close. He was surprised cops didn't pull more people over just for their looks. This motherfucker was probably just like the person who had travelled up McCullough Avenue from the Southside when Carter's family first came to San Antonio. His sister was twelve back then. The person offered her a ride to the convenience store. He took her to the rock quarry, shoved a gun in her throat and raped her. It had been a culture shock coming from a small town in Minnesota.

Carter slowed further as not to make eye contact. On his right was Don's Super Auto. He had sold some advertising to Don a couple years before when the economy had been good. Carter had been working for the local newspaper back then. Don's had a big, neon superman "S" logo above the garage doors to the body shop. His family, old Germans, owned two blocks of this part of Fredericksburg Avenue – and another block all the way down where the pristine cobblestone walkways and refurbished signs, bus stops and ceramic decorative inlays of Colonial Spain attempted a renaissance of the area where the south mouth of the avenue bled into the beginnings of the outskirts of downtown. That area was also near Jefferson High School with its neo-classical dome roof, that wasn't much smaller that the actual memorial in Washington DC, and was positioned amidst a wondrous, individually designed cottages in a neighborhood where stone and gardens dressed each home with an unique signature. Sadly now that is a district plagued by armed robberies. Maybe "Good, Old Don" would buy some advertising thought Carter? Fat chance. Don wasn't interested in a rag like the Thrifty Nickel. Carter kept driving.

Advertising was suffering in the downturn. A profession that already frustrated Carter was twisting its blade from subtle hatred to outright contempt inside Carter's heart. He despised the difficulties and tact required to wrestle money out of small business owners. The Thrifty Nickel was already at the bottom of the barrel as far as advertising gigs. Carter had sunk to a new low. Still, it didn't cost much to put an ad in the Nickel and there was always someone who wanted cheap advertising.

Carter had searched this block at least three dozen times like a hawk seeking the its prey while he had been looking for Miguel's place. He was not going to find it on this day. Not selling something, especially after a week or two, despite being in times of economic hardship felt like a moral failing. Sales had a way of brainwashing a person. It is a culture of hype, intensity, demands and dreams. Carter had the gift for it at one time even though it began as an alien and loathsome endeavor. It used to be said that the best salesmen were Communist propagandists. In the one way Carter's natural willingness to engage his fellow humans had been perverted by a series of sales managers who indoctrinated him in the mandatory survival ethic of sell, sell, sell – "always be closing..."

It was like an addiction. Carter knew it was wrong to judge himself solely by his sales performance, but it was happening even as a shred of his true dignity was aware of the self-deception. If anyone were to blame for what would happen – it was those sales managers.

Carter had once envisioned a hope. A grand idea to form a National Sales Union that would save the hated "backbone" of the American economy – the countless out there, like Willy Loman, on the frontiers of business where item or service was traded for cash. Sales, sales, sales – it was damned thing. Anyone who had gone a month working as a non-insured, commissioned based independent sales contractor making $150 in a slow month while listening to the owner of the company talk about buying his third boat could sure as hell understand the better intentions of the Unabomber's war on capitalism. Yet, the truth was Carter could not afford to raise enough spare cash to build a website to attract promote his "Union" so the chances of him one day standing on a table and hearing hundreds of sales folk chanting, "Union, Union, Union," were slim.

Carter was shaken from his thoughts by an actual, physical revelation. It was something he had not noticed before on his hundreds of travels up and down Fredericksburg Avenue. It appeared like Alice's looking hole or a cosmic window in space; a business driveway with a small sign that had an arrow on it pointing away from the street and saying, "Body Shops." Carter swung a sharp right into the driveway. Fredericksburg Avenue was coughing up one of its hidden gems in return for Carter's diligence. The driveway, concrete paved, lead back to a series of open aluminum garage spaces.

Garages typically could garner some clients; the ratio was usually that one out of twenty would spend $50 to $75 on a small block ad and then perhaps renew it for a few weeks. Carter was surprised to see that the driveway lead to a large series of aluminum garage buildings. He had no idea of any of it was there. It was at first like finding a Shangri-La of potential revenue. It was the mother-load of aluminum buildings. The yards went back at least two football fields. The series of large buildings each divided up into two, three or four shops. The only marker that told the outside world that all this was there was the small sign off Fredericksburg. Carter found a parking spot where it looked like nothing would crash into him. He pulled the emergency brake, looked around once more and then with a solid push rolled his legs and belly out of the Honda, which despite his extra weight, was too close to the ground for people over six feet tall.

Carter surveyed the lay of the terrain. He saw two dirty-faced mechanics looking at him from inside an open aluminum garage. One had an oil gauge in his hand as he was wiping off sweat from his brow he then cocked back his head to check out Carter. The advertising salesmen moved toward his prey slightly waving a folded Thrifty Nickel newspaper in the air. One mechanic automatically moved away where Carter could no longer see him. Carter approached closer.

"Hello," he said hoping the man understood English.

"How are you?" replied the remaining mechanic.

"Great – listen are you interested in increasing your business – it's real affordable advertising.

The Thrifty Nickel: Only $50 an ad and it goes all over this part of town. It'll get you some new customers," began Carter's pitch.

"No... No sir – we're not interested at this time, but you can asked around maybe someone else is," said the mechanic as he replaced the oil gauge back in the car like sheathing a sword.

"Okay – thanks – I'll just asked around at these other businesses," agreed Carter who had lost all aggressiveness for sales long ago. If someone did not seem interested right away Carter rarely pursued overcoming any objections they might have. He moved along.

He had discerned that likely each of these aluminum garages were a different business. That was surprising. There might be twelve or more businesses back here he thought. Could be something to pick out of the bunch he thought. Carter walked along the driveway that connected the aluminum edifices. The next two were locked up. The fourth had a pair of feet dangling out from them. Carter moved in. The man's legs were under a car. They were twitching slightly from the work he was doing on the engine of a 1967 Mustang. The car was primed gray and full of flaws. It wasn't going to win any beauty contests in its current condition.

"Hello – hello there how are you?" said Carter to the rest of the body he assumed was attached to the waving legs, which he skipped over to avoid tripping on.

"No sir – not here we don't want anything today," bellowed the voice from beneath the Mustang.

"Okay thanks," said Carter as he moved on.

He turned a corner where the driveway widened. The flags on the large aluminum fort startled him. Barbed wire formed a necklace of twelve-foot high walls that hid an encampment in the far alley of this secret business park. The fortress sported surveillance cameras, colorful flags that seemed to be from various Latin countries and even a couple of sentries who lingered on the corner parapets of the facility. The large aluminum gates, at the moment, were open like the jaws of a shark. Someone was doing business there assumed Carter as he went up to the gates.

"What do you want," said a man in overalls who popped into view from the side of the gate.

"Oh hey there I'm with the Thrifty Nickel," answered Carter.

"The Thrifty Nickel! It's okay Miguel – send him in," said another man who was sitting on a lawn chair near the front office.

Miguel gave flinty eyed assent, which Carter took as permission to move inside the compound. It appeared to be a fancier auto body shop than the others. The man who called Carter was sitting under a stylish green veranda with a life-size, hand-painted ceramic cougar sitting to his side. He sucked on a tall red drink with an umbrella swisher sticking out of it.

"Hola amigo – how are you today?" greeted the man.

"Doing well - how are you sir," replied Carter who was always at once refreshed and suspicious when a business owner greeted him affably as compared to visa versa. It usually meant he was about to pleasantly be sold some hubris of commercial conceit; a showing off of the other man's success with little promise of buying anything from Carter.

"Your with the Thrifty Nickel – a fine little paper. Glad you came by," said the man.

"Nice operation you got here," said Carter.

"Gracias senor," said Roberto Garza, the owner.

"How's business?" inquired Carter.

"Business is bueno – muy bueno," smiled Garza.

"Great. It could always be better with some advertising," suggested Carter.

"That's true, but we specialize my friend. Customized SUV's. Come see," gestured Mr. Garza.

"Great I'd like to see what do," said Carter mustering as much false exuberance as he could bear in order to play along.

Maybe he'd get a referral out of it in the least. The man got up and pointed his fat hand toward the wide aluminum garage in the center of the gated portion of the complex. Together the two walked toward this inner section of the compound.

The man lead Carter inside the large main work area where large pieces of quality metal parts and tools hung from the rafters and walls like bulky necklaces and earrings. Three SUV husks were anchored on platforms in the center of the room like elephant carcasses caught in trees. A few mechanics moved about the hanging SUVs like worker bees buzzing with power tools and adding sturdy "meat", in the form of metal parts, to the developing carcasses in a rapid feast resembling some blend of engineering and reincarnation. This looked like a high-end operation from what Carter could tell.

"Twice a year we caravan our special SUV's to the southern border of Mexico and Central America. There is an auto auctions right where the jungle roads begin. It's quite profitable," bragged the shop owner.

"I see. Wonderful work you do. Are there any other aspects to your business?" asked Carter as he ran his hand over the smooth surface of a nearby automobile hood.

"Funny you mentioned it. In back is a junkyard. We're looking for spare parts to salvage and that's where you may come in handy to me," said the owner.

"Really – I'd love to help," replied Carter hastily.

"Yes. Well you can put an ad in the Thrifty Nickel. It should read..." Carter scrambled for his notepad and pen as the owner spoke with his thumb and right pointer finger stuck together as he whirled them in figure eights, like a butterfly's dance.

These darting fingers moved through a pattern that consistently waved nearer and nearer to Carter's face as the man spoke:

"... 4559 Fredericksburg Avenue. Rims and wheels for sale. Saturday morning auctions. Also Looking to acquire used SUV's – contact Jesus at 210-589-3692. Yes that should do it. Did you get all that," finished the man.

"Yeah no problem. Got it," Carter read it back as the man listened with is head angled at a forty-five degree angle and his chin pointed above the horizon.

"Excellent. How much to run it for six weeks?" asked the owner.

"Ah that would be... $350," said Carter.

The man reached in his pocket. He pulled out a wad of cash, all one hundred dollar bills, whose circumference was too large for the man's hand to completely encircle. It must have been over $30,000. Carter had never seen that much money in one place. It seemed more than any man had a right to hold at one time. Still, Carter held his breathe. The man flicked off four one hundred dollar bills and handed them over to Carter.

"Put the extra $50 on my tab for future ads will you?" said the man.

"Certainly sir," replied Carter.

"Come back in three weeks," said the man.

"I will. I will," answered Carter.

As was his custom Carter took the money, gave the customer his receipt and got out as fast as he could. He didn't want to linger in case buyer's remorse set in. The hundreds glowed in his hands. They meant a thirty percent commission for him. He had not expected the sudden luck when compared to how the day had started. He was not one to look a gift horse in the mouth or press his fortune. He decided to forgo calling on the other businesses in the complex and made his way quickly back to the Honda. He had come to believe he could not have that kind of success repeat itself within the same day. Having it though gave him an excuse. He'd celebrate. He sometimes liked to celebrate.

Carter knew a neighborhood that was a nearby and had a place to go. His sales manager had hounded him down enough in this area that he knew the places of retreat that could also serve as a reward on day's like today. Every area a salesman canvases has secret hideouts of pleasure and comfort. Fredericksburg Avenue was no exception.

Fredericksburg was not the worst of areas from a sales goal standpoint. Usually with effort he could ring three to four hundred dollars out of it in a month's time all in bit sales of about $50. The big haul from the chop shop gave the itinerant salesman some breathing room. The Crossroads Mall was at the corner of Fredericksburg and Loop 410 just ahead north. The Mall was the main oasis in this district. It sported lavish terraced, landscaping which lead to a series of sunken fountains and was a tranquil spot to grab a bit to eat and a soda or the perennial Texas favorite; an iced tea. Iced Coffee was making a comeback too. His mother used to make that years ago when he was kid. That was before she died suddenly when Carter was little more than a boy. Funny, iced coffee only brought back good memories. He sometimes now ordered one from the McDonald's drive threw. Today though would be iced tea.

Crossroads Mall used to be called Wonderland Mall. It used to have a beat and rhythm, but recently had descended into an odd and pathetic caricature of commerce. It was home of the Bijou Theater, the only place in town that played foreign and independent movies on the big screen. The theater rested just inside the massive glass mall entrance where the sunken fountain base pooled its water. From there one could travel to the food court or go up the giant escalator to the main shopping fronts. The rub of Crossroads Mall was that only fifteen percent of the storefronts were occupied. It held an odd mix of a rap clothing store, a Quinceanera dress rental store, a perfumeria that specialized in elaborate generics and foreign scents, a textile shop, an MD, a nail salon, an educational supplies store, a Hobby Lobby, a Burlingame Coat Factory and a Merwyns were virtually all that was left inside the husk of the once thriving "Wonderland Mall".

Recently there had been an inner city drama charter school and a martial arts dojo, but they were now gone. Even the military recruitment office had closed it doors here. Perhaps this no man's land remained as a buffer between the old and new parts of San

Antonio. It had to be plain as to avoid envies and hostilities. Maybe it was a place for daring diplomats of the north, south and west side to détente. There was the newly added Norris Mini-Convention Center, which stuck to the side of the Mall like an artificial lung, and hosted bi-monthly job fairs where no one ever got a job, except when they were solely looking for medical assistants. At least to date the place had never claimed a riot.

Carter liked that Crossroads Mall was always empty. He needed the space to let his distempered vibes absorb out into the architecture. When there were too many others around they acted like emotional radar sending back the vibes, like echoes, until they landed on his nervous system making for grand confusions and irritations. At heart he had become a wild animal.

This Mall was a grand contrast to NIOSA, the yearly festival that was going on each night. Carter had not been to that in nearly thirty years when he got severely beaten one night in San Antonio. Still, the drumbeat and deep hunger of NIOSA {Old Night in San Antonio} reverberated though the daylight of the city during these times, the echoes of jammed crowds, beer warped minds, groping and coughing on each other as they ghoulishly wandered the dark street of the old town center now propped by hanging paper lanterns, concessions stands, loud speakers and rows upon rows of port-a-potties: A brawler's paradise and a night when a man or two could end up with life sentences in prison. A gala for has been Charro Queens and gang mamas with their breasts on parade, a den for lurking swine flues and ancient desires of cannibalism that could surface at only moment amongst the throngs wearing SPURS and DALLAS COWBOYS T-shirts. At NIOSA people moved like magnetically guided bumper cars through a sea of humanity where ordinary senses did little good and one is moved by the masses.

Then, as Carter was remembering this unpleasantness, as if the universe was conspiring to offer an option of joy - a funny song came on the radio from a local, prankish Disc Jockey Mike Roberts of Magic 105:

"Here's a funny little local favorite – this one goes out to all folk with hubris out there, that means too much pride for ordinary folk like and me – listen and chuckle:

20

Tommy Lee Jones, Tommy Lee Jones One of San Antonio's very own
More than one Oscar he should own
Mention any part
He'll jump on it and do it smart
Tommy Lee Jones, Tommy Lee Jones
If you see him in a local bar Be wise and stay away far
Tommy Lee Jones, Tommy Lee Jones
Like Texas he needs space to roam
Dare to talk to him and he'll look you in the eye
And curse your mama's soul till you cry
Tommy Lee Jones, Tommy Lee Jones
One of San Antonio's very own
His neighborhood is his kingdom
The cops watch his house for him everyday
If you stroll your car near for a peek
Be ready to pay
Tommy Lee Jones, Tommy Lee Jones
More than one Oscar he should own
He loves local lore, his flicks help bury the dead
But if you live in this town
Watch that he doesn't bite off your head
Tommy Lee Jones, Tommy Lee Jones."

Carter easily parked in the wide-open mall lot. It was a short jaunt to where he could descend the well-crafted stairs by the big fountain. A breeze pushed a spray of water onto his face from the fountain as he descended. He picked up his descent to a light jog due to the invigoration of the water and the thought of the new money in his pocket.

Boom - a worker pushed into Carter accidentally from around the corner at the base of the staircase. He had been holding a weed eater and when the men collided the he pulled the trigger of the weed eater, it went off, it blared a loud screech and the sharp wire spun its rapid rotations, the man jumped back and released his hold on the trigger, the machine stopped, but had startled Carter and as he moved away his mind went back to that night when he took the terrible beating.

He blamed it on the Viking guffaw he made in the middle of the crowd, he had been happy, but the glee of the laugh offended some nearby Latinos. That's how he remembered it. He had been drinking, but wasn't a rough drunk. They came at him to censor him and more. He had gone beyond acceptable Tex-Mex mannerisms. He would be punished. The crowd was indifferent to his plight. The smell of fajita meat exuded from the skin of the bystanders as they mass around beer ticket stands to carry off rolls of red tickets, loosely wound and with tails hanging at least two feet long. Vague music blasted from the speakers that were everywhere, the sound attacked the center from the periphery and encouraged frenzy. The scrutiny of this inquest had become "how down you are" with the real people, but Carter did not know that. He'd get his warning. The assassins off in the dark, the making ancient recipes from grandmother – it had brewed and needed a victim. NIOSA would offer Carter that badge of honor with each fist and foot stomp he took that night. Pregnant women waltzed by his broken body. In the back of his mind he thought he heard the sirens of a 1957 Le France fire engine fly by. It's all on parade here if you can read between the lines - It's all part of the show.

Coming back to the present as best he could Carter found him self-aware again and just inside the lower level entrance to Crossroads Mall. He went to The Juice Stand and ordered a large strawberry and partial banana smoothie. He liked these 75% strawberry and 25% banana. He also ordered an iced tea for the caffeine.

The sound of it, "energy booster", made him "feel" healthier. Besides he was easy.

There was no one easier to sell than a salesman. Carter's Ninjitsu sense must have been activated though when the weed eater almost sliced him because as he turned, with his strawberry and banana smoothie in one hand and his iced tea in the other, to begin to find some seating he was sure he would see Jack Pearson. Maybe it was an unusual squeak from Pearson's wheelchair that he had vaguely heard or some unconscious calculations of the odds since every third or fourth time Carter went to Crossroads Mall he ran into this crippled follow. Jack Pearson liked Crossroads Mall too. It was close to where the terrible automobile accident had happened six years before. That accident had made Jack a multi-millionaire and also gave him a lot of time to burn. His lawyer Murphy Bander secured a thirteen million dollar settlement from the company that owned the eighteen-wheeler that so damaged Pearson. Jack and Bander split the settlement amount 50-50.

Generally speaking Jack Pearson thought that it was worth being crushed by a truckload of California grapefruit in order to gain 6.5 million dollars. His life had never been the same and despite many men's experience about losing use of their legs he could still achieve an erection and satisfactory ejaculation. His love life had not been much before the 6.5 million, but it had picked up considerably since the accident. Jack Pearson had no problem with waitresses: Mexican-American or otherwise.

Pearson noticed Carter, but wasn't about to roll out of his way to greet him. The two were acquaintances. They had shared several amiable conversations over the last year after having bumped into each other in line at the Bijou Theater one afternoon when Carter had been playing hooky from work. It had been a revised showing of the movie BRAZIL. Today Carter, in his exuberance from the day's sale felt friendly and with only a moment's pause, due to his instinctual caution, waltzed over to the food court table where Pearson parked his Sememax 7000 Deluxe series wheelchair.

"Hey there Mr. Pearson. How are you?" greeted Carter.

"Not bad," said Pearson.

"Mind if I join you?" asked Carter.

"Help yourself," replied Pearson.

Carter sat across from Pearson who was looming over a beefsteak sandwich.

"Keeping busy?" Carter asked curiously – he knew Pearson had some money – enough not to work, but assumed some social service had donated the chair. He thought maybe Pearson combined his disability with a small savings from a past settlement and barely made ends meet. He thought Pearson's rudeness was due to misery, not the power that comes with real money. He knew too that Pearson was strangely informed about the goings on around town. Carter figured the guy had plenty of time to read and talk to people that was for sure – he should know what was up in San Antonio. The area surrounding Crossroads Mall had its share of unemployed, mischief-makers who could transmit gossip. Carter didn't know that Pearson moonlighted as a private investigator and had more than a few friends in the know.

"Oh yeah I have been busy – just like Fredericksburg Avenue – may seem low key, but I get busy," said Pearson.

"I know what you mean. I just ran into a character down the street. Some sort of body shop where they customize high end SUV's," mentioned Carter.

"Roberto's," informed Pearson.

"You know em?" asked Carter.

"Sure. Roberto does a lot of business with the legal community," said Pearson. "Yeah I bet lawyers like to drive fancy SUV's," said Carter.

"Not the lawyers – their clients. Those SUV's are drug runners – armor plating, stash boxes, extra fuel tanks, bulletproof glass – the works. Did Roberto tell you about those auctions down at the southern tip of Mexico?" inquired Pearson.

"Yeah he did," answered Carter.

"That's who buys there – the Cartels – they send various emissaries to those auctions and stack up on highly durable SUV's for those perilous jungle roads," stated Pearson.

"Huh – I thought it sounded fishy," said Carter.

"Fishy – a friend of mine – real sweet and reliable girl who works as a real estate secretary – she was driving the other day by the airport – turning the corner in a secluded industrial park and..."

"I know the place," said Carter rapidly interrupting..

"... and saw a cop car on fire with about six hundred bullet holes in it. Like from machine guns. Man, we're in an all out secret drug war here in San Antonio with the Machete 13 – Mexican Cartels and who knows who else – probably a secret police force here too and none of it is being reported in the papers, on the radio or on TV. Makes ya think," continued Pearson.

"There are a lot of new brand names in cop cars these days," added Carter. "You notice that too," agreed Pearson.

"City Marshall, City Constable, Highway Patrol Transit..." listed Carter.

"County Police, County Constable, Metro Police..." added Pearson in synch. "Homeland Security, State Patrol, San Antonio Police, State Police, Texas Highway Patrol, County Sherriff, Undercover Patrol, School Police, Airport Police, among others, not to mentioned two dozens types of unmarked cars - everything from Suburbans to F-150's to Mustangs to Chrysler 300's," offered Carter.

"Have you noticed how San Antonio has added a black and white pig mobile division to the old blue and white cars? Just like L.A. man. Getting ready for the war..." said Pearson.

"It's scary," said Carter.

"Scary – did you hear the news about that bow and arrow killer?" said Pearson who seemed to be able to change the subject as if using a remote control.

"Yeah that was pretty weird," commented Carter as Pearson took another bite of his beefsteak sandwich.

Carter was wondering how serious a person or what side of things Pearson really sat on. He was more informed than the ordinary gossip, but also somewhat paranoid sounding. His conspiracies did not exactly jive with Carter's own. This meant Carter either had to adapt what Pearson was saying into his own schema as truth or partial truth or reject it as lie. Also Carter believed people who can change subjects so quickly seemed unpredictable. He looked, scrutinizing more closely, at Pearson who was wiping a gob of beefsteak sauce off his cheek.

Most of San Antonio had heard about the seventeen-year-old boy who climbed into his neighbor's window and shot her with an arrow to the forehead. It was a deathblow. The lady turned out to be the esteemed matron of one of the city's most prestigious Tex-Mex dining establishments. As with most of the best Mexican restaurants – Chango's – had started out with a small taco shop on the poor Southside of town. With an excellent work ethic and quality tacos it's reputation and wealth grew to where the owners were able to open fancy dining halls on the wealthy Northside of town. There the same food was served at two and half times the cost and the place became all the rave of newspaper reviewers. It was a story told ten dozen times with ten dozen Mexican-American food oligarchies.

"Hmm... yeah something likely fishy about that bow and arrow killing," Carter put out there to test the water's of Pearson's thinking.

"Not necessarily," said Pearson.

"Ever hear about the City Medical Examiner doing stuff not exactly on the books?" queried Carter.

"What da mean "not exactly on the books?" asked Pearson. "You know shady," said Carter.

"Not really," said Pearson.

Yeah, Pearson was hard to read.

He was in a way like parts of San Antonio itself thought Carter – though not all of San Antonio. Carter glanced away and his gaze landed on the rolled fat of one of the many women in San Antonio who wore their clothes skin tight even though they had gained sixty or more pounds since high-school. The look might be more a statement of ease than sexiness, but Carte was not certain. The look was relatively new. It could have been an expression of Hispanic comfort and a safety to be casual. Twenty years before it wasn't seen. San Antonio then felt more overtly threatening, like a Wild West town stuffed with enclaves of gangsters and evil sheriffs, where rednecks cruised the streets with shotguns, fully visible, on their rear window racks and cowboy dancehalls were loaded at night with palpable tension and outright brawls. There was a vibration on the street in those days, an aura of pending violence based on a 50-50 race split with no leader, no guidelines from one dominant culture. The hegemony back then had been up for grabs.

Those people, the rowdy white ones, had all left San Antonio. It was a Mexican town now; more like a Spanish Colony than the Wild West. For most citizens, in most parts of the city – on most any given day - a certain order had replaced the tense air, but with that order came a sort of peevish Inquisition, the subtle criticism that a high-school kid might imbue in the workplace if they were boss; using preferences in hiring and promotion and laying out the juried law as well as general customs. Carter had questions about his future in a place where such a great shift had taken place. George Lopez said there would be big changes. Carter thought comics might be prophets as well. There were more sudden gun battles, murders in the night and unfair judgments, sanctioned or informal, and bribes to escape these judgments that Adam Carter did not understand. These were the things Carter feared.

Yeah, if there was one quality that defined the New San Antonio it was mockery. And Pearson had it too. He must have been raised here thought Carter. It was the thing, that quality: mockery, that Carter was at war against. He didn't think he really liked Pearson all that much. The Lord would call Pearson, like others around this town, "Pharaoh" one day and dole out a greater judgment. Carter thumbed his Quixote.

"Why do you always carry that book around with you. Is it like your baby blanket?" said Pearson.

"Cervantes has a lot of wisdom for a place like San Antonio," said Carter.

"Oh yeah – like what," jibed Pearson.

"Well," Carter opened the book randomly, "Here Sancho Panza tells a story of when a farmer once invited a gentleman to dinner, "just as the two of them, as I have said, were going to sit down to the meal, the farmer insisted on the gentleman's taking the head of the table, and the gentlemen like-wise insisted on the farmer taking it, for a man's wishes should be obeyed in his own house, But the farmer, who prided himself on his courtesy and good breeding, steadfastly refused, until the gentleman angrily put his hands on his shoulders and sat him down by force, saying: "Sit down, blockhead, for wherever I sit shall be head of the table for you."

"Hmm. That's weird," said Pearson.

"Yeah a little bit," affirmed Carter. "Hey it's starting to drizzle outside," observed Pearson. "We can expect a lot of traffic," said Carter. "Yeah San Antonians can't drive in the rain for shit they'll be wrecks all over the place," stated Pearson.

Pearson raised his seat in the Sememax 7000 chair to a pitched angle. The 7000 could do that. At $12,000 per unit it could do a lot of things. Carter finished his smoothie.

"Maybe I'll ask around the courthouse, casually, about this Medical Examiner," said Pearson.

"Okay," said Carter.

"I'll let you know what I hear. It seems like you like to be in the know," said Pearson.

"Yeah that'd be cool. Just don't use my name okay," said Carter.

"Of course not. I'm a pro. Here let me program your number into my cell," said Pearson.

Pearson was thinking Carter had something, he was certainly crazy, but he had something. This could be used for his network. Carter was wondering what all the connections were to the legal system that Pearson always referenced, but did not feel the need to ask as he dictated his number "210-XXX-XXXX."

"Ever go to the Havana Bar?" asked Pearson.

"Been there a couple times," said Carter. "Okay then let's plan to meet there on Friday – say around 8pm and we will compare notes," said Pearson.

"Ok sounds good," agreed Carter who was generally very lonely anyway.

Though this situation did not seem like some cure for loneliness, rather it seemed like to the two were entering into a pack of some sort. It seemed warranted. Carter was intrigued. That was Pearson's intent, he always liked to initiate new informants at the Havana Bar because of its air of mystery and suspense. It was his RICK'S from CASABLANCA and he left Carter that morning wondering what would happen when they rendezvoused at Rick's as Carter was a man who had a sense of fate about him. This from Pearson's experience was an unpredictable: a thing not necessarily to be trusted and not necessarily good.

CHAPTER 2

A Mexican Childhood

Growing up on the outskirts of Matamoras was tough. The Mexican border town had a long history of strange people and events. Events there came to a head in the 1980's when a white college boy from San Antonio was drugged and tortured to death by a small, black magic cult. Black magic was part of the fiber of the area surrounding Matamoras. The old Indians from the region had a line of freak shamans, perhaps genetic mutants, who did not have a heart for treaties with the body of mankind. There were still a few survivors of that tribe who for centuries passed on dark beliefs and practices. The Catholic Spanish blood that mixed with these people did not dilute that twisted heritage very much. Matamoras had been overseen by a series of particularly wicked priests whom allowed bent interpretations of the Church to further seep into local lore. The new blend served to aggravate the innate perversions of the region. The fruition and pinnacle of this fiendishness was Timbero Mantos. Timbero was born in 1976. He came into the world as the offspring of the marriage between Jorge Mantos and Lupita Garza. Traditionally the name Garza reflected people in Mexico and the southern United States that most often became paragons of good citizenship. Garzas were many times found as successful business clans in any given district. In the least one could find a Garza practicing honorably in function of public notary or county assessor. The calm name of Garza did not arise suspicion in society. Its lineage elicited few "beefs" between folks. Even the stauncher Texas bigots mostly had few bad things to say about the "Garzas" in their counties. Quiet and wise, Garza's, were largely facilitators of self-knowledge and community cohesion. They were happy to label the region that held San Antonio as Central Texas, not South Central Texas, as to appease the Anglo sensibility of hegemony.

Now, in Timbero's case, it was likely the Mantos line was where the trouble likely came from. Though Jorge Mantos, devoted husband and gentle father, was most virtuous – if genealogical scientists were to go back a few generations to the point where the evil priest Don Gonzales raped, the already deviated amateur

29

sorceress Isabel Lupita Nacodogches {a name who locals would recognize as polluted with the most diabolical Indian blood} – then the source of Timbero Manto's resurfacing oddities could better be accessed.

Timbero in his teens had found books that inspired him. They told about the old ways. He researched further and in secret began his practices. He was most dangerous in many ways, but not the least in that he was a self-taught occultist. Personal whim and rhythms were what decided his private atrocities and their frequency. They were not always rooted in the grounding of the community as was could be said for his ancestors use of the black arts. Now Timbero worked for other people, but that was only his day job.

Driving up I-37 from Corpus Christi to San Antonio Timbero was fighting terrible feelings inside. His hands constantly rubbed up and down the side of his jeans, or twittered with the radio or unnecessarily adjusted the rear view mirror. It was getting more difficult for him to control his need. He had obeyed his master's with expert proficiency. They were not at all displeased with his performances. He knew though that he needed to "fix" again. It was coming faster this hot summer and the desire was changing into the lust for new types of objects. The lust was impossible to refuse. It was amazing he had fooled his masters for so long. They had no idea of his complete needs. Usually he could get it done in Juarez without much notice. Something though had triggered inside and he needed to do it in America this time.

Timbero turned the large, round wheel of the vintage Cadillac to the right and pulled into a Valero gas station. He parked at the pump. The car was a 1982 wide ride. White in color and with two odd distinguishing features on the tail end; an oval license plate guard that read "US Submariners – The Silent Service" and a smallish sticker of a skeleton in a purple suit eating a jalapeño. This part of Hwy 37 was pretty barren. Dust, skies and a small amount of traffic were all there was. Timbero had bought the used car in Corpus paying cash and using fictitious identification. It was the same M.O. he used each time when doing a run to San Antonio. There one of the Cartel's chop shops would take care of the Cady and reassign Timbero another vehicle for the more precarious return journey. Still Timbero was meticulous. He used an old Philips head screwdriver to remove the "Silent Service" license plate guard and scraped off as much of the purple sticker as he could. Still, a little bit of the purple coat and red jalapeño was too embedded to remove.

Timbero had an assignment to carry out in San Antonio before dropping off the Cadillac at the chop shop on Fredericksburg. His cargo was in the trunk. The less conspicuous the car was the better. Big cars could still be seen all over Texas so he was okay on that point. He scrubbed the sticker one more time very hard then went inside the store.

He bought an 89 cent can of coke in the Valero shop and winked at the cute clerk while leaving fifty cents in the well of desperation; the "tip jar" resting on the countertop that had become fashionable in all sorts of places that they had never been before. Timbero liked to fill his movements with little gestures that would get him noticed, but not remembered. He felt like it kept him invisible: that and the crucifix of St. Peter on the cross that had been blessed by spells.

The store clerk was not what he wanted, nor was the coke that he tossed in the back seat unopened, as he once again sped up I-37. He could feel the land becoming more northern. The south felt more compressed compared to the feeling of expansiveness as one moved north. Timbero was proficient at pretending to like things that everyone else seemed to like. He believed, correctly, that people mostly forget the ordinary. The drive to San Antonio was as uneventful as Timbero had hoped. The only difficulty was that without distraction or need for applying his skills of subterfuge Timbero had too much time to think about his personal needs. The itch was burning. He grinned again on how he had been last able to satisfy it in Juarez and the grin soon became a deep glee that sunk into his heart as he reflected on how no one, not even his masters amongst the Cartel knew about his secret. He faintly recalled how heinous the world might think his private acts to be, but quickly ignored that train of thought as he replaced it with selfish visions of how good it was to do that one thing that he liked so well, with such great passion. He knew on this trip he would quench that need with an American. Just like his master's message in the trunk, Timbero wanted to expand the range of his desires. It was only fair for as they say, "As above, so below."

He saw the tell tale sight that he had arrived fully in San Antonio proper. The bulbous Tower of the Americas plotted in Hemisphere Plaza – central downtown. It was 587 feet of structure that stood above all else in the San Antonio skyline. I-37 travelled through downtown on raised highway platforms. Off to the right Timbero passed the latest shortsighted monstrosity bequeathed to the taxpayers of the city by the its council planners – the Alamodome; a stadium that looked like a post-cubist work in the shape of a skewered and splayed Armadillo laying on it's back. Alabaster securing cables were fastened to the erect "legs" like dissection pins while the beige brick and greenish windowed core lay helplessly flat against the ground. San Antonio was forever conflicted between building its infrastructure versus catering to its substantial, 87 Billion dollar a year, tourism industry. The military spent 15 Billion a year in San Antonio from its four bases, but they came from all over the nation so as far as getting them to go to the Alamodome to route for the "home" team – fat chance. That was one reason San Antonio didn't have a pro football team that the dome was meant to attract. Medical development and research thrived as an endeavor of commerce. It did not hurt in this regard that San Antonio held the title of the 2nd Fattest Metropolis in the United States. The heart stint had been invented in San Antonio.

Timbero knew the area well. I-37 would take him directly to Loop 410 where the new overpass would cut in front of the airport then deposit him right on the McCullough Street exit. His destination, North Star Mall was there on the left. The Mall had once been the pride of the city. It still was a keen shopping spot. Before the city expanded to and past Loop 1604, North Star Mall had been the beacon of civilization at the northern tip of the city's development. Seventy-five foot steel cowboy boots in front of the parking entrance in front of Loop 410 signaled quality Texas shopping. North Star Mall had expanded in recent years with additions of trendy stores like the Cheesecake Factory, The Apple Store and several chic clothing brand stores. It had Nordstroms, Dillard's and Macy's. Yet, it now bordered on an inner city housing and school district that received ghetto funding. It was more central city now than Northside. Still, it was the best location for the Cartel's gift to the "pinche" Americanos because of its accessibility and status that was at once mainstream and elite. Timbero, because of his first hand knowledge of the United States, was allowed to pick this mall as the delivery point for his overseer's message. In a way North Star Mall was still the heart of the city despite greater developments such as the lush outdoor mall, La Cantera, out I-10 and off Loop 1604 near the University of Texas at San Antonio and Fiesta Texas Amusement Park just before the hill country.

Timbero reflected on the Alamodome as he past downtown. He had a keen assessment of the ways and status of San Antonio. He never studied civic and urban demographics formally, but he had a refined perception due to his special way of paying attention. In his business he heard what important people, people in government, thought about matters. He knew the Alamodome was San Antonio's latest attempt at enticing an NFL franchise to the city. He knew that this fiasco came to a head, with serendipitous delusion, when Hurricane Katrina forced the New Orleans Saints to play in the Alamodome for several "home games". Ungracious to the fallen city of New Orleans, San Antonians and certain city leaders attempted a coup by putting forth enticement to the Saints to abandon New Orleans wholly and relocate to San Antonio. It didn't happen and San Antonians would be wise not to wear their "Alamo City" T-shirts while strolling late at night on Bourbon Street for all the acrimony that gambit fostered between the two cities. Only the Spurs would remain as a sports team of any note in San Antonio and with Tim Duncan, Manu Ginobili and Tony Parker aging that dynasty looked to be coming to an end.

In Timbero's mind San Antonio meant one thing. It was a major city inside the borders of the U.S., in which a gang member from the Mexican Cartels would maneuver with impunity. It was a "Beaner" town, as Jesse Jackson might call it. Timbero smirked at the thought. Insult the bean and you insult the Mexican he thought to himself in a moment of odd, personal humor. He had no real affinity for bigotry other than using the prejudices of others to manipulate them into one's own will. He knew how powerful racial preferences were for most common people. He thought maybe it was a side effect of his "quirk" that he did not harbor such judgments. He did not know for sure because he had never met another of his kind as to determine if, by and large, people with the same private desires as himself shared in such freedom from bias. He knew he was different. Of that fact he was deeply aware. He used his awareness to protect himself.

Timbero steered his car onto Loop 410 from I-37 and quickly exited on the McCullough ramp before taking the first left at the light, near La Mansion, and driving alongside the underground parking for Dillard's at North Star Mall. To his left was the abstract Wells Fargo Bank building. It was one of the first pieces of new architecture in San Antonio. Timbero remembered that it had been a local branch, Mercantile Bank, back then when it first was created. He remembered architecture and the names of old businesses and the faces of many of the dead.

He turned the Cadillac right on Rector Street at the end of the underground parking lot and drove along the back side of the mall until just before San Pedro Avenue, which lined the far side of the mall. Here he took a right into the mall parking lot and made he way to the highest ground of North Star Mall. Timbero kept heading for the highest point on the hill. From this mall entrance the lots spread out before his gaze like the vista of a desert expanse. The cars were as great blankets of sand from which the hot Texas sun burst off its reflection. Timbero's sharp eyes, one whose eyelash was peculiarly white, peered through the desert for an oasis. Gotcha. He saw one or two within reach – empty parking spaces. A free space was not far to the left – two lanes in. Timbero's calculations assumed no other car could get there before his Cadillac. Spinning the wheels quickly by pressing a heavy foot to the gas pedal he made it to the parking spot, as if it were a professional sport, before any other. He shut down the Cadillac and spun freely out of the car as he often neglected to wear his seatbelt. He went to the trunk. The lid opened easily with crisp popping sound; a combination of age and quality of the vehicle. As Timbero grabbed the large white bag with both hands he thought back on the prizes he collected therein; the one from the border patrolman – he had been snacking in his car out in the desert, the American Sheriff's deputy – he had been lured by Lucinda the whore to a cheap hotel room, the Mexican soldier – the fool thought he would be receiving bribes when he entered the back room of Toro's Liquor Hall, the DEA agent – believed falsely that Timbero was an eager informant as he rested next to him in the Cartel owned barber chair, the Mexican police Captain – abducted from right in front of the police station and brought the old warehouse and the Mexican Judge – convinced he was meeting an American attaché at the men's club – only to be kidnapped from the gymnasium locker room, smuggled unconscious to the old warehouse in a towel cart: Six in all.

Timbero pranced with his gifts into the busy mall entrance. It was a hot day before Easter in Texas and Timbero was happy to be in the air-conditioned shopping zone. He had a special glee knowing the fruits of his talented work were about to be delivered.

Timbero glided with the white bag between the movements of the crowded mall patrons. His destination was merely another fifty yards ahead in the open area of center court. The Easter Bunny photograph display was amply decorated with giant colored eggs, a center swing where the man in the Bunny suit was perched and a long line of families waiting to donate gifts, get a picture taken and sign for a big prize. Timbero deftly slipped to the side of the lines where a small wooden fence surrounded the Easter scene. Timbero charmingly dropped his white bag amongst the numerous donations bunched in a large pile to side of the swing and photograph area.

Timbero sneered as he left the mall with thoughts of his gifts being received. He made sure to window shop briefly before exiting as to appear like he belonged and was in need of the same sort of commodities that normal folk generally valued. It was Penelope Walton who eventually opened the white bag that evening. She screamed so loud that a child nearby, the daughter of a shop worker who was waiting with her father as mother closed the shop, began crying. Penelope, an Alamo Heights matron fond of donating time to good causes, was not used to finding six, severed human heads in the Easter donation pile. She dropped the bag getting a splatter of blood on her right forearm.

The next person to open the bag was Detective Julian Cordoza of the San Antonio Police Department. He was the one who found the note.

It read, "Take one of ours and we'll take six of yours." The war had expanded.

The *JUAREZ FILES* next day ran the head line:

Message In a Bottle, Not Exactly, But Close

The JUAREZ FILES were Barry's local version of his media idol, Jack Cafferty, of CNN's *Cafferty Files*. His editor at the San Antonio Light allowed Barry full reign in this editorial column. Barry was popular with the people and had a knack for discovery big stories before anyone else. That was a rare an invaluable instinct in the press. Most media people were followers, they followed the story, Barry was one of those rare birds that found the story. Not everyone, especially amongst his co--workers, liked the narcissistic reporter and his style, but he had to be tolerated and even encouraged for business sake. That day's editorial on the "6 Heads" went on to say:

Drug violence in San Antonio, Texas has taken larger dimensions since yesterday Monday April 14, 2009. Likely it was one of the Mexican Cartels vying for supremacy on our borders and beyond, right into the heart to our state. The message; a gruesome one, six decapitated human heads delivered to North Star Mall – awfully so – as they were left in the Easter donation gift drop for Mrs. Penelope Walton of Alamo Heights to not so casually find. This gimmick of intimidation is straight out of Shakespeare or some B rated horror flick, but no this actually happened here in San Antonio. What did the message mean? Who were the victims? Let's start with that –

Readers may remember the shooting of a Nueva Laredo drug lord by DEA and FBI agents last month while on sanctioned bi-nation raids between the governments of Mexico and The United States and the proposed Inter-Cartel Treaty to be voted on next month by the Congress of the United States. Clearly the message is: if you come in our backyard again, if you attack one of ours, if you sign that Treaty then expect more blood. Do not bother us on our home territory and we are more powerful than our government and maybe yours... we are not afraid to defecate on your front lawn.

Among the "6 Heads" one of the victims is expected to perhaps be officials involved in fighting the drug trade who have gone missing lately including an American Sheriff's Deputy, Pat Sanders, who had a big arrest last spring of a Cartel shipment. Apparently the Cartels want to replace that photo of Sanders on the cover of NEWSWEEK standing on a pile of wrapped cocaine and marijuana six feet high with this, their latest image for the press - his severed head. Forensics should confirm all identities within two weeks.

Folks I knew it's gruesome, but it's war on our doorstep. It must be taken seriously and not shied away from. This reporter urges you to write your Congressman to ratify the Inter-Cartel Treaty and in short "go after the bastards".

Barry's article went on predicts the identities of the other men who died standing up to the drug lord's, in some fashion or another, be it through service to justice or betraying a bribery system in place that they were an accomplish of. Then Barry went into an explanation of the three most powerful Cartels on the Mexican border and provided names and backgrounds of leaders and suspected affiliates. The hometown, ace reporter was determined to sink his teeth into this story. Barry had been laboring for decades in San Antonio all the while desiring promotion to the national media scene. This story had advancement written all over it. He knew the bigger he could make the story the bigger he could make himself. It almost had the whiff of Pulitzer on it. Yes, with a Pulitzer, he could write his own ticket.

The article continued:

How long do we in San Antonio have to bear the crucible of the most heinous forms of brutal "bullyism" by the dregs of that cesspool government south of our border? Do I sound harsh against the homeland of my ancestors? Well, if so too bad. We're Americans here and if I remember we are a people of backbone. Besides, Pancho Villa's revolution kicked out everyone from the intelligentsia and middle classes with integrity from Mexico long ago. These Cartels are fond of knowing no law. Well, there is one question left: What will our LAW do in response to their actions? The choice is clear. Ratify the Inter-Cartel Treaty. Send them running south of Mexico and to infinity and beyond. San Antonio has seen too much spill over – too much nesting of these banditos. I vow to name names. I vow to expose. For as long as it takes the Juarez Files will be dedicated to the eradication of the pest of drug thugs – and any enemies from within or without of our society who side with them. Remember the Inter-Cartel Treaty is as American as Apple Pie. It was written and sponsored by Senator Mitch Murphy, war- hero and board member of that most American of corporations: General Electric. If the General and the Hero are ready to stand up to these villains then the least the rest of us can do is give them our vote!

Juarez over and out – stay tuned, until next time...

CHAPTER 3

The Lady Sometimes Wears Red

Dr. Julia Brown came to San Antonio three years after her divorce. It had been a bitter time. Her revenge, if only unconsciously, was to move the young children as far away from their father as possible. Trinity University seemed like a good nesting ground for a distinguished, tenured history professor. The University had been founded on a prominent hill, that overlooked what was now downtown San Antonio, by Presbyterians around 180 years before. It had grown into a premiere, small-scale liberal arts University. The campus housed a few quality departments, fantastic amenities and functioned as an active lecture circuit destination. The incentives Trinity University was able to offer Dr. Brown for leaving the east coast was generous. They overpaid on moving and relocation costs, gave immediate transfer of tenure, had a signing bonus, extended research leave plan, publishing and editorial assistance, two paid researchers, a corner office with windows that was 2 and 1/2 sizes larger than anything on the east coast and not to mentioned the house they had given to her, for extended use, in the luscious, vintage Monte Vista district that cloaked the elite University's perimeter in a combination of ivy, kudzu and classic stone homes whose only downsize was a scorpion or two living between the mortar work.

Yes, San Antonio seemed a fine, sunny place to raise Beth and Michael; now eleven and fourteen respectively. Dr. Brown thought Trinity would be the right college for Michael to attend in a few years, he seemed more of an athlete or social carouser than intellectual to her. He was not the type to dare moving far away. He had local friends that he seemed to value highly. No, he wasn't, in her estimation, the thinker that she had been at his age. She who had climbed the slopes of the stringent standards of the east coast, first prep school and waves academic competitions and foreign language development. Then, Columbia University where she obtained her undergraduate diploma and then one of her first graduate degrees. She was just the type to be snatched up by the admin at Trinity U.

She was kind by nature, effective, humorous in a way that youth could appreciate and just enough of a class snob that her D's and occasionally F's would most likely fall on those who came to Trinity on grants and whose grammar skills betrayed a less sophisticated upbringing than say a son of foreign Prince or American CEO. That's how they rolled at Trinity U. This deference to power was mostly unconscious on the part of the professors who by and large prided themselves on their academic integrity, but also on their station near the upper classes that Trinity afforded. It was Dean of Academic Affairs, Lori Nesbouton, who was aware of how to exactly calculate this game for profit and who to hire that would play the game well.

Trinity, with its Olympic swimming pool, dozens of tennis courts in multiple locations, solar paneled heating system and high end dormitories, was for brats that needed the credentials, but did not necessarily have the gusto to take on an Ivy League education. Trinity's niche was to pamper the world's prestige classes during their college careers: the sons and daughters from marginal monarchs, sketchy dictators, the newly very rich, old American wealth that somehow was not the YALE or HARVARD set, or the children of powerful, yet slightly dull industrialists. The professor's were the pawns in this game even if they did not know it.

In Dr. Brown's case vanity and old hurts brought her to South Central Texas. In regards to her son, she was actually projecting her negative feelings about Don Baxter, Michael's father when she considered Michael's weak intellectual foundations. She was competitive, leaning to the type that liked those around her to be a little less. This likely could be blamed on the great devotion she had given to her father and the need to stand out above his first child from a previous marriage. It was one of a number of blind spots the otherwise brilliant professor possessed. She had to be the best.

Make no mistake she was a great mind. Several professional communities knew this to be true including, but not limited to the criminal law world, the realm of third world election monitors, as well as the patent and commercial invention arena. It did not matter that Trinity was in a sense a step down from east coast academic excellence because Dr. Brown's freelance work and the reputation she had thus garnered more than makes up for the transfer in campus status. Already in the few years she had been on the San Antonio campus she had lured a higher level of fellow professors and guest speakers to participate at Trinity. This was recognized as a value by the admin and they knew her for what she was, a leader in her field. With some much certainty there was bound to be shadow.

Dr. Brown knew about some of her blind spots. Whenever she was blocked or unsure of what to recommend in one of her papers she went online. Sometimes companies sought her advise on obscure or particularly difficult historical justifications for say, perhaps - a new medicine that vaccinated populations from a deadly disease, but possibly caused sterility in .0087 percent of the population over forty. Or the issue could be that a defense attorney in Georgia needed a historical profile, sociological opinion and statistical analysis of common criminal deviations occurring in socially disadvantaged African-Americans whose entire line had never risen from working in the equivalent of small sweat mills. Once in a while the questions were even more complicated, requiring outside the box opinions on morality. In such times, when these puzzles stumped or stalled her, Dr. Brown opened up the questions, in paraphrased form, to the devoted readers of her anonymous blog, "Big Questions, Possible Answers."

The blog handled many areas of Dr. Brown's needs. If she was having trouble with Beth at school then that went into the blog's queries. Its readers were diverse and appreciated the quality and breadth of the host's mind that interacted with them. Lately, Dr. Brown had been deeply disturbed by her growing awareness of the hundreds of murdered and disappeared women from the area of Juarez, Mexico. Dr. Brown had become aware of the unusual proportions of the crimes only a couple months ago. Her knowledge of the region, though she had picked up Spanish her first year in San Antonio – it after all being very close to Italian in which she was fluent, was limited. As a neo- feminist, fully aware of the contradictions of the gender politics, she still had concerns about the disproportionate anti-female views in the Hispanic culture. It was a somber illustration to her of this lack of valuation for women that Mexico had allowed such a travesty to be "gotten away with". How could so many women die or vanish in one place without a greater outrage from many sources? Why was it not big news? She blamed American media as much as anyone else. She did not have the time right now to sabbatical to Juarez in order to investigate, so for the moment she was compiling a dossier on the cases as well as an open discussion on "Big Questions, Possible Answers". In the past such limited efforts by Dr. Brown had solved entire cases. Her energy and attention always seemed to make things happen. It was a gift and her Catholicism would say it was from God. Still, she wished she could do more. In the least it was time to update on the blog about this situation, it was not time for her regular podcast, but Dr. Brown could add blog text. Likely some regulars, who had her sign in on their alert "pop ups", would show up and comment in real time. It always happened like that. Even though she had solved crimes nationally, helped solidify international treaties, aided in corporate mergers as well as solved complex historical and philosophical academic problems, Dr. Brown, was likely more popular in "unknown blog" form to the general public than by her actual name and accomplishments.

She sat at her desk, her dark good looks unnoticed by actual eyes, brushed back her hair and began typing on the computer keyboard. She had the best high speed at home, it only took brief seconds before she was logged in and blogging:

Legion:

{Julia's Brown's online cover name}: Whose out there today? I feel like adding some comments from my latest research on the Women of Juarez. What a farce that the government of Mexico has closed its investigation on the latest killing. At least 18 girls have been identified missing in the past 14 months. These women share some similar characteristics: pretty and slender, with dark, shoulder-length hair, at least nine of them vanished while shopping downtown or looking for work. Most of these women also come from impoverished families residing in the outskirts of the city. I am leaning toward a tacit confluence of criminal, social, class and racial prejudices that have turned this area into a hunting ground for several non-connected, yet overlapping and complicit sources. Though under current International Law this circumstance may not be considered actionable on grounds of mass murder or systematic biased killings I believe it to be the pivot point on world demographic gender balance and equality.

Red Herring:

You have to be a professor with the way you write? But, yes a hunting ground is exactly what Juarez has become. A place for men with indecent, specialized tastes.

FemNazi:
Yeah - is this kind of treatment the women in the States can look forward to with the Latinization of America? I think so.

Will Rise:
Don't be too sure all the murderers in Juarez are Hispanic.

Legion:
I've thought of that – it's somehow even more disturbing to think that perhaps Anglos are traveling to take advantage of that "killing ground".

Tomorrow:
Or being sponsored to come.

Will Rise:
Are you a conspiracy theorist Tomorrow?

Red Herring:
Or a cop?

Tomorrow:
Is that projection Red Herring? I've had my suspicions about you...

FemNazi:
Hey ANIMOTY everyone!

Legion:
FemNazi is right – come guys – or gals as it maybe...

In fact "Tomorrow" was 13-year old Randel Hartman, a bored chess prodigy from Wisconsin whose mother did not monitor his Internet friends very well. At seven, Randel had mastered eighty percent of the gambits used by the Russian Masters over the last fifty years. He was hailed at twelve for winning the United States Juniors Championships by "envelopments that could have defeated Napoleon at Austerlitz and offensive originality worthy of a Super Bowl Dynasty". That was how Ben Burkheim reported the event in AMERICAN CHESS. Randel, unassuming about his chess prowess, attributed his wins in that tournament to extra helpings of sugary FRUIT LOOPS in those mornings before play commenced. He had been on a very self-aware sugar buzz the entire event and played unusually aggressive.

Despite all his early triumphs Randel was a lonely boy who had no real friends except the adults online who, not knowing his age, treated him like a peer. He retired from chess after the Juniors Championship to focus on having a "normal" adolescence. It had been anything but. A date was as likely at this point as an encounter with an extra terrestrial. After so many years attending chess tournaments, talking with girls seemed as difficult as splitting the atom with a set of Ginsu knives. Randel's mother did not encourage her son to do anything particular. She was lenient in all aspects, one of the last followers of Dr. Spock's "let children find themselves" theories. Randel found it hard to understand social interactions as easily as he did chess. Sports were also out. He didn't like swimming at all. He excelled at math and science as second nature, but was completely befuddled with history and English though insight into the psychology of killers strangely came innate to him. His contradictions left him confused about his own identity, yet his opinions about others were mostly sharp and correct.

A point in fact would be that his online buddy, RED HERRING, was indeed a sort of cop. In fact, Daniel Lebowitz, lived in Jerusalem as a retired Israeli Defense Force Colonel. His function had been as Military Intelligence Advisor to the Internal Security Department for Israel's southern districts. Daniel was a widower with no children. He, unlike Randel, still read chess manuals to improve his Sunday games in the park against fellow retirees.

Legion:
You mean to suggest that men of power are invited, as a special perk from some dominant interest like a corporation or government, to come to Juarez to be able to indulge in awful acts against women that fulfill their angry fantasies?

Tomorrow:
Exactly "invest in our Maquiladora and your CEO can hunt and rape a Mexican girl".

Red Herring:
Worse things have happened.

Will Rise:
It's too much to comprehend and hard to prove.

Red Herring:
I could see tacit approval from the Mexican authorities as a subliminal message to the government of the United States – something like – "help build our nation with incentives and trade deals or else this sort of bloody mess would grow and spill over into your country."

FemNazi:
That's sort of what I was getting at earlier. Those fuckers.

Will Rise:
But does real life work like that? These are likely, mostly, individual operators who have a motive, strange and vicious desires and an obscure, yet isolated address.

Tomorrow:
Legion do you think our looking into this can help solve this?

Will Rise:
Not likely comrade – how old are you?

Legion:
Well, I was hoping to contribute to the body of knowledge about these cases and hence
perhaps make a difference. I've sort of done that before.

Red Herring:
Hmmm... Professor or detective or...

FemNazi:
Listen to this I just found it on the Net:

Diana Washington Valdez, an investigative reporter for the El Paso Times, has covered the {Juarez} murders for three years. In her book Harvest of Women, Valdez contends the killings are part of a circuit of parties hosted by prominent Juarez citizens:

"The best information we have is that these men are committing crimes simply for the sport of it," she tells Burnett. "We know of people who've told stories about escaping from certain parties, orgies, which some of these people were present -- they were recognizable people from Juarez society, from Mexican society." In particular, she names two men with ties to the Juarez drug cartel.

"The authorities know who the killers are, and nothing's being done about it," Valdez says. "We have two issues here: people who are getting away with murder, and... authorities who have become accomplices, and so this has become crimes of the state."

Will Rise:
Sounds sort of like anecdotal evidence, not sure rich people would be so public and in it for pure pleasure as a group. I think I saw that movie in 1976 anyway.

FemNazi:
Hey since 1973 over 400 women have been killed there and over 70 still missing. Some engine is driving that machine.

Red Herring:
Maybe the crime is people in Mexico buying the allegiance of Alcoa, General Electric, and DuPont – all who have factories in Juarez through giving them something they can't get anywhere else.

Tomorrow:
An offer their perverted hearts couldn't refuse. Hey Red Herring you don't think like an American – your not are you?

Red Herring:

I never kiss and tell.

Will Rise:
Seriously folks, that almost has a ring of truth to it. Corruption and power lead to terrible vices.

Legion:
We need to keep digging folks – it's all speculation at this point – at least as far as I operate. I need direct source material, deposed confessions or eyewitness accounts to take this beyond my generalized sociological premises. I wish I could go down there for a few weeks and talk to people.

FemNazi:
That sounds dangerous. Are you that kind of person Legion?

Legion:
At times.

Julia Brown loved this group. It gave her a perspective lacking in her professional peers and she could entertain way out thoughts and their accompanying tributaries precisely as she could not in academic circles. It was all under the cover of an online blog. She loved it.

In reality, FemNazi was the closest to her blogosphere call sign: Sarabeth Johnston lived in San Francisco, had done two semesters at Berkeley in the eighties, was politically active in feminist activities, owned a cat, had tried being a Lesbian in the nineties, hated the patriarchy, but tried to like people. Sarabeth worked three part time jobs, had no expensive habits and had a social network of friends and compatriots that made life in the Bay Area pleasant. She had tuned in long time ago to finding her true self and the lifestyle of that journey, if not leading to total self-knowledge – had paid off in a peaceful existence. She had a heart to serve others and this blog was one of many great avenues for her concern.

Will Rise was a former NFL special teams player, Ben Moss, who after early retirement from a knee injury, dabbled in white supremacists groups in his home state of Alabama before giving up on racism to open a small bait and tackle shop with his last savings from professional football. Ben was fond of journaling quotes from scholars of the ages in his notebooks. The Internet had done what pro football should have and opened him up to a world of many ideas, from which he changed some of his fundamental Christian and racial leanings. He did enjoy some of the latest research coming out of David Duke in Rome that compared the polyglot empire of ancient Rome to the same declining influences here in the United States, but could no longer stomach open spite against a person simply because of their skin color. The fact that global, interracial porn had softened his racial bigotry was just another benefit of the educational properties of the Internet. He considered it a spiritual awakening and now only dated black woman he met during his monthly sojourns to Atlanta.

FemNazi:
If you do go there be careful. Those bastards who run that place are no friend to people who care about women. Many government officials and high members of the Catholic Church in Juarez, Mexico blame the women for bringing this upon themselves by wearing short skirts. Those motherfuckers.

Will Rise:
I'd back ya up Legion if you went. Though look what happened to Dog the Bounty Hunter when he went down there trying to clean up a pervert. It's dicey overall.

Red Herring:
What are the chances of getting someone from the inside, with a guilty conscience to confess?

Tomorrow:
You know that is possible – most of these killings involve long periods of imprisoning, torturing and raping these women. Even mutilations. That would produce a guilt complex in some that would be bound to come out at some time.

Red Herring:
How to coax the queen out with the castle?

Tomorrow:
Sirkorsky seventh paradigm moves are the most effective ways generally.

Red Herring:
Someone knows the Russian chess masters?

Tomorrow:
Try to forget I said it.

Legion:
You guys are on to something though. Getting to this through a source that knows something, but feels they can redeem themselves if they let it out - might be the only way. It's something to look for. If we generate enough dust someone may ask to come out of the smoke.

Tomorrow:
The more I think about it – I think finding this missing link is about the only way to penetrate the aggregate core of this problem. The methods of killing are too alike, so are the commonalities of attributes like "slenderness" in the victims that do suggest a bonded culture, with common knowledge and access to this "sport". You can shed two to four percent of the 400 victims to standard murder rates for any like given region and perhaps another percent or two to lone, "opportunist", copy-killers, taking advantage of the climate, but the degree and method of the aggregate suggest the logic of conspiracy and in the least the tacit approval of the state.

Red Herring:
The logic of your mind Tomorrow is making me more curious about you.

Tomorrow:
I am certain you are not a Native English speaker. Somewhere from the Middle East is my guess.

Red Herring:
Hmmm.

Legion:
Back on point I think Tomorrow has it close to right. This brutal phenomenon is passed down by a sub-culture, intergenerational. It's ritual for some pack. And with that there has to be a family storyteller – somewhat on the outside of the whole mess, but with enough damning details to sink that ship. Now only to find him. Well boys and girls we should scan the Netwaves for that type of person. The more we create an information storm the more it has a chance to create a feedback loop to us.

Red Herring:
There are some formal sources on that too that I can look into...

Legion:
Some fieldwork will advance this when possible. Anyone able to get to Mexico easily?
Actually there might be someone already in the prison system in the States that could be approached with a bargain specific to this issue. A person the local wardens didn't think to ask for these cases in Mexico and in turn the prisoner thought any information of that sort had no value to Americans for a leniency trade. Anyone know any officials in the border States?

Will Rise:
I'm a little east of all that.

Tomorrow:
Yeah sorry.

Legion:
No worries I'll get on that. But you all look for openings too. We've got quite the assignment. By the by I'm going out tonight for a night on the town.

Will Rise:
Getting back into the dating scene. Tomorrow thinks your recently divorced???

Legion:

Tomorrow are you some kind of psychiatrist? Well no – FYI – not dating – just checking out the local scene. Fairly new to the area and have not been out much.

Red Herring:
Have fun Legion. Be careful if you run into any hoodlums, don't openly ask them your questions. There's better ways to do that as well.

Legion:
We can get into that later – detective...bye all..

All:
Bye bye.

Julia did not really want to go out. She wasn't much of a social butterfly these days. Since the divorce she had thrown herself even more into her work. Work had always rewarded Dr. Julia Brown amply. She was fortuitous in that right away all arbiters of prestige and social gatekeepers instantly recognized her talents and bestowed, non-begrudgingly, alliances of status and position. In return Dr. Brown never let professionals down. She consistently delivered results in teaching, mentoring, writing, organizing or consulting. Her opinion always fit the facts in a way where superiors and decision-makers got the answers they needed to make their lives easier. This was an invaluable commodity in the marketplace. Still, over the last several years Dr. Brown was becoming increasingly aware of areas of life where she has large gaps of ignorance. It wasn't just with men. She began to realize there were significant ways of seeing the world that in no way conformed to the orthodox opinions leaders valued so much from her. And understanding this new way of seeing would require more than a tertiary study of Buddhism. She knew it would require immersion. There was a new mysticism to life that she was discovering. She began to label this form of knowledge "other expertise".

She saw it at times in the common understanding of her automobile mechanic and once in a while in a visiting priest. It was something her elite education had not taught. It seemed to be something that the privileged generally were not exposed to.

Ironically, it was her blog that gave her increased insight into these areas of life where fellow professors and people of civic importance declined to acknowledge or investigate. Some of her key blog comrades revealed hints of this "other expertise" in odd, often one-line, answers to questions Dr. Brown thought might require lengthy and detailed essays. Dr. Brown had come to one conclusion on the matter. This "other expertise" was not simple folk wisdom. It was a specialist skill, perhaps closer to occult or shamanic insight, and as such not a view held by the majority. It had to be sought and coaxed from oddballs and loners in the field.

Her former husband, Robert Brown – she kept the name – might have begun the lesson in breaking the barriers that had once prevented Julia from noticing "other expertise". His philandering, unknown to Julia for years – showed how apparent synchronistic values could be totally false. How one could live for years under a delusion. Bob had always called her, "Dr. Wife" – Julia took it as a criticism of her unstinting devotion to career. When he left her soul opened up to new things like a broken dam spews water. She was lost. Her professional front was easy to maintain, but she no longer trusted any anchors and foundation from her former world that allowed such a delusion to nest for so long in her home.

It was the kids that insisted she get out more at night to social events. They probably wanted the house to themselves as much as anything. They were both just old enough to enjoy that. Professor Hatkins recommended Julia visit the Coca Club for some fun. He said it was "sophisticated, yet local" – whatever that meant. Julia thought it better than to trust his judgment as he taught sociology, but what the heck she wanted something new.

Dr. Brown wore a full, casual cut, evening dress. She wasn't about to show off, though she had the figure that could. She was not against most forms of exploring and that was what justified this expedition. San Antonio proper was a tough nut to crack. She had been at Trinity University for going on five years. Usually in that time span she would think to have cultivated quite a number of important local contacts. As it were local consulting jobs were near impossible to get. She did not need the money, but the locals should have been eager to get someone of her global stature in problem solving, yet this was not the case. The locals, for a city of two million, seemed like an exclusive club afraid of outsiders. It was something Julia had never encountered before. She needed the sense of contributing to her local community. It made her feel grounded and safe as well as provided her access to people of local influence to call upon for referrals and eventually, when she gave enough to the relationship: favors. She had to influence and effect her environment. It was in her nature. This basic social schema was being denied to her in San Antonio. She was now determined to tackle the local environment on her own, guerilla style. No more network luncheons, community groups or chamber meetings. She would form bridges with the people on the ground and make waves until the larger spectrum saw her value. It was her natural response to generate a sense of purpose and security in her immediate surroundings. She would begin by challenging the sub-strata of the city, where access was readily available just by showing up. This would provide good "Intel" that she could not gain from the heights of hill, on which Trinity University so comfortably sat. She would find the core of this city and meet its possessors of "other expertise".

The buzz on campus was that the rest of the San Antonio was a ghetto of uneducated Hispanic clans and Texas "old boy" gentry best to be avoided. Julia knew enough anthropology to know this could not be the truth. Something was cooking out there that was very human, universal and essential to the make-up of the culture at large. Osmosis was happening, though "Trinity Hill" was unaware of what was absorbing into them – what was ultimately transmogrifying them into a new being: a larger entity of citizenship. Julia knew it. She felt it. Now she was going to name it.

Dr. Prosus, from the Literature Department, claimed that beyond the walls of Trinity, San Antonio had no mind. That snob did not know everything though Lit Profs tended to believe they did. Actually all in Julia's world tended to be snobs, including her, though she was willing to break out of that mold. What distinguished Dr. Prosus among his peers as a snob among snobs was his grand ability to carry out his over-opinioned persona 24 hours a day, seven days a week including in his discussions with his children, his lectures to the paperboy and when casually talking about film with whatever professor was standing next to him while pissing in the John.

Speak of the devil, there was Dr. Prosus driving from campus in his BMW. Julia waved as she walked onto campus and past his 900 series southern German made auto as it cruised past the water fountain, sprouting forth, from the side entrance of the street where her "gratis" house existed. She decided to drop off a book at the library before going out on the town. She felt obliged since it was Friday night and it would be past due by Monday. She hesitated slightly as she was dressed for an evening out and seeing a student might cause an awkward thought. Maybe she should dash to her office, change in work duds and complete the historical cost analysis of desalination systems used in the Mediterranean that was waiting on her desktop. The Economic Development Bureau of Cypress had commissioned her for an independent study of this issue. And to think she was having a hard time getting work consulting for Helen Thompson Media of San Antonio on how local businesses could benefit from BRAC – the Base Relocation and Closure program of the U.S. military that was driving growth and expansion to San Antonio's Fort Sam Houston. No, the Cypress water system paper could wait until Saturday afternoon and Sunday. She knew herself enough to realize as well this was her old defense mechanism at play. It was a hesitation, an excuse to jump back toward work when the opportunity to expand outside of the job was right at hand. It was her old dichotomy: tentativeness and fierceness.

As she walked the part of campus that lead to the library, happily absent of students, a sort of ode formed in her mind made of opinions, facts and supposition she had gathered about the campus during the last few years. There was none of that polluted feeling you got, even on the best of the east coast campuses. Trinity University's grounds might as well have been a state park. It was clean and the buildings were sterling. The tower was to her right. Fashionable at one time, now sealed because of the shooting that took place on the Austin State campus years before. She could see the Dean of Students office as well: Jolene Mission – a well-read elderly lesbian, known for bringing dollars to the school, and occasionally putting a little too much pressure on young female professors to belong to her book club. Any rumor of impropriety was unfounded as Mission's offerings were more so cloying and grandmotherly, than any actual play at sexually crossing the line. There was Gordon Perry's office; the single British import to the faculty who had made a name for himself writing two mammoth biographies of a once popular English novelist. Perry, a short man

54

with a twin brother that scorned the arts, had a definite complex that Julia had yet to decipher – pleasant fellow though overall. Then she walked by Daniel Stoessel's office; all of these professors had their abodes on "star row" with broad windows facing the main grandly landscaped, promenade that led to the library. Stoessel had escaped the Nazis before the Holocaust. He then ended up in the States as an advisor at the United Nations and consulted for some high-ranking Presidential advisors. Unfortunately, Stoessel had made the error of using UN funds to support lavish trips for his young mistress. The students liked him though because he told a good story and graded most easily.

Julia moved into the library itself, the outer shell being a reflection of the complete campus thus constructed with overdone red brick, the inside of the book reservoir centered on attractive browns and greens, yet the main stairwell was coated with a giant, absurd black and white mural, done by an independent artist, that claimed to explain civilization with imbalanced representations of Picasso bulls, Ex-Presidents, the moon landing, Hollywood stars and asunder. She walked past the mural, ignoring as much of it as she could, and dropped her book at the circulation desk where the young student eyed her fashionable appearance for a moment, then a moment later Dr. Brown was back out into the courtyard toward home. On the way she observed the blobs in front of the auditorium, to the right, these abstract sculptures did no service to the school.

They looked like vomit twists on the otherwise pristine landscaping and their grays and bronzes had no aesthetic or rational place as compared to the backdrop of the ubiquitous, evenly placed red brick.

Julia walked back past the west fountain entrance to her car. On her way, her neighbor from three houses down, Judge Bustamante Pena was jogging by. He looked like an adorable, round ball. His bulbous head had proportional symmetry to gratuitous circular gut. His shorts went far past his knees and at five foot three he resembled a darkly colored gumdrop. He was much different than the long legged, Nordic runners Julia was used to seeing back on the eastern campuses.

"How are you this evening Dr. Brown! You look lovely," said the judge in a wave that was at once commanding, flattering and creepy.

It seemed to her that the Judge, prominent and seemingly satisfactorily married, had the "hots" for her though he never did anything except give an extended greeting with a smile as wide as the Rio Grande. The Judge was a little bit of sphinx to her. She wondered if he had some "other expertise" of his own. She had to admit a weird attraction to the man as he had an odd gravity that called her. It was like he had the latent power of a veteran who had seen lots of close in combat.

She considered asking the Judge, known to be very powerful in local politics, about assisting her in how to go about finding a leak in the Cartels that may speak about the murders in Juarez. Some her fellow bloggers suspicions may be correct though in that criminal gangs have nothing to do with the flagrant murdering down there. That could be anti-drug trade propaganda starting from US backed interests or forces inside of Mexico? - the message being - "See they rape children as well as peddle dope" or "it's not us – it's those filthy drug dealers". Still some criminal must know something or the Judge might have contacts within Mexico that knew something? But no, Julia's instinct rejected asking Pena for help. She thought it violated her maxim of mixing neighbors and business. Or maybe it was something else. Still, it was her instinct and that was what she trusted.

Julia went directly to her vehicle: a 2008 black Lexus. The radio was played some heavy metal music. Michael was in a hard rock phase. It seemed to be popular in San Antonio so she assumed it helped him blend. She had dropped him off that morning at Pat Hilleveler's dojo. Michael was into martial arts these days. It helped him with the anger from the divorce though it seemed a little odd and intense to Julia. She quickly switched channels, but remembered how the other morning Michael had laughed at two local radio buffoons, Lyle and Hahn.

There was some interesting discussion though on their "Weekend Intelligence Report". A young man was insisting on the abundance of police corruption in the city. He implied several other things as well. It interested Julia as possible truth. This was the type of information she wrote about in other places. In order to know San Antonio better and to have San Antonio know her better this was the type of "retail investigation space" she could corner. On top of the specifics of such cases Dr. Brown could add interpretations of

56

cultural evolutionary theory. The boy on the radio sounded vaguely educated and could not be placed as a disaffected youth. He was not the blue collar masses nor part of the establishment. He would best be caste in the social outsider mold.

Often, Dr, Brown discovered, these types had insight into the larger social milieu of their time and place. It was a lead.

The man had implied ethnic preference and both conscious and unconscious determination selection of such a melting pot of Hispanic and Anglo influences, as was San Antonio. Historically the Texans had taken this territory by force from the Mexicans. There was of course divided loyalties of ethnic Mexicans who fought on both sides, yet now majority incentives were allowing Mexican-American identity a resurgence. The fact that this was spilling out in open dialogue on the public airwaves through semi-educated voices was a new phenomenon of acknowledgement of the natural progression of subtle cultural hegemony. Julia stayed focus on the goal for the evening, going out and having some fun, instead of jotting notes on her current train of thought she put more attention into applying fresh nail polish. Julia knew she was getting closer to the heart of San Antonio.

Julia perfected her looks as much as she intended too for going out that night. Back outside her house, it was night, she got inside the Lexus and drove after configuring the GPS.

It wasn't long before her thoughts turned back to the women of Juarez. She could use Judge Pena's attraction to her to coax any connections on the subject he may have. No, that wasn't wise. He'd expect more attention in return. Damned she was pissed about it though. She has never heard on the east coast that over five hundred females had been murdered in one city, right on the U.S. border, and no one caught. She wanted answers on that. If she played her cards right maybe she could create an overall theory and profile to tie it all together. Maybe some local authorities would use that to track down the killers. It had happened before. In the least with the Internet maybe someone local in Juarez would come froth with valuable information. She'd start a website for leads when she nailed down the profile and statistics of places and when the next killing might take place. It would take two or three months of very hard work, but she'd do it.

She then began thinking of the magazines that would pay top dollar to publish her articles on San Antonio's demographic structure, strengths and plights. It was a big story and the more she thought of it she realized San Antonio was the center of giant shift. The center of population in the United Sates was moving to the Southwest and San Antonio was more of a key city than most people understood. It would have to be supported with evidence, dissected and categorized with scientific theory and quantitative statistics, but it was something significant and Dr. Brown was on the cusp. Her thinking kept expanding on the subject, tying in what loose ends and strayed parts that might elaborate the theory. What role did racism play in all this? How about money or political demographics? What about sexual instinct? She was feeling her own as she put on a little extra lipstick whole peeking in the rear view mirror. She could write an article that Texas Monthly published. That would be an opening into the local scene. First things first – she'd hit a bar.

CHAPTER 4

The Night Life

Adam Carter did not often go out for a drink. Especially since it was only Wednesday. Still, the stress of late and the excuse of celebration after his first modest sale in weeks warranted something.

The Jones Bar was the spot Carter decided upon. His apartment was located in a sea of complexes surrounding Churchill High School. This area was once the most prestigious neighborhood in North Central San Antonio. Lately, Carter's neighborhood was under siege by gangbangers. Many were Hurricane Katrina refugees that relocated from New Orleans after the disaster. The apartment complexes were sub-divided into gang and drug zones. Fences between complexes had sections cut out to create pathways for Speed and Marijuana traffic and local skateboard troupes. In the parking lot behind Carter's apartment rested an old red Monte Carlo {Starsky & Hutch style} with white {Reverse Nike} swoosh. It was an odd relic for such a crime heavy spot. The collectable never moved. It seemed a monument to drug corruption in Carter's mind. The car sat there like a reminder of impotency. The great American cop show was a fiction. It could in no way combat the horrid deterioration of the neighborhood. The car seemed a trophy to the enemy. The mockery probably explained its longevity. It was the criminals Mount Rushmore – none would dare tamper with their public trophy.

Just last week, in the middle of the night, there had been sixteen gunshots fired in the air outside of Carter's apartment. He was still shaken by the memory of it. The apartment manager said a visiting cousin had been angry with his relative who was a tenant in the complex. The only new businesses opening in the area were convenience stores run by Arabs. They amazed Carter with their facility to penetrate any neighborhood. They picked up just enough Spanish and ghetto talk to purvey any local need. They were wondrous, if unethical traders. All items sold at their stores were handed out in the same black plastic bags. These black bags as well carried away the wide variety of pornographic material they distributed. The magazines included every fetish from barely legal to

59

mature women – any color you liked and even a few homosexual rags were visible on the porn shelves.

The Arab, it seemed to Carter, had a gift for reading individual vice and combined it with local lingo as to increase "add-on sales". One might hear, "Hey hombre care for some miniature cigars to go with that twelve pack while you watch the futballers?" – which would perfectly appeal to the vanity of some newcomer from Central America. The prices were robbery. One though could have a small, but interesting conversation with an Arab clerk if the line of customers was not too long. Generally it was more difficult to start up a talk with a fellow American citizen, who happened to be a stranger, than with an Arab. Native-born Americans were paranoid these days. Carter liked talking to new people in one-on-one conversations. Especially when they were friendly. Carter gained a little insight into Arab culture from his visits to the convenience store. Their attitudes seemed to fall somewhere in between the European/American and the Latin in qualities and expression. He did not have time or inclination to submerge into it any further. He was Custer in San Antonio, fighting off the invasion until it consumed him.

Churchill High School itself still somehow held the neighborhood together from total eclipse like an anchored ship in the eye of an immovable storm. The young people provided commerce and a sense of life. There were enough cops, overseers and storeowners looking over the welfare of the students that the neighborhood was not turned into a complete hell. The school building, decorated with giant British flag painted on the side of its squared roof, was about two miles from North Star Mall off Blanco and West. Ave. It was almost half way between the Loops of 410 and 1604 with Blanco connecting those highways. Castle Hills was still only blocks away from Churchill. It was a town within a city. Texas is famous for these. Due to strict zoning regulations Castle Hills had not changed its small, but elite town feel in forty years.

This "fiefdom" contained the exact number of businesses as it had twenty-five years before. Even the gangbangers did not speed through Castle Hills. Its two patrol cars were consistently doing fast U-turns to pull over the next car that went three miles over the limit; one after another. "Starsky & Hutch", the star cops, were alive and well in Castle Hills driving like Hollywood stunt men and handing out moving violations starting at $120 a pop.

The Jones Bar, was not in Castle Hills, but was nearby just off West Ave. about two blocks further east off Blanco. It had the opposite of a "Castle Hills" feel. It carried the theme of "Margarita Ville, Florida" with beach balls and sun umbrellas – posters of girls in bikinis and iced cold beer. It was popular, though smallish enough to almost be dingy by virtue of how cramped it was. One metal sign on the corrugated tin lined walls that "outlined" it's exterior read, "LONE STAR BEER – if you can't find it your in a foreign country." Texas has the official slogan of "the lone star state".

Carter parked strategically in a spot with enough space between itself and any other cars as to not get a possible door ding. He went toward the Jones Bar feeling like John Wayne from the Old Westerns. The small success from the sale had him pumped up. He opened the doors to the joint with bravado and walked inside. Who knew maybe tonight he would meet a girl?

Inside the Jones Bar was a mild crowd. Maybe fourteen people talking in various groups. There was no one singing karaoke or dancing. Carter decided to sit at the bar after surveying the scene.

"Can I get you something man?" said Tito the bartender, who recognized Carter as someone who came in once every two or three months.

"Oh yeah. A beer. Budweiser," answered Carter.

"Bottle okay?" responded Tito.

"Sure," said Carter.

"Great - coming up," said Tito who was the type who had to answer every phrase spoken to him with some words however brief.

Carter remembered that Tito liked to talk from the last time he had been to the Jones Bar. The two had never talked beyond initial greetings in the past. Most of Carter's drinking over the last year was done with misery on the mind; this would be the first with a slight hint of celebration. Tonight he would not mind talking a little with someone.

Tito brought over the Budweiser to Carter within twenty seconds.

"You come in once in a while. I remember you," said Tito.

"Yeah I'm not a big drinker," replied Carter.

61

"That's understandable, but you like to get out every now and then," said Tito. "Yeah just a change of scenery," agreed Carter.

"Got a lot on your mind?" asked Tito.

"Ah – a little bit – lot going on out there you know," answered Carter.

"That's for sure," agreed Tito.

Carter was surprised how intimate Tito had gotten in a short time. He had seen this before from bartenders. He was getting uncomfortable and his plan to be happy shrank. He decided to throw out a general concern that might put the man off the trail of his real personal demons. Perhaps if he said something odd then Tito would leave him alone altogether, dismissing him as a quack that could not be understood.

"Dude do you realize if only the country would have paid attention to the moral of the first half of the movie "The Magnificent Seven" back in 1960 we could have avoided the whole God-damn Viet Nam War," challenged Carter.

"Kennedy must have only watched the second half, that's when they twisted the story into something like the triumph of the outsider heroes. At least Yul Brenner was in it. He did something noble at the end of his life when he went on TV looking awful and warning how bad cigarettes were," answered Tito.

Shit, thought Carter, this cat knows history, politics, flicks and saw the socially conscious side of Yul Brenner.

He wouldn't be so easy to shake.

"God damn right – God damn right – it's clear from the first half that no good can come when a bunch of gringo cowboys go to some poor country and though skilled – they are outnumbered and even turned upon by the locals they are trying to help... - no reason to fight – no reason at all," elucidated Carter.

"Yeah then Hollywood adds the fantasist's second half – we're the good guys win out, save some people and prove the moral. They should have stopped in the middle when the gringo cowboys were rounded up and captured like fools. That's the real ending of those sort of things," prophesied Tito.

"Exactly," agreed Carter, amazed at this bartender's insight and depth, "Hey I got to piss."

"Be my guest," said Tito as he pointed the way.

Carter got up to go to the restroom. It was an ordinary piss for a man of his age: a little slow, but it all came out okay. As he relieved himself he studied the poster on the bathroom wall. It was an uncanny reflection of what the interior of his soul had become.

It spoke of him. In the poster a decrepit matador, wearing ragged outfit, held a shredded red cape as he feebly lured a miniature toy bull, made of empty beer cans whose only mobility to charge were harmless looking roller skates. The matador, with his posture that was meant to dare, was merely a mockery. This was what really hurt Carter deep down. This silly caricature was how he felt, and ironically it was how he perceived the self-effacing, impoverished personas of Mexicans when he first encountered them in his youth. The gritty soul must have been there back then, but it was covered up with Uncle Tom-like buffoonery. That clown act was gone now. The Mexicans were the majority and their true face for good or ill was what they led with in most cases. The old mockeries sometimes resurfaced in jest slightly or as a reflex when an old member of Hispania encountered an old guard white bigot. Tito seemed to perform a balance of this charade, enjoying dashing between the elder generations obsequiousness and the new edge. It was intriguing. Carter knew enough to tell Tito was playing a game with the facts and perceptions. In fact Tito was the alcoholic third son of an aluminum mogul from Del Rio, Texas. Tito wanted to be a stand up comic. He considered these performances practice for his act and beyond that being generous soul and black sheep of the family would go to large extents to people please.

For Carter, who since boyhood had difficulty with change, the new world had turned upside down as if overnight. He had been in the north for seven years and out west/northwest for ten years before that. It was not like this yet in that part of the country though the embers of change were evident. The problem for Carter was that he needed people to be weak, or at least many of them, so he could pretend to be powerful; if it was all the display of theater, of "Toming" in some form, then that was okay with Carter. It was enough to make his ego feel safe. That game was cracking in America. Minorities were becoming majorities and homey didn't play that. In a way Carter was no better than an Old Master's overseer: His persona lingering uncomfortably on the fence, milquetoast, between Mister Fletcher and Captain Bly. Closer still

Carter needed someone to be pathetic alongside. His soul was Peter Loire carelessly holding a small revolver, hands shaking. He had to constantly guard himself. In fact every group; women, blacks, gays, Mexicans – they were all claiming great strength publicly and this strength seemed to need a weak enemy to vanquish and Carter's type was it. White people distrusted Carter because he was smart and the rest sensed this and gang-tackled. Carter zipped up his fly and went back out to talk with Tito. His mood had changed again. He wanted to talk to the bartender. At least Tito knew how to chat it up half way properly.

Carter was happy to see none of the other customer's had taken him away so he ordered another beer to keep Tito's attention.

"How about a Corona?" ordered Carter.

Tito served another beer. It was his ten thousandth, but no one was counting. No door prize bell rang for that moment in history, even Tito didn't know he had hit a milestone.

"Try a little Mexican this time," said Tito a he handed over the beer from south of the border.

"Why not," agreed Carter.

"That's what she said," joked Tito.

"Ha ha – very funny," said Carter.

"You want to see why we are losing the drug war?" asked Tito.

"Okay," said Carter.

Tito took out his iphone. Carter marveled at it. This bartender, Tito, had an expensive $500 tech contraption – again it hit home, despite the day's success, all were doing better than he. His ability to get too high from a minor win was dangerous.

Tito pushed a few buttons and up came a UTUBE video of a dancing Mexican Federali Policeman. He was spinning wildly around a large sombrero while tossing dollars above his head, which flapped around his head like flying leprechauns in a poor Irishman's dream.

For a moment Carter saw it – the innocent childhood glee of the dancing Mexican policeman – carelessly giving in to corruption for that simple sake of personal happiness, Jeffersonian perhaps, in a world drug war much larger than himself that was not worth any sacrifice of his own. Why not? We should all be so lucky and carefree. Take the money and run, do it for your family, damn the larger consequences – no, no, no it was not the ethics of his own internal dialogue, no, no – he must reject this view...

Carter exclaimed, "what a dumb son of a bitch – think of how many murderers he has let slip into the U.S. with their filthy drugs."

"I didn't say it was pretty. It's the face of war," said Tito. "Oh yeah a real war it is," said Carter.

"Hey nearly 17,000 have died in it since 2006. 45,000 Mexican police have died in the last twenty years, we lost 58,000 soldiers in the war in Viet Nam – it's almost the same number – ratio wise. You can't argue with that," declared Tito.

"Maybe not. You know San Antonio hasn't been the same since the drive-ins closed down," diverted Carter put hoping to lose Tito with an odd train of thought.

"Oh I see you blame the Mexicans for all this – well Mexicans can be tricky, but it was not the loss of the drive-ins where the Mexicans really took over this town, it was when the young stopped going out to party after the killing on St. Mary's Street began to shut a lot of things down," explained Tito.

"Yeah that was pretty bad, St. Mary's Street was like a mini Bourbon Street four nights a week," agreed Carter surprised Tito, a Mexican, was going with him on this train of thought.

"Yeah the town lost its balls for mixing after that ugly affair. It's a graveyard down there now. Used to be big business. I was working down there that night when the killing happened on the street," revealed Tito.

"It actually occurred in alley beside Huey's – that's the place where those two college kids got jumped, near the garbage dumpster in the back of the parking lot," recalled Carter.

"Well that was not the whole story," said Tito, "the white guys taunted the hell out of those Southside Mexicans first," assured Tito.

"Oh yeah – still you don't murder someone," said Carter.

"It started out as a simple fist fight, then got out of hand... You can't mess with the passion of folk from the barrio like that so easily. There are consequences," said Tito.

"I guess a lot of things start out like that and go wrong," said Carter, "but it was more than symbolic – whites and Mexicans were in a real fight for that piece of property down there – it was nice, party real estate at night and classy dining for business lunches and perfectly located in the center of the city between the north and south side – it was like a game of chicken being played down there that kept escalating until some suckers got waxed," remembered Carter.

"Sam Stamper wasn't a sucker," interrupted a beefy man-boy next to Carter. "Who's that," said Tito.

"The guy killed on St. Mary's street that night, he was a friend of mine" he said. "Oh – sorry about that – it was an ugly mess," consoled Carter.

Tito moved off a little bit to tend to other customers.

"Yeah is was nasty. Sam was a good guy. He was a really good guy and didn't deserve what happened to him, but it was a long time ago," he said.

"Hey what do you do now?" asked Carter changing the subject as he noticed how unusually big and muscular, yet short this man was.

"Oh I'm Tom Pettinger by the way. I do some personal training. Lately been selling quite a bit of Florida Coral Burials," said the guy.

Tom's friend, a beefed up clone, rejoined him from his trip to the restroom and sat on the bar stool on the side of Tom. Then Carter put it together, Florida, personal trainer, short, massive and a friend with the same look – these were steroid junkies.

"Coral Burials. I've never heard of that," said Carter eyeing the man's bulging neck whose veins looked as if they would pop out at any minute or at least send the tight gold chain around his neck spiraling off into orbit as it burst loose from its burdened clasp.

"Man they are the latest thing – super cool stuff – when you die we take your remains out to the Coral off Florida's south coast on a 48 foot yacht. Your remains are exquisitely placed in a lead lined and gold rimmed submersible urn, after cremation of course, and we dive down to place them in the underwater "seamatery" surrounding the beautiful rejuvenated Coral. See look at that," said the guy as he flashed a photo from his iphone that showed an underwater "seametary", complete with gaudy statuary of the ancient Greek God Poseidon with several nymphs.

The site lay in front of the natural wonder of a wall of live Coral. Color fish of all ilk and size darted amongst the burial ceremony of about twelve mourners and a reverend in scuba gear.

"If you don't scuba you can still go visit your deceased relatives last resting place with a tour on a mini-submarine," said Pettinger.

"Huh, that is pretty cool," agreed Carter who was noticing how these pair of steroid men had tropical shirts and shorts sporting bold colors that likely matched the vibrancy of the underwater gravesite.

"Might you be interested in a plan for such arrangements for yourself?" asked Pettinger's buddy.

"Yeah I might," said Carter.

"Cool – give me your cell number – I'll plug it into my iphone and set up a meeting with you when we can both check our schedules. I think you'll be pleased with the pre-planning it's not much different from a regular funeral home. What's your number," said Pettinger.

"Ah – 210-555-6767," answered Carter.

"Cool got it. Listen man we gotta jet, but we'll catch on the flip side," said Pettinger.

"Okay sounds good," said Carter.

The two men left the bar.

Tito returned to Carter moments later.

Carter was flipping through his copy of Cervantes' famous book Don Quixote.

"Did you know Texas has executed three cannibals?" said Tito.

"Had no idea," said Carter.

"It's true," said Tito.

"It's a weird place full of death and destruction and maintenance – a lot of maintenance," said Carter.

"Never thought of it like that – but that is exactly it," said Tito.

"Hey I might win a couple of free tickets for the Spurs game tomorrow night – if I do ya wanna go? It'll be nosebleed section, but it's the Spurs," said Carter.

"Thanks man, but I can't – my cousin is having her sixteenth birthday party – I said I'd show up, but thanks," said Tito.

"Hey Dick Beak get over here," said a new guy who had walked into the bar and was referring to Tito and his obviously big, hooked shaped nose.

"My friend how are you," saluted Tito as he went over to the new man immediately.

Tito passed on attending the most popular "local mass" with Carter at San

Antonio's number one religion – The San Antonio Spurs. Carter failed to make a pal.

Likely Tito was just spouting his philosophy that night or being entertaining. Tito was a guy who enthusiastically greeted a man who called him "Dick Beak" {Tito did have a large nose} but would not go out to see the Spurs with Adam Carter. Carter felt abandoned. As he did in such times he mumbled aloud his reading of Cervantes' text, opened randomly, as if it were prayer.

""*Observe Sancho*", *said Don Quixote, "that virtue is persecuted wherever it exists to an outstanding degree. Few or none of the famous heroes of the past escaped the slander of malice. Julius Caesar, a most courageous, most wise and valiant captain, was branded as ambitious, and not over-lean either in his clothes or in his habits. Alexander, whose exploits won him the title of the Great, was said to have been given to some measure of drunkenness. Hercules, the hero of the many labours, is said to have been lascivious and effeminate. Sir Galaor, the brother of Amadis of Gaul, is criticized for having been over lecherous, and his brother for being a blubberer. So, Sancho, among so much slander against good men, what they say against me may pass, if it is no more than you have told me.*"

'*Ah, there's the trouble, damn it,*" *replied Sancho* 'Is *there anything more, then?*" *asked Don Quixote.* 'There's *still the tail to skin,*" *said Sancho.*"

A man's voice broke into Carter's thoughts. "Like books huh?" said the man. Carter came out of his reverent daze, but still hadn't focused – then again: "I said you like books huh?" repeated the man.

Carter looked to his right. An older man had sat next to him.

"Oh yeah a little bit," answered Carter.

"I don't have much care for books. I like a good movie once in a while, but most of them are unrealistic," said the man.

"Yeah I know what you mean," said Carter.

"You been in the service?" asked the man.

"The what?" said Carter.

"The military. I guess not," said the man.

"Me – no, never, but my family had been in going all the way back to the

American Revolution," said Carter.

"Really wow. See people who been in the military know what's real more than the rest of folks. Even if they hadn't been in war, they still know a little more," assured the man.

"I would imagine that is right," said Carter.

"It is. I was in war though, killed 7 men on Iwo, 2 of them with my bare hands and a knife, didn't get no real medals, well actually came back with two "medals", "metals" in my left arm that took this chunk of flesh," the man showed Adam Carter the missing flab of flesh where there should have been a triceps' muscle, "and the "metals" that embedded in the right leg – oh yeah I got proof too – see here," – the man pulled down his shirt to reveal a necklace of smashed bullets that had been removed from body during combat surgery.

The old man flashed a wide grin: an earthly and potent grin, nearly the embodiment of malevolence; a grin that a man so old should not have been capable of. It was as if the furnace of Hades was fueling this old timer with power based on years of bragging about death and never grieving it. Adam Carter noticed as the braggart's pronouncements spewed forth, the way this man's sleeve, on the left arm, flapped copiously from having too much open air between where the fabric was and where the missing flesh should have rested.

"You know we even skinned a Jap on Iwo," added the old man.

This guy was barbaric thought Carter and something about his words was making him feel violent. At the same time Carter was rejecting this man's words he was conjuring his own images of violence that would be justified.

"Hmmm," mused Carter.

"Yeah I don't know why you offered to take that Spick to a basketball game? Take me, I'm a genuine hero," said the man.

"Oh – I don't really have tickets. I was just trying to be nice. I knew he'd say no," said Carter.

"Oh," said the man.

Carter realized the old guy had just called Tito a Spick. It made him sick. He glared briefly at the old guy. As if feeding off Carter's growing negativity the old one continued jabbing.

"Sometimes I'd look to go up to all the Spicks that run this bean town and give a big Nazi HOOYAH!! in their faces – the arrogant bastard wetbacks," said the old guy.

The old guy had made Carter viscerally sick. They should outlaw drinking for certain people. Why was the old creep drinking at all thought Carter? He had seen drinking destroy. Had he mentioned drinking destroyed his mother? He was angry. Why did he have to see that old man at all?

It was the racism that made him sick: the name-calling. Carter didn't call names. It was not hatred that fueled his dislike of the status quo, it was his send of divine injustice. Carter's belief was pure, it was obvious God or nature had made him more sensitive and intelligent than others. That should be honored. He should not live a life of hardship, but rather society should recognize him. He even believed, divinely, that everyone should be recognized. But in no case should he be at the lower end of the hierarchy. He actually blamed the situation on Hitler. If he had not terrorized the world with the belief that blonde haired, blue-eyed people were supreme – then there would not be today the vast, if unconscious, hatred and persecution of blonde hair, blue-eyed people.

In any case there was no need for name-calling, blonde jokes or even hatred in his world schema. It just was fact that he had a natural goodness and intelligence, but it wasn't being acknowledged. There was Carter's schizophrenia. The two things he could not hold in his mind at the same time. He thought he remembered a time when the races were like ships and whales on the open sea, the water was for everybody and even though whales and ships were of equal heft, they shared the water and did not collide without purpose. Now the relations were more like cars and pedestrians in the sprawling strip center parking lot. There was a constant shuffle for supremacy and before long there were inevitable crashing into each other.

"I'll take a Spick over a Nigger though any day – so fuck basketball anyway," blurted in the old, foul man.

"Excuse me I have to go," said Carter leaving and extra dollar on the bar for Tito he got up and left.

"Feeling sick are we?" the old man called after him. Carter was out the door. Why hadn't society given Carter a license just to murder foul creatures with mouths like that? Murder them on the spot. Those air takers: Sub-humans – Iwo Jima or not. Carter wanted no part in their open conspiracy of name-calling. Carter and these sort of bad mouthing beasts were not the same. Carter clutched Cervantes closer and made it into his car.

Alone in his car Carter felt better. He placed Cervantes on the passenger seat. His life was not philosophy or words. It should be understood. It was not public debate. It should be religion taught early on in the home so people carried it out in public without debate. Carter was special god damn it and people should know it!

His cell phone rang. "Hello? Hello?" no one answered, but he heard voices.

"The Councilman wants the job done tomorrow night," said the voice at the other end of the phone, but he wasn't calling for Carter.

Carter recognized the voice. It was the steroid guy he had just a chatted with in the bar Pettinger, something or other, who was into water graves.

"Why can't the Mexicans do it?" said the Pettinger's buddy.

"Cause they want him scared not dead," said the guy.

This phenomenon had happened before to Carter. Not with such drastic language at the other end. The last time this happened he heard some rich father yelling at his teenage daughter that, "I can go in any room in this house, anywhere I like cause I pay for it all. Why don't you want me to go in your room? Did you buy another pair of $150 sunglasses? Stop buying $150 sunglasses!"

It was a butt dial; an accidental calling of a number, often recently accessed, and plugged into your cell phone's memory. Some kind of karma was dicing out all sort of intrigue at Carter this week – he listened on – the massive glut muscles of the steroid freak must have betrayed him:

"I guess they might want to set up the reporter to eventually land him on their payroll someday," said the buddy.

"Now your learning – the guy we rough up this week could be our associate next week – that's how these Mexicans roll. Ya gotta go with it," said Pettinger.

"Hey its more work for us – I won't complain," said the buddy.

"That's the idea," agreed Pettinger, "hey have you seen that Steve Winwood CD?" asked Pettinger.

"It's over here," said the buddy. "Thanks," said Pettinger. "At least we won't have to meet up with that creepy Chink med examiner on this one," said the buddy.

"Got that right...Hey oops – hello – hello?" said Pettinger.

Carter hung up.

He shouldn't have been listening: Silent, frozen panic. His phone rang. It was the steroid freak calling him back. It was easy to see what number had been "butt dialed" and how long the call had lasted. If Carter had hung up right away nothing would have mattered. He was busted. He didn't answer. He'd pretended he didn't hear anything. They'd never look for Carter anyway. He hadn't heard any real details had he? They didn't know him anyway. Tito knew nothing really about him. He hadn't paid with credit card had he? Would they cruise the neighborhood? These guys were gangsters. He kept running into criminals. Was that the advertising business or the poverty that brought him so close to this group? He had just seen the reporter with the councilman. They had been talking about the medical examiner. People on both sides of the law were onto each other. A showdown was coming. This sounded like the stuff the wheelchair guy, Pearson, was into. Maybe he'd bring it up to Pearson when he saw him next? Maybe. Maybe it was best to try to forget about it? Pettinger hadn't left a message when he called back. Maybe Pettinger was going to forget about it? Carter wasn't going back to the Jones Bar anytime soon. Maybe never.

It had taken Tom Pettinger years to build his cover identity in San Antonio, Texas. He had been a fairly big shot in Orlando, Florida before unpleasant circumstances with the Russian mob made him flee to his grandmother's house in San Antonio. He was familiar with Texas since childhood and he had made a few border runs into small Mexican pharmacias to load up on steroids to sell to the gym market back in Orlando. It would be easy to judge Tom Pettinger's story by evaluating the surface, but as with most things it dug deeper than just the surface.

Tom Pettinger's father was fluent in several languages including Vietnamese, which he used in the jungles to extract information from prisoners. The closest Tom Pettinger came to this sort of daring, his father having risen to Colonel in Special Ops, was enlisting in the Air Force and functioning as an electronic radar specialist. He had talent with gadgets, but no one ever praised him enough in that area for him to do anything legitimate with it. Drug dealers had praised Tom's daring graciously over the years. It was them that he needed to please deep down as surrogates to the absent praise of his father. The Pettinger didn't praise much as a whole, but Tom was the type who especially required positive reinforcement.

His family was so self-consumed they weren't even greatly aware of this fact. His family had always felt a little ripped off since back in the 1800's they sold Ringling Brothers Circus some key pieces of land in the Carolinas on the cheap.

Tom Pettinger had gone outside the normal standard sets of bravery to find himself. His crazy boldness clicked full on in the mountains of Columbia, where the Russians sent him on a mission to check out a possible cocaine supplier. The banditos put a hood over his head and raced him up a hairy pass on the sides of steep cliffs to a manufacturing facility. At the mountain factory – the hood was taken off, the machine guns lowered and Tom Pettinger's eyes rested on the Holy Grail; a stack of cocaine seven feet high. Impressed with the suppliers facilities Tom went back to Florida to give the go ahead to the Russians that this source was worthy of doing business with. Yeah Pettinger was an addict. Perhaps the impossible legacy of the Founding Fathers made all Americans addicts who used because they were unable to live up to perceived expectations. Lots of business owners who thought slavery should make a come up actually liked it that way. Make em' for it and make em' work hard.

It took only two years living out of his Grandmother's house in San Antonio for Tom to established his steroid posse of white males who were driven by envy, thrived in the party scene and were willing to break the law to gain power. The boys in Pettinger's pack were all between 20 and 30 years old, were capable grass roots drug dealers and twice their normal size from vigorous regiments of weight lifting and heavy duty steroids. They bonded on their feeling of superiority and their lust to be near a very strong, power source without paying too many rookie dues. Though many were from middle class backgrounds, none had developed legitimate skills and education as to gain access to privilege by traditional routes.

Serving the Mexican Drug Cartels was an acceptable option for them. It gave them money and connection to people who could make things happen, but also people who needed them for their own special status as insiders in American society. They were highly valued because they were willing to break the law to get ahead quickly.

Tom wasn't sure what to do about the nerd who seemed to have overheard some his dealings during the "butt call"? It was likely the guy couldn't figure anything out and if so wouldn't do anything about it. It was best not to hunt him down and give cause or leave clues. "Doors not opened, don't have to be closed". It was an old saying of his father.

Everything about Tom Pettinger was fake, cautious, perceptive and needy. One of the bumper stickers on the sports car he drove, often much too fast, read, "Native Texan". He decorated his grandmother's living room with fine replication sketches of Medieval Art next to gaudy, faux Swedish horse statues and an imitation print of George Washington crossing the Delaware. He hated Obama, but loved to do the "fist bump" with his buddies. He never read a book that didn't involve how to make more money, but he could occasionally spit out a Freudian analysis of a slip that would cut a seasoned intellectual to the marrow.

CHAPTER 5

Big Irish

Walt McKinley was six feet six inches of Scotch-Irish mustard. His great great-grandfather had come to Texas with the Tennessee Volunteers under Davy Crockett that held out at the Alamo. A quick engagement with a prostitute in the El Bexar Hotel, before being slaughtered by Santa Anna's troops at the gates of the old Mission, produced Walt's great grandfather and the San Antonio line continued from there to present day. Now, the memories that great battle and all the love making that happened in the El Bexar Hotel, all that once hallowed earth around the Alamo, is continuously trampled by the feet of hundreds of thousands of tourists, year upon year. There are many who believe the grounds of the Alamo to be haunted by ghosts of the slaughtered dead from that great battle. One sensitive to such otherworldly vibrations can discern this by walking near the outer walls of the old Mission called the Alamo.

Walt's red-haired line was old school San Antonio. They were South Side Anglos, with a sprinkling here and there of Hispanic genes "blended in for good measure". They held onto blue collar and city jobs of increasing influence generation after generation. These old salt types were folk who had learned to put up with the slander of the Northsiders and the hushed-toned views of TV newscasters and the treason-like print from the Hearst paper about how dangerous and unlivable the South Side of San Antonio always was. They knew the South Side was the heart and soul of the city. It was community with memory and roots. The District by Old Windsor Park Mall had plenty of proper families. It didn't matter that many were Anglo because the culture was so fluid that shared values and community exchange took dominance over any sort of ethnic rivalry the media or chicken shit Northsiders liked to stir up. No matter that Windsor Park Mall had remained an empty, eyesore shell for over twenty-five years – renovation of the South Side would come in full one day. The Toyota plant had come. King William's District had resurged. The river expansion was planned for going south as well as north {that part had already been built}. It was true that South Side developments had created isolated neighborhoods.

Neighborhoods whose regeneration possessed only limited beneficial spillover to the community at large. A lot could be blamed on the growing emergence of nasty, authoritarian Neighborhood Planning Committees that hogged the good development. They had no embarrassment about telling less attractive businesses in their neighborhood, though area favorites or landmarks, to bring in the bulldozers if it meant a piece of the action.

Like his father and grandfather Walt McKinley worked for the city. It was a solid living with enough pay and pretty good benefits for those who could survive city politics, budget cuts and endless revisions by City Mangers that came to power with each new mayoral administration. The McKinley's were survivors. They knew how to play the San Antonio game. In fact their line helped develop it. They were backbone people. Over the years they attended social lunches with big shots of all ilk that demanded obedience and deference. They knew how to keep a tight lip. If a family got known well enough at these mixers, and consistently refrained from insulting anyone, they could move up in San Antonio. The McKinley's were masters at this art. They were alike to a crew of eternal worker bees, vigilant in their task holding firm the family stations, with perhaps incremental gains from year to year. They did not hold pretentions of vast increased in status. They were resolute and hence always on the proper docket. When the wear and tear of the game playing got to them they knew how to retreat into the private and ritualized joys of family. One remedy for their souls was "Sports Sunday" on television. On Sunday the males of the clan got together, drank beer and riotously ragged on all the pompous pigeons of the city that they had to listen to that month. It was a decent trade off that elevated their standard of living each generation.

Walt was accustomed to mixed crowds of all walks of life. He knew how to patiently maintain deference to all majorities and superiors, speaking seldom, smiling often and joking about the wider American mainstream culture as depicted on television where they weren't really like San Antonians altogether. Walt could worship good enchiladas, praise the rodeo and the city's professional basketball team; The San Antonio Spurs, never take Selena the Tejano singer's name in vain, talk occasionally about his high school football days with fondness and let people know that he worried tremendously about the future of his children and yours. If you had a cause he supported it. If you wanted to friend on FACEBOOK he did it. Actually, by the time the family genes manifested into Walk McKinley, even though he was 6 foot 6 inches tall, the old fire of the rowdy Tennesseans who came to the Alamo had pretty much trickled down to a pilot light on an old gas stove oven. Even beer did not bring out much of his clan's biases on Sundays. Most would call this progress, but others may say that none would ever build a shrine to the new McKinleys.

Walt was on the inside of the system with the fluencies and expertise of a true native. When out with the boys who worked with him at the city he always drank the regional brew, Shiner Bock, though for the last few years he had taken to consuming Fosters Lager in the privacy of his home. He could evade entrapping gossip with wink and generally expected a clear shot to a comfortable retirement. He knew the players of the main game in San Antonio: The break down was easy; several powerful, old Protestant – many Presbyterians families – controlled the heart of the city, with alliances to organized Catholics forces and the help in civics from "outside hire" or homegrown talent that helped the infrastructure move along. Below this level though was seedy, yet significant network of city officers, judges, police and local powers that could be very nasty. How these groups kept things going was mysterious, but with the advent of new criminal elements that heavily infiltrated the management core and democratic pushes from grassroots Latinos the mix was getting a shake-up.

Walt McKinley was a quiet epicenter of all the forces that made up San Antonio. Being a city Health and Standards Inspector he got around and saw much of the mechanisms of the town. He was like liquid glue bonding strange and differing alchemical pieces that needed connection so the place could keep its history. He had made a name for himself with the newspapers and local TV news for his crackdowns on buffets in San Antonio in the 1980's and in general was an influential cog in the wheel.

Friday seemed like any other day for Walt. He had a note to check out some new portable taco stands on the Southwest side of town. They all checked out fine for cleanliness and paperwork. It almost looked to be an early day to head back to the downtown offices, but a truck that had the word "Bread" written on its side caught his eye. It was parked behind a pool hall. There had been some problems last year with bars running mini-kitchens without licensing. Walt was one to check such things out more closely. No one was in truck, but the back door to the pool hall was slightly ajar. A mangy dog running loose crossed his path as he walked to go inside the establishment.

Once inside, a knife quickly came at his side, the switchblade cut a small portion of the fat on the "spare tire" of his gut, though Walt had darted aside enough that the wound was minor, though the blood covered the lower part of his shirt rapidly. Walt swung his clipboard at the man and bashed the side of his head before he felt a thump on his back as another man, unseen from outside, charge him and with such a great force that the tackle propelled the giant Scotch-Irishman through the swinging doors of the kitchen and out into the main pool room where the two fell on each other in a scramble. Walt rolled violently, crushing the man's cheek with his elbow and spinning up to his feet faster than a guy his size should have been able to do. It was then that Walt, the tenured city inspector, was awakened by the full recognition of being in the wrong place at the wrong time. The big man was in trouble. Six more men, gang members, were amassed around the pool table over-looking a large stash of weapons and drugs. It was not the place for a guy with a button down shirt, a city badge and who had been holding an officious looking clipboard to be the center of attention.

"Vato must die," said one of the men.

In fact it was the meeting of two small gangs and a deal. The man who spoke took the leadership and spoke for all. Maybe it was lucky for Walt that part of the deal meant no had a loaded gun on them? Maybe.

Three of the Mexican guys pulled switchblades and snapped them open, two more grabbed pool sticks and the sixth a bar stool. Something inside Walt clicked; there was no time or way to run. He charged, yelling like a wild boar, into the men – swinging his broad framed limbs chaotically and smashing the nose of the guy holding the stool, then a flicker to his left and he had another small knife wound to his upper back, screams from all and his fist came down with a crack like a hammer on the top of the knife wielder's head who just stabbed him, the man fell limp, then a pool stick broke over Walt's shoulder, but Walt took the remaining piece of stick out of the man's hand and thrashed it across another's ear – the attackers were blending together, it was impossible to know who was know, more yells and cursing began, then another knife at him, this time he blocked it with some move he might have learned from the movies or as a child taking karate at the community center, it was all instinct, yet one thing was true - in that moment he was more alive than any of his clan had been for the last hundred years, then another knife thrust – this one wounded, and caused terrible pain, as it caught the full side of his stomach – yells and attacks, swings and misses, blood going to the floor, Walt was choking one man and kicking another, there was much blood, in that second Walt felt like Gibson in BRAVEHEART, but this wasn't a movie – a guy from behind, the one from the kitchen hit him full force with a iron skillet in the back of the head, his grip loosened on his foes and he fell to one knee. Several struck him at once with assorted weaponry, it was near the death blow, he managed to retrieved one of the dropped knives and slit a man hard and good, before finally, completely falling to the floor and being pounced by death.

CHAPTER 6

Man On The Run

Barry Juarez wasn't the first reporter on the scene. Still, it looked like nothing had been tampered with by the cops and he was one of only three let inside to observe the crime scene. This was definitely one Barry could play up in his "Cafferty File" style investigative and opinionated reporting. It was a bloody mess and that would insure popularity. It was drug related so that made it Barry's main beat and it had the touch of something one could put their imagination to. How in the world had a city health inspector walked in on two Westside gangs trading loot for stash? There were a number of ways Barry could take this as he wandered in circles in the alley behind the crime scene, while formulating his weekly column through spoken word into his hand held voice recorder:

"Giant Southsider, the city's Walk McKinley, health inspector found dead in a pool of blood, police sources say he fought fiercely with up to seven vandals as our hero wounded at least three, based on the blood spattering before being sent to Southside's Valhalla – it must have almost been like that scene from the Green Beret where the big sergeant fights nine Viet Cong alone in the jungle. Afterward John Wayne comes on the scene and says the sergeant must have killed them all or they wouldn't have left "this" behind as he holds up the fallen soldier's M-16 rifle. Though in this fight, here in San Antonio, our "sergeant" didn't take them all with him. We are losing this fight – losing because the bad guys took away their dead, their drugs, their weapons... we good citizens are the General Custers. We are the ones who are paying..."

Or maybe this one needed to be played with a different spin – like the one that got Barry the City Desk Award last year:

"What was a City Health Inspector doing in the middle of Westside drug deal? How much do we know about Walt McKinley? Was it a deal gone wrong? Victim, accomplice or coup against the inside man? Just who are the masterminds behind the city's drug problems – does the search need to go into the city itself?"

Barry didn't have to decide right away how to spin this one. He'd do a little more research and then see what fit best for the best result. He had to get downtown fairly quickly. He was scheduled to meet an informant at the Gunter Hotel. Barry was planning to gain some info on the machinations of the City Counsel. It had become a more powerful, and in ways a more secretive body, over the last decade. Barry was suspicious and needed more data on the individual council members. These were not as accessible as the last wave. There was something more mercenary about this bunch. It resembled what Barry had noticed as a general trend of society overall. The informant said he had some details about BRAC, the military base relocations and closures, which might prove of interest to the reporter. Funny thing was that council seat where Ft. Sam Houston was located was held by a young Yale grad that seemed a stand up sort of person. Then again the military was big bucks, the third biggest contributor to the local economy after tourism and medical – so anything was possible. Any informant who could afford a room at the Gunter might be somehow near the inside of whatever was going on. Info from the inside was always best.

The drive to the Gunter was an odyssey through American style. The first neighborhood Barry had to drive through was sandwiched between the Westside and Downtown. It was a blue collar stretch of properties that held on to their pretenses of civility, but in reality creating numerous defense systems by deploying a minefield of hexes and barricades in the forms of lawn gnomes, bird houses, police and fireman residents, dog walkers with sticks, teens savagely playing basketball in the street under a portable hoop, ex-army NCOs' speed walking while carrying batons, lawnmowers left in the front yard, miniature fences with small spikes on the tops and extra cars in the driveway.

The fools could not hold off the inevitable thought Barry. This neighborhood too would go down to poverty and crime. Marissa, his lover, had said Barry was a self- hating Mexican. The only truth Barry could find in that statement was that he hated all people in this part of the country who did not want to vigorously improve and reform their lives and society as a whole. His family had been

Canary Islanders. They were Spaniards, some of Sephardic Jewish heritage, who had settled San Antonio for the Spanish Crown in the early days. Barry still had their pride. A testament plaque to the Canary Islanders, the first 13 families to settle San Antonio, was in front of the main Courthouse downtown. It did not mean anything to Barry that being a "Canary Islander" had become somewhat of a San Antonio joke as every other family claimed descent from these harbingers. Barry knew the truth of his roots. He was of Canary blood. His people had greatness and wanted to build something great. Now most Tex-Mex folk were a bunch of holy-roller Jesus lovers who chased stories of Chupacabras on the holidays – thought Barry snobbishly: too much tainted Indian blood. They needed fewer switchblades in high school and more Mark Twain thought Barry. He really belonged in the Manhattan market. A Pulitzer would do it for him. He needed enough of a sensational, true story to create enough of an even more sensational lie, then the critical mass of readers would send his reputation through the roof, the waves of which would be felt across the nation.

Quick swerve to the left, Barry was almost done in by a mad rushing VIA bus, he didn't have time to get the number, but he knew the line. He thought he put them in place last year with his article on how the public bus system was losing it's legitimacy with rampant accidents involving driving into pedestrians, taking off before handicapped passengers fully unloaded and generally running over poor people and commuters alike. Video-texting of pornography by bus drivers was the main culprit in his featured case. Via transit system was yet again an example of a San Antonio mega-project rolled out with superlative pride that within years had descended into a fiasco.

Entering downtown took some care, but Barry's alertness from his near miss with the VIA bus was a sufficient precaution to attune his senses for the task. Downtown San Antonio was not really difficult to get around in. The lanes could be a little narrow, especially the beautiful ones created with cobbled stone. Handsome bridges passed above the River Walk. Horse carriages, out-of-towners from around the globe with cameras, strange circular and orange modern sculptures that camouflage the downtown McDonalds, large convention centers, luxury hotels designed to look like Old Mexico, rolling, rounded rock with vine coming up from the River Walk that engulf various quaint shops for old coins or old world delis. Barry, while driving over one of the picturesque bridges, glanced down to the River Walk and amongst the tourists and momentarily saw the Devil, Mephistopheles himself, fishing into the greenish waters. He took a double take and this Satan was gone. He had these hallucinations sometimes. He understood it came with the territory when one had creative genius. Still, he needed to talk to Dr. Fishman about increases his meds.

Yes, San Antonio, a city that was really as lovely as it was meant to be: An old colonial, frontier village, which sprouted a modern city directly from its core. Barry, for a moment had the thought, that perhaps it was the "Jesus under Glass", a replication of Christ lying in a glass box, at the old Mission San Juan just south of downtown that emanated the fertilizing manna that propelled San Antonio forward, manna scoured from the souls of Indian slaves that had been held on that ground, whose life forces kept pushing this city toward its manifest destiny, stolen from the grasp of Santa Anna's Mexico to be someday reborn into a New Spanish Empire, perhaps with the old house lords of the Sephardic at its helm? They would turn the old courthouse with the red brick and green tiled roof into the new City Hall. Barry dreamed on, in dialogue that would make great writing for his column, as he past the Alamo and then the Menger Hotel, where Teddy Roosevelt gathered his Roughriders, the men that he brought to Cuba who inevitably charged up the San Juan Hill. Though Barry had just learned that some historians report that the Roughriders stalled at a certain ridge leaving the accompanying Buffalo Soldiers to finish the dirty work atop the crest of the hill. All this was fodder for his columns, which were famous for their literary embellishments that fell in line with his devoted training in the New Journalism. Barry, above all, clung for hopes of career aggrandizement. Delusion or no, medication or not, these crazy thoughts were the poetry that had made Barry Juarez San Antonio's most well known writer. Well, there was that infantile former middle school teacher who wrote those squalid fantasy books about the Greek Gods and that pretentious writer who relocated from New York City after writing supposed high literature about the histories of his family's roots complete with a channeled ancestor from the caveman times. What bunk. Barry Juarez was the name that the 700,000 plus people who read the local newspaper knew.

Barry's thoughts floated deeper down on the river to a place known as Dirty Nelly's – the shoebox size piano bar where it was okay to shuck peanuts, as many as you could eat and throw the husks on the floor or at the piano player, if the evening was really late and full of wasted folk. That was the bend in the River Walk that made it to the silver screen. Before the Spurs won their 4th National Basketball Association Championship the only countrywide media San Antonio had received was the silly Universal Pictures movie Cloak and Dagger. Right in front of Dirty Nelly's was where Dabney Coleman chased spies up and down the river in that not so stellar spoof. It hadn't captured a fraction of the natural beauty that was San Antonio. What a waste of scenery. Again anything to do with San Antonio got the short shrift. All San Antonians thought that way. Well, at least with the honor and integrity of the Spurs, San Antonio had gotten noticed somewhat in the limelight.

The diligent reporter pulled his car into the parking lot of the Gunter. He had formulated enough descriptive literature in his imagination for backdrop in three columns. He used to take notes on such streams of thought, but had learned it was all there, in his mind, when he needed access to it later while sitting in front of his MacIntosh.

The Gunter, another classic downtown hotel, did not stir Barry's soul very much. Barry had heard the stories. The Gunter was haunted. If you came late in the evening you could see the old night manager rooming the reception area, looking over the shoulders of workers, tapping his finger on his wristwatch when they were slow and expressing displeasure at the new fangled types of computer cash registers that had replaced the old style, fat and golden push key registers from back in the day. There were darker stories too. In the 1930's a woman was murdered in a room here and supposedly chopped into pieces before being put inside a suitcase. It had been a big scandal. Barry though did not pay much attention to ghosts. He saw nothing, but facts and his own twists on them. He strolled through the lobby of the Gunter without the slightest chill of the supernatural being present. He took the elevator to the third floor and went down the hall to room 309.

A simple knock: It wasn't very musical, but the door opened. A hand reached out and grabbed Barry's arm, he was tugged violently inside the room and then strapped to a chair with a belt. The thrashing began before the words, then the words said, "Your gonna back off the city investigations Juarez. Then later your gonna listen to us more. Or you won't like what happens. Got it Juarez?" – the voice was experienced and serious.

Barry Juarez was paying attention.

After these words came more beatings. The beatings were strategic. Heavy, swift and violent blows to his arms above the sleeves and on the sides of his back. There'd be no visible marks. Barry Juarez registered that too. Tom Pettinger's father had used this technique in Viet Nam. You beat.You tell what you want. Then you beat again to let them know how serious this is and that it will happen time and again if you don't obey. It was effective torture.

"See how I beat you first Juarez without asking any questions, you don't even know why this happening?" explained Pettinger.

"Please what do you need?" asked Juarez.

"Oh you've got some ideas Juarez," told Pettinger.

Another hit.

"You know there are some people you should leave alone. Not ask questions about," insisted Pettinger.

"I get the picture man – Barry Juarez gets the picture," said Barry Juarez emphatically.

"Do you Barry Juarez? Do you. Not just saying that," coyly responded Pettinger. Another few hits.

"Yeah man I get it," assured Juarez.

"I hear pride in there Juarez. Your pissed. You want revenge. Just think I will let you go and then forget about this," jibbed Pettinger.

Another hit.

"No man, no man I don't," said Juarez feeling the pain terribly.

"Okay we're finished with you Barry – for today – I think you understand our meaning. I think you know what's going on. I think you got the message," said Pettinger.

"Yeah I got," said Barry.

"Okay. Here's a knife. Cut yourself free in five minutes – five minutes got that?" said Pettinger.

"Sure five minutes," agreed Juarez.

"Okay, if we see you're headed in the right direction over the next few weeks you'll get some perks – maybe some leads of some great stories even, and then over time you might get a request from our people. I think you understand me," said Pettinger as he handed the reporter a knife.

"Sure, no problem," replied Barry. "See – he says no problem. The man likes opportunity," said Pettinger as he walked out of the room 309 of the Gunter.

Barry waited for two minutes then began to cut himself free. He had played their game. He felt the pain. He was afraid, but Pettinger was right the first time. Barry Juarez had lied. These bastards were not going to get to Barry Juarez. He'd have his revenge on them and that was for certain. They'd learn his game if he had to bring down the whole god damned Mexican Cartels single-handedly then that was what was going to happen. Snap. The ropes busted loose and Barry Juarez was free. He rapidly removed the blindfold from his eyes. The room was spinning. He had never gotten a good look at the décor inside the room. It antique looking and did seem ghostly. Now, after the beatings, the old hotel seemed a very unfriendly place. He hated it and what had happened to him there. He spit on the floor. The humiliation burned. Some of his flesh was now part of the ghost of this building. He clutched the knife and moved toward the door, he exited room 309, thinking he may have to stab and kill someone outside to get away. Damn those fuckers. He wanted to kill them. He opened the door, but there was no guard outside the hotel room door. They had sounded white. That surprised him. They had been bulky, overly muscular – he had felt that when they were restraining him. The accent did not sound like it was of local origin. He'd find them. Maybe set it up where the cops killed them in a shoot out? No one fucked with Barry Juarez.

Some facts came to Barry as he rushed out of the Gunter and to the newspaper's office. The white guy, the leader had used "whom" twice – that was proper usage. It was as if he had made a point to use that language: as if it meant something to him to be correct – perhaps in the eyes of someone who he knew to be highly educated. That was telling. It means he likely had a marginal secondary education, but associated with people who did have an education. He wanted to be peers. The muscles would be out of place in that crowd though. Those were contradictions that narrowed down significantly the odds against finding this culprit. Maybe the classic or swank bars like the Bombay Bicycle Club or Stonewerks?

That thug, who admired education or not, obviously worked for drug dealers so likely dealt or at one time dealt in drugs. He probably was used to working the college crowds and nightclub scenes. Not tall guys, this from where their chest rubbed up against him when they first grabbed him: Steroids, yeah steroids that was part of it – that explained the strangely sized muscles on a last criminal with an ego complex. That fucker also knew what he was doing when it came to torture. All the strikes and bruising would be in places that would not be readily seen by the public; shoulder, back, upper arms and upper legs. So, they did not want anyone to know what they had done to Barry. The message was for Barry Juarez alone. They wanted to convert him to their side. Those fucks thought he was easy.

Maybe the guy had had military training or was trained by someone who did? That would explain the method of the abuse. The technique was very much like what 3rd world governments used on their people. This was someone Barry Juarez could find. He'd lay low for a while and keep gathering information then spring on them all at once like he did with his expose on the Sheriff and that crappy animal inspector a few years before that.

No, the Sheriff was a warm up. This take down would be his masterpiece. The previous destruction of villains was merely practice. He was turning on his grand scheme – he was conjuring his vast vision of payback and it felt sweet already. It didn't hurt that if he could write some of the headlines for it then his fame, plus his revenge, would be guaranteed. This was at once personal and ethical. He had some ideas of what type of players would be needed to make this orchestra sing. The Cartels thought by now he was pushed over to their cause or at least to silence, but that wasn't the case. Wasn't it after all that great San Antonian newsman, the sports guy for News 12 – Dan Cook, who coined the phrase, "The Opera Ain't Over until the Fat Lady Sings..."

CHAPTER 7

The Loner

Dropping the six heads at North Star Mall was the main mission for this trip to San Antonio. Still, Timbero had other things to do while in town. He'd function as back- up, clean-up, special envoy, secret agent and double crosser if they needed him too before he went back to Mexico. San Antonio had a mighty network of operatives for his Cartel and other Cartels and these gardens of villainy that needed constant tending and plucking.

Often these needs were in flux so there was one place Timbero went to get new instruction while in San Antonio: The house of the Teacher.

Yet too, he would likely have some time for himself in between all of his job responsibilities. The heads at the mall and the subsequent terror and news they had caused served to increase the wish to partake in his private fancies. He had an idea of where to go for what he liked. Money was no problem. He was paid well by his bosses. He was an appreciated specialist and planned on treating himself like a top man while in San Antonio.

Timbero did have to check in with his handler, The Teacher, before getting the days of leave time. He had to be debriefed and informed. It was through the Teacher that he would receive his new vehicle. Things were routine, but changes happens. Timbero's particular Cartel had the deepest pulse into the city of San Antonio. Surprises were few. Still, workflow updates were part of the territory for any "corporation".

The safe house was on the Northwest side, past 410 and Fredericksburg, where no one would expect. It was where the modest, new middle class couples bought their first homes. It was nice. Some had pools. The one where the Cartel kept the "Teacher", on Viking Court, did not have a pool, but the kitchen was well furnished and garage had an automatic opener. The Teacher was an information source and transmitter. He sometimes passed on orders. He sometimes did other things. Timbero would meet The Teacher in an open lot. There he left the old vehicle. The drive to Northwest part of town was pleasant, the highways seemed longer and wider with vistas in each direction, but Timbero was fighting terribly with his personal itch. He needed some flesh soon.

The switch point did not have any suspicious looking people lurking around.

Timbero left the big car and walk to the Teacher who was parked in a older model Ford truck.

"This one mine?" asked Timbero.

"Yes it is," said the Teacher.

"Good I was in the mood for a truck," said Timbero.

"Any special reason?" asked the Teacher.

"No just a mood," said Timbero.

"Maybe you should fill it up with piñatas to take back across the border," said the Teacher.

"That an idea. Hey is there any new work for me while I'm here," asked Timbero.

The Teacher began driving.

"No, we want you to lay low for a couple days then go back. Our message was loud. Just lay low," said the Teacher.

"Okay," said Timbero. "Come over for drink though before you go," said the Teacher.

"Thank you," said Timbero.

The Teacher drove the old Ford to his house on Viking Court. He pressed the button to the garage door, it opened, and he parked inside next to his Honda Accord. Inside the garage was a thick, steel reinforced door with multiple locks that led into the safe house. It was an imposing sight and one immediately realized this was no ordinary house. From the outside the house had no distinguishing marks. In the neighborhood the Teacher passed for a retired person, a widower who liked to keep to himself. He was in his sixties. He began opening the complex door. Timbero said something in Spanish.

"You know we must kept to English here Amigo," said the Teacher.

"Yes, of course," replied Timbero as he was let inside the steel door into the house.

The two moved to sit on the comfortable leather couch.

"So it went well?" asked the Teacher.

"You read the papers right," answered Timbero.

"Yes it looked like it went well," said Teacher.

"It did – no one noticed me," assured Timbero.

"Good. By the way did you hear what happened to some boys of the Piedras Cartel's local gang when they were dealing with some of the Banditos?" inquired the Teacher.

"No what happened?" asked Timbero.

"A city official, actually a food in inspector, stumbled on one of their transactions on the west side. It was a bloody mess. The guy put up quite a fight from the reports though he's muy muerta," announced the Teacher.

"Huh – interesting," commented Timbero.

"Yeah. Keep an extra low profile this run as eyes and ears will be up," said the Teacher.

"No problem," replied Timbero. "We're gonna have these Gringos where we want them soon," said the Teacher.

"Better than the Italians ever had em," joked Timbero.

"The problem with the Italians was that they wanted to be like the Gringos, deep down – they wanted to be accepted. We don't have that problem," instructed the Teacher.

"No we don't. Once we get to the tipping point this pretty shithole will be ours again," said Timbero Perez.

"You're a "Wise Latina," said the Teacher playfully as only he could to this killing man and get away with it.

"Reconquista," said the killer.

"Let's have a drink," said the Teacher.

"Gracias," said Timbero.

The Teacher poured two drinks.

"The heads were the perfect message," said the Teacher.

"Yes they will think twice," agreed Timbero.

"All we need to do is get the people afraid of us, we need to show them we are harder than their police, we are bloodier, that we do things that most humans would not do and that we never have fear, this even in their home, then they will give us whatever we want," assured the Teacher.

"They all ready feel guilty for calling the ones here Tex-Mex," added Timbero.

"Your funny Timbero, very funny," said the Teacher.

The two men finished their drinks.

"Another one?"

"A quick one then I go."

CHAPTER 8

Bing Wiz

"Who do we have on the phone today," asked Lyle.

"Could be anyone," responded Hahn.

"That's for sure. Come on San Antonio what's ya got for us," cajoled Lyle.

"I think we have someone Lyle – it's Jose on the line," said Hahn.

"Jose how ya doing man?" asked Lyle.

"Not bad Lyle not bad at all I just wanted to put something to rest," said Jose.

"Hope it's not your Aunt Bertha," said Lyle.

"No it's not Bertha," said Jose.

"Well that's good," said Lyle.

"Remember the other day when your question of the day was what do you do when you get home from work and your wife doesn't want sex," said Jose.

"Who could forget it?" said Hahn.

"Well I want to answer that one once and for all – let me tell you if I am the man..." said Jose.

"We hope you are..." joked Hahn. "and I work 40, 50, 60, 70 hours a week, I pay the bills, I provide the car insurance, I buy the food and pay for the house, I am out there busting my ass five, six days a week then I get it whenever I want it – no questions – if I come home there's no "she's not in the mood" like you all were talking about the other day... you got it," ranted Jose.

"Yes sir," said Lyle. "and I mean it. She cooks, she clean and most of all she gives me sex whenever I ask – I'm not messing around with that – if she thinks she can hold out on me she's got another thing coming," said Jose.

"Judas Priest fan here folks," said Hahn.

"No kidding... when I want it is when I want it and I'm the man of the house providing everything then she knows she's gonna give it to me when I need it – got it!

No ifs, ands or buts about it – that's the law of the land..." stated Jose.

"Well San Antonio you heard it here – our gentleman caller has made the case for getting it whenever you want it," said Lyle.

"And put it to rest once and for all I'd say," added Hahn.

"Thank you sir – what da think Hahn was the question to inflammatory?" asked Lyle.

"Not for him – he had his honest answer and the rest of us will have to wait for the blog vote to see how the majority of San Antonians feel about it," said Hahn.

"At least we hear at 99.5 KISS The Lyle & Hahn Show don't have any ditto heads listening to us," said Lyle.

"Amen to that brother," said Hahn.

In order to know San Antonio it helps to know Lyle & Hahn. They performed a daily show on the popular rock radio station weekday mornings. They had been at it for over twenty years and knew the heart and soul of San Antonians. Spoof and comedy were a big part of their repertoire, but also passion. Their passion was for local issues, sports, music, dirty innuendo and San Antonio gossip.

Several influential people were listening to the two long time popular morning DJ's from San Antonio, when the weekend Intelligence segment came on. Adam Carter, on a lark, made an attempt to reach out with his message. Professor Julia Brown was driving her son to his karate class, and reporter Barry Juarez was listening in his car as well. Dr. Brown's son liked these jokers so she listened to try to get inside her teenager's mind. These two radio jocks were the fools who had the giant billboards posted around town with themselves in S & M gear, complete with red rubber balls gagging their mouths, while a woman in black leather stood over them with a whip in her hand. The ads had met some controversy from proper matrons about town. The professor hoped this attitude did not sum up San Antonio or her teenage son:

"Well hello San Antonio – proud home of the second fattest citizens in America," announced Llye as the show continued.

"Hey man we're are proud of that fact here, it means we all have enough money to eat well, we are doing well here in San Antonio," added Hahn.

"That's right Hahn so well we can afford the best diabetic and heart disease care in the nation," retorted Lyle.

"Hey that's big industry," said Hahn.

"Your right lets not knock it, an extra carne guisada taco is always worth the calories isn't it. Hey folks in Radioland it's that time in the day – for the weekend Intelligence Report. What do we got?" asked Lyle.

"We've got Adam on the line – let's see if Adam can report the seen and unseen doings of the city over the weekend – what do you got Adam?" said Hahn.

"It's not good guys. The city's fallen, its on fire," pleaded Carter.

"Fire on the city – tortilla city is burning heh?" said Lyle.

"Complete chaos is creeping big time upon us," assured Carter.

"The six heads wasn't pretty business," said Llye.

"That's only a small part of it," urged Carter.

"And how to do you know this Adam?" asked Hahn.

"Yeah what's your profession Adam – seismologist?" asked Lyle.

"Advertising," said Carter.

"Then you see the worst of it my friend. I sympathize," said Hahn.

"Yeah that's worse than being a cop for seeing into any local heart of darkness...

Advertising geez sorry man," added Lyle.

"Do elaborate Adam won't you," continued Hahn. "Yeah what's your beef," stated Lyle.

"Did you two hear about the cop car that got shot up and was on fire near the airport last month?" inquired Carter.

"Nope," said Lyle.

"Machine gunned – hundreds of bullets in it and police stooges viciously warding off any citizen witnesses," said Carter.

"Inside scoop – Adam's got some eyes ears in the city," said Hahn.

"Yes and you can't trust the lawyers or judges here in Texas," said Carter.

"Well Texas is where they killed JFK," commented Lyle.

"Hey be careful guys we don't want too much trouble here," chastised Hahn.

"What the heck are you afraid someone's going to follow you to your car after work?" suggested Lyle.

"Your right Lyle no reason to get scared now - go on Adam we listen to it all here on the famous one and only Weekend Intelligence Report," said Hahn.

"Anyone looking into the vast networks of illegal doings there. Mexican Drug Lords infiltrating all walks of our society. Nasty stuff. They're taking over," said Carter.

"Hold on Adam are you saying Mexicans are taking over San Antonio?" asked Lyle.

"Paranoia Alert," said Hahn.

"Think it's a joke? Have you started putting two and two together with all this high ranking violence going on?" said Carter.

"Come on man, talk yourself off the ledge – this is America pal," said Lyle.

"Yeah home of melting pot and equal opportunity Burrito..." added Hahn.

"Of the color blind where we are all just trying to get along," continued Lyle. "Think it's that easy! Skin for skin I tell you and this country will be tested like never before," said Carter.

"Is someone a little burned out around here? Was that John and the Bible man?" said Hahn.

"Let's hear the guy out and maybe help him out and back to the fold Hahn. Hey Adam no one said it was easy buddy, but it is necessary – civic rights man, the grand dream, true human brotherhood – we are more right than we are wrong," said Lyle.

"Ya, that's right Adam we don't do discrimination - it's all Tex-Mex here," added Hahn.

"Hey it was you who put it together that I was talking about Mexicans when I mentioned the drug dealers – is that stereotype or politics. A fact is the first thing that comes to mind. Still, think it's a joke. Have you seen the Mexican Worker's Party flag? Substitute the falcon for a swastika and you've got the colors of the Third Reich. A new fascisms is on the way babies," listed Carter.

"This guy's trying to get clever on us Lyle," said Hahn.

"Thanks for the report Adam hope you work things out – now onto other news..." continued Lyle.

"Did you hear about the City Inspector killed the other day," interrupted Carter. "Okay you want a debate – sure there's been a lot of violence lately – it happens in cycles," said Hahn.

"And you don't think rogue elements are infiltrating deeper and deeper with each wave violence," said Carter.

"Hey it's the nature of change," said Lyle.

"Yeah it's the American Way - home of equality and the Giant, extra super spicy – a melting of all ingredients indeed – land of the colorblind and free - we're... we're all just trying to get along," said Hahn.

"You think it's that easy. You fools. Anglo culture has been holding onto a greased pig since we got here and we are losing hold of what we never had a hold of in the first place and we're losing it at exponential rate," assured Carter.

"Exponential rate huh – you almost sound the educated type," mocked Lyle. "Didn't say I wasn't," said Carter. "Doesn't sound like you believe in the American

Dream though bub," said Hahn.

"Another joke right. You know let's see what Cervantes says – I sometimes do that," said Carter.

"You mean the one armed Spanish writer who fought in the battle of Lepanto," said Lyle.

"Precisely. I happen to have his work Don Quixote right here:

" "I cannot persuade myself that all that is written in the previous chapter literally happened to the valorous Don Quixote. The reason is that all the adventures till now have been feasible and probable, but this one of the cave I find no way of accepting as true, for it exceeds all reasonable bounds. But I cannot possible suppose that Don Quixote, who was the most truthful gentlemen and noblest knight of his age, could be lying; even if he were riddled with arrows he would not tell a lie.." "

{Chapter XXIV. In which a Thousand Trifles are recounted, as nonsensical as they are necessary to the True Understanding of this great History.}

"Do you still think I am might be making all this up?" insisted Carter.

"Are you telling us Adam that you open up that book randomly and look for some divine judgment by matching what you find with the current situation in your life?" asked Hahn.

"Well... I find that it works," replied Carter.

"And you're the good Don Quixote in all this I suppose," added Hahn.

"Adam my lost friend I think you need professional help, you might have Augsberger's Syndrome or something," said Lyle.

"God Bless America," added Hahn.

"Look Adam no one said it was easy. But it is necessary – Kumbaya and fraternal love, peace and goodwill man – it's worth striving for. San Antonio's great – forty-four percent of our listeners are Hispanic," elaborated Llye.

"Sure they are," said Carter.

"That's enough of you Adam – we don't tolerate blatant racism here – it's all Tex-Mex here buddy," cut Lyle.

"Yeah good luck and out," said Hahn.

"Well, thanks for that report on the street Adam hope you enjoy your lithium, and now onto other news," said Lyle.

"America was set up like a Ponzi scheme by greedy usurpers to be milked by the rich until the rest of us were left stranded in a wild land!" Carter was still on.

"Hey Chuck I thought you cut that off – cut him off," said Lyle.

"Sorry about that folks – the last vestiges of the old insanities heard here live on the radio – but as you can hear we still own the station and got the last words... onto other news – did you hear that San Antonio Spurs guard Tony Parker will be featured in a new H.E.B commercial without his bros Tim Duncan and Manu Gino..."

CHAPTER 9

The End Of It

It was the strangest of dreams that night, in the dream Adolph Hitler and Jesus Christ were simultaneously encouraging Adam Carter to continue on his path of defiance and seeking answers to his misguided intuitions. They told him the visions were backed by otherworldly sources and on the right track to destiny. He woke up feeling empowered that day – like the peak of yang before the dimness of the yin begins to descend.

Unconsciously the dream signaled Carter was peeking in his silent rage. Again none listened, nothing functioned as an outlet for his pain, though now he had gone further than ever before by claiming some of his views to the world on the radio. It made him paranoid. He felt like someone would be coming after him soon and he had better do a big act. Still, there was no support and that is what he needed to do anything meaningful. He was a nut. He knew that's what they thought in their compromise with evolution, their sacrifice for social harmony, there willingness to gloss bold fact for a pay check, their bow to "the go along to get along" attitude of the power structure that needed the transition in human mass to happen without revolt. The power structure didn't care about culture and feelings – it needed bodies to rule over and to fight for it. The power structure was anonymous and ubiquitous. It made decisions without men, it moved with its own force through history and it had decided that mixing humanity was the best profit margin and control factor. Enforcing this collective will was what governments knew how best to do. The people were the battleground of its mandate and weaklings like Carter were the natural losers. Carter's hand was tired from scribbling these random notes and more. He rolled out of bed and walked to the bathroom.

He looked in the mirror. He knew he was practical and real and scientific. He wasn't a redneck. He needed the educated and the semi-educated to believe him and they didn't. He wasn't putting much stock in Jack Pearson, the guy in the wheelchair guy he was supposed to meet again, and the only one who had half a conversation with him about what was real. Pearson seemed shady. What Adam Carter wanted was a responsible discussion that would help him find his place again. Now that some of the genie was out of the bottle and there were no kind ears around to fully hear him out – panic set in big time. His emotions shifted fast, too fast for normal. Even for Adam Carter this day would be extreme. He needed expression.

His hands that had just been busy scribbling mental notes wildly, now needed something else to occupy that space. Cold steel. Hitler would have approved if not Jesus. The old revolver was a gift to his grandfather from a compatriot alongside him from the war. Even though outdated, Carter had bullets for this gun. He put them in. It was as if an automatic program was setting itself off inside him, something that had been there for this moment, like destiny, from the beginning of time. It was as if he was seeing the things that had already happened, like a vision, before his eyes. It was telling him what to do. He would return to the place of the shame that sent him careening down on this path – the local newspaper.

He left the apartment thinking about Tito the bartender. He had thought he had really connected with Tito, but that was a lie. There were no friends or family to call out to and those radio guys were assholes to him. It was time to spend a little extra of his money first. He would play. Perhaps that would fix things for a bit. He got to play only about three or four times a year. The one hundred bucks would be worth it. He had gotten lucky with the Fredericksburg Ave. sale. Maybe some law of threes would happen and more good things would come? Maybe with enough fun he would forget about the newspaper for today? Why not test his luck?

Carter sat in his car and before turning the key he picked up the ragged copy of Don Quixote that lie on the passenger seat. He again opened it randomly, like an I Ching reading, as to make sense of what might be.

"And then he proceeded to relate to them, in great detail, the lady Dulcinea's enchantment, the events in Montesinos' cave, and the instructions of the sage Merlin for her disenchantment – the affair of Sancho's flagellation. Great was the pleasure the two gentlemen received from hearing Don Quixote relate his extraordinary adventures, and they were alike surprised at his extravagancies and

at his elegant manner of recounting them. One moment they thought him a man of sense and the next he slipped into craziness; nor could they decide what degree to assign him between wisdom and folly."

Kim's Salon, the name sounded neutral, but if one knew what they wanted they could get more and it didn't take long to get there. Carter frequented this place every four or five months, when things got bad and when he could afford the pleasure. He liked the Asian girls. They gave him a sense of control. He wanted to feel bigger than those around him.

The bell rang as he entered. "Hello – long time no see," said the Chinese girl who remembered him.

"Yeah just need a massage," said Carter.

"Very good, no problem come this way," said the woman who was a little older. San Antonio was where the old massage specialists were sent when they couldn't command the high dollars of the richer cities like LA, New York or Houston. Carter followed.

"This room – lie down – be with you in one minute," said the woman as she pointed to a massage table in a plain room decorated with a radio, a photo of an old country house and a stack of towels.

Carter got naked and laid on his stomach. The woman came back. "You comfortable – very good," she began to touch him and spread oil over his body.

It felt good. It had been six months since someone had touched him like this. Times had been tough and no one wanted a loser. No money – no honey. Carter hadn't had a girlfriend in eleven years. The oil soaked into him. Hmmm – it felt good. The lady covered his body, her hands touching most of it, the oil soaked into his neck, back, arms, legs, one foot, his right one then the lady moved toward his left foot, some imbalance in Carter's body made him react, instinctively he did not want her to touch his left foot... Carter rolled over onto his back before any oil touched his left foot. He gave half a smile and pointed toward his cock. It was hard. The women knew Carter; these girls had great memories for customers, and she knew what he wanted. Her hand like a magical feather began to stroke him until he finished with a "happy ending". She never once touched his left foot. It was one of those times when Carter came quickly. Sometimes tensions made the process take up to twenty-five or even thirty full minutes of stroking his member before he was satisfied.

There was more ease today. Something about the chemistry of his body that day was ready for a fast release. The juxtaposition of his total body covered in oil and the absence of oil on his left foot somehow made sense to the electric reactions going on in his brain. Completeness was felt. Connections, almost mythical, and comfortable were made.

As the girl had serviced him the thoughts of high school, a girlfriend from those days, he remembered enjoying reading the Iliad – how funny he was like Achilles – this mother of the flower spa had coated his body, in this rebirth, yet one spot, his left ankle and foot was left alone. If the oil were magic protection then he was doomed, like Achilles, by the one spot. His left-brain was active with imagery of himself as the hero with the massive shield on which was painted the story of civilization. Achilles the protector of beauty stolen, the rescuer of maidens, the champion and the one who defied Kings – why not he Achilles, why not? When he finally burst with relief, in a gush of coming, at that moment he forgot the humor, forgot high school and forgot thinking about the enjoyment of the Iliad and the lack of wisdom of proceeding into the world with a vulnerable left foot.

It was strange after leaving the spa, Carter felt a little like he had a hangover. A slight depression set in. Perhaps buying something would help? He had a little pocket change leftover. The only place he could go was a thrift store. Maybe he'd find a treasure? Maybe he deserved it? As he drove emotions changed. The sexual experience, the great pleasure, accentuated its briefness and limited frequency. Overall he was denied such human expression consistently. He would not have that again for months, maybe a year and even so it would just be with a whore. Anger. Carter would never find love again. He was cut out of the equation – at least in his mind until maybe perhaps Affirmative Action was dissolved. Maybe then they would allow the white shamans back in the workplace; the big men who didn't take shit. The smart ones that could call corporate bluff, rally the troops and look the boss in the eye? For years though he'd always been one of the ones that lost out – didn't get the interview cause someone needed the quota. It was no secret. At the fucking newspaper he had been literally one of two white men in the ages of twenty-five to fifty in a company of hundreds. It was obvious.

Official stats for San Antonio put the Hispanic population at 53% though it was in reality closer to 68% and in a bigot's mind like Adam Carter's it was 88%. How could it be fair according to any standards that the large media company only have 10 to 15% of its people be Anglos? Reverse discrimination was getting out of hand and it was the dirty little secret everyone was terrified of talking about. If you did, the feeling in America was, you might get sent to the gulag. Adam Carter remembered his gun. Just like John Wayne he had a gun, a six-shooter.

But he had just gotten off. They couldn't stop him completely from powerful functioning. No they couldn't. Though the fact was in this obscenity that the brawn & cunning of the Anglo Saxon was losing its love of country, its might, it's expression. There was price. It was factual turning and some would feel the changes. Maybe it was for the good overall and throughout time, but for now Adam Carter was suffering badly. The sensibilities of his ilk had made the laws though this was losing hold. Maybe they, the high ones of his kind, would wake up and see they travesty being done to their shamans, their holy men: These, the first causalities aware of the big change.

They might coup. They might steal a nuclear bomb. No, what Carter called the Greedoligarchy was winning with its Bully Broad Academies and the inferiority and ant- like industriousness of the new one mind neighborhood authority. The new law that was taking over had no spirit. It had no culture. Law did not see it's holy men.

In his bowels, Carter's contained fury, was churning like Hades' cauldrons. The worst of notions that had been simmering for years, escalating their heinous boiling forth. It was surprising. Usually Carter was lazy in the morning, but alchemy, transubstantiation was occurring. The sense of perceived injustices rolled through his mind like dancing Panzer tanks at Radio City Music Hall show. His vivid memory did not help matters as the faces and words of each superior, co-worker, client and bill collector who had mounted their compiled assaults on him flashed, white hot, through his minds' eye. Like a perfect portrait each of these offenders faces were completed by sinister and devious smiles. The loss of his old newspaper position to a younger, darker and female person seemed the final stamp on his rage. Still, he decided to give it one more chance, even though he had loaded his pistol. The pistol that was hid, tucked away in his belt. He thought a trip to the Goodwill Store might cheer his emotions enough not to carry out the massacre at his previous place of employment. He thought to himself about the phrase used by Lincoln that we should be "guided by our better angels".

His minds' own combat had distracted him as he had been driving. There had been some small detail in his mind all day, ever since the moment he awoke, it was like a tiny puzzle buried somewhere deep inside his unconscious that he could not locate. Throughout the day, every few minutes, the memory of that little puzzle he was supposed to find would pop to the forefront of his thinking – only to be mused upon momentarily then forgotten with the realization of its impossibility. He could not even find the puzzle, much less the answer. It bugged the back of his mind all day. He was now far on the west side of the city, having circled a good part of Loop 410 during his ruminations. There it was though. A Good Will. How reliable it was. He parked in the rear of the strip center.

He walked toward the Good Will. For a moment he felt like a dude's dude in a dude's time: A real man. Maybe this was his puzzle? Walking down Guadalupe Street, like a real man was never an easy thing to do. It was rough here. His puzzle might have been a mistake. Before Adam could get to the front of the Good Will, the safe part, where people could see him from inside and from the main street he was cut off. His strutting had gained attention from a local. Out of the corner of his eye Adam saw a teenager, easily 17 or more, tracking him on a bicycle. The bike itself was meant for an eight year old so the sight on one level was absurd: this big body of a Mexican teen on a little boy's bicycle. Adam looked the person in the eyes. That was the mistake. The troubled man keyed off on this as a sign of defiance, of mammal aggression. The man on the bike moved in. He wouldn't stop staring at Carter, straight in the eyes, in the most menacing manner and Carter in turn could not take his eyes away from the man. Carter slowed. The man began circling Carter on his small bike. It was absurd, but absolutely real and terrifying. Carter noticed the man was truly mad, the kind of madness that was genetic and added to by heavy drugs, it could all be seen in the man's eyes. Carter could read those eyes like a case file, but that file did not matter, file were far away from the fact of moment and the crazed man on the boy's bike circling and circling like Comanche or

102

Sioux riding its pony on the old, great Plains and about to converge on some lost wagon of settlers. The madman continued his Southside war dance around Adam Carter. It came out of the wildest blue and could not have been more horrifying even if it been designed by Vera Wang on crack. The madman was not going to back down. That was evident. Carter was no Bernard Goetz. He wasn't going to just shot this man. He felt his heart for a moment. He averted his eyes form the man's gaze. It was enough. The man trailed off on his bike away from Carter. He just wouldn't be the first to back down. Carter had to show submission. The experience brought out in Carter conflicting souls, the combined persona at once of MLK and Bernard Goetz, Captain Bly and Fletcher Christian. He at once wanted to preach songs of love and salvation and at the same time blast the goddamn motherfucker away. Instead he deferred and the fiend, his adult body scrunched up on an 8-year olds' bike frame, let him go.

The city was on fire with insanity. Every inch of it was a combat zone in the new war. San Antonio was an identity war matrix. Adam Carter's mind was burning. He was angry that he may not have been tough enough for this war, but once this war was realized as truth it must be fought – he heard the ballad of the 7th Calvary in the back of his mind – da daa naa naa naa, na na – maybe he had found his puzzle. Some puzzles, likes driving a car through stops signs, right turns, stoplights, and left turns, were easy. The puzzle of music and destiny was the real trick thought Carter. Carter had graduated to the big puzzles, yet none were there to give him a diploma. He was alone with George Armstrong Custer.

It was a Friday and the shopping should be good at the Good Will. People dropped neat stuff off at the end of the week. Still, he wasn't on the good part of town and didn't really think he'd find any treasures at this thrift store. He always fancied that he might stumble on some collectable worth having when he came to these places. Maybe he'd find something worth some real money? One never knew. Some relative of his used to say that, but at the moment he did not recall who that had been.

As he approached the entrance to the Good Will he began feeling the gun in his belt. It had suddenly reminded him starkly of its presence. It was as if it were talking to him. "Never fear friend, do

103

not worry, I am here if you need me, I won't let you down, I am tougher than they are – don't worry, don't worry, don't worry..."

Carter grimaced and made his way closer to the doors of the large thrift store.

"Damn those motherfuckers – I told that Bitch she'd better make it right – I don't care whose cousin she is..." the voice was of an old woman on a cell phone, "my baby will cut that Bitch if she don't do it – you hear! You tell her that – motherfucker, tell her that," shrieked the grandmotherly woman like a siren calling down a curse on the grounds of the second hand establishment.

What the fuck was this thought Carter as he passed the woman while into the store? He tried to block out as much of the harsh sounds as possible. Next to the old woman was another with a small child. Why were they talking like that in front a baby thought Carter?

"You wait little mami, grandmother is almost done talking, we'll see the toys soon – okay little mami?" said this woman to the child.

Why did they train them so young to be "little mothers and fathers"? It was brainwashing for multiplying and breeding. It was so anti-population control. Why wasn't that group of activist's complaining about these people always calling their small children mami and papi? They were the babies for fuck sake. Not the adults. This sort of pride was outrageous thought Carter. Carter went inside the Good Will as fast as he could as to not pollute his ears with the vulgarity.

Inside, on his right, were three aisles of gigantic bins stuffed with a range of every newly acquired product. It was a rag-tag, jumbled mess of shoes, toys, books, home items and sporting paraphernalia around which were lined dozens of hungry shoppers darting their arms into the bins like beaks of frenzied cranes in a lagoon pregnant with fish, the scene looked like a production line wacked on hallucinogens all searching for a single gold bar that was rumored to be buried in a heap of trash. Carter had a slight panic attack looking at the voracious example of human consumption. He made his way as fast as he could to the far left of the store where items where items were structured on "regulation" size shelves. He glanced at the line of prints hung above the shelves on the wall. There were copies of a couple of mid-17th century masters, a Nagel, plenty of cheap boat scenes, several 1970's bull and matador renditions on poster, along with an assortment of depictions of streams, mountains and cabins.

Then he came to the book section. That was what interested him. The books were surprisingly organized considering the carnival at the other end of the store. This area was as well pleasantly unpopulated. Ease overcame Carter as he eyed through the hardbacks in the non-fiction section. Nothing incredible jumped out at him. Carter moved to where the fiction was located. He peered through the titles. It had to be something inspired for him to choose it. He wasn't seeing anything right away. Sometimes science interested him, sometimes the classics. He did still occasionally read religion and of course sociology. It was unlikely an author of fiction though could pry him fully away from Cervantes. He had left that book in the car though now he felt the need to touch its pages like a child's blanket. He wanted a sense of safety. Then he worried something might happen to it there, alone, in his car?

"You know all these people want the novel, but they are only worth the short story..."

A disheveled man was speaking near to where Carter was standing. He was older, gray haired and twisted with shabby clothes that were once fairly nice and was holding an ancient briefcase with scuff marks across its bow and aft out of which papers poked out the edges.

"You know U.S. Grant failed as a hardware store owner before he became the great general..."

The man was not directly speaking to Carter. Carter moved away slowly. "Nothing has been the same since 1947. That's when they created Israel. That shook the cosmos and spoke of the beginning of the..." Carter moved a safe distant away from the mumbling man.

Near him now was a fat girl in a wheelchair who caught his attention. She moved along with a special glee. Carter was curious to investigate its source. He approached from an angle that let him peer at the girl. She held a book in her hands - it could not be – but it was – it had to be – a Harry Potter 1st edition from the England release. Carter recognized it from a TV program he had seen. This was the blessing that Carter had been waiting for to change his life. This is what he deserved. The book was worth real money and this fat, crippled girl had it. Carter acted.

"Excuse me miss – gosh you've got the book that my daughter wanted me to get for her Birthday," Carter lied.

"Oh do I," she said.

"Yes. Listen I can't find that book anywhere – it's really important to her. I'm sure you understand – do you think I could purchase that book from you say for ten dollars? It would make her very happy," asked Carter.

"I'm sorry your daughter doesn't have this book yet, but I can't let you have it," replied the girl.

"What? Come on how about twenty dollars – that's four times what the book is worth – okay?" Carter demanded.

"Um no – no thank you. I hope you find something she likes," said the girl as she began to wheel herself away.

"Damn it!" yelled Carter.

Then he acted decisively. He grabbed the book from the girl using full force. She yelled.

Just then Patrolman Marissa Gomez had turned the corner of a nearby aisle and saw Carter standing above the screaming young woman.

"Hey stop right there," yelled Officer Gomez.

Carter's head bolted up. He looked straight into the Officer's eyes. Everything that had been bad for so long came together in that moment, all Carter's feelings of fear and guilt, he was trapped. This meant more than just grabbing some book. He could see in the policewoman's eyes that she recognized this too. Carter spun on his heel and began to run for the exit. Officer Gomez sprinted like a tiger after him. Just before he reached the doors of the Goodwill, Carter turned again in a swift motion, pulling his gun, and turned toward the policewoman. Carter's left hand had dropped the Harry Potter book. The moment froze. Carter and the policewoman were the stars of this stage. All the people in the Good Will were reacting spectators to their drama. Carter realized in that instance he had never really wanted the limelight, but it was too late. The assembly line of shoppers were yelling and ducking under the crowded Good Will bins. A clerk went hiding behind the front counter and began dialing 911. The girl in the wheelchair peered around an aisle corner to see what was going to happen. The disheveled man was kneeling and scribbling notes furiously with a pencil. Everyone in front of the Good Will had run away. Officer Gomez proficiently crouched to a

106

one knee shooting position while she fluidity drew her service automatic as fast as any gunslinger from the olden days. Carter realized he was going to be shot. He realized he had a gun in his hand. It was as if before the gun was never real. Officer Gomez fired twice. This was impressive. Most cops in a firefight unleash all 16 rounds of their automatic because of the hysteria of the situation. But Marissa's lover, Jenny, had taught the young cop self- restraint through years of expert cunninglingus practice. Carter should have been lucky, but as well Officer Gomez was a precise shot. The two bullets buried themselves in his torso. Carter smashed against the glass door thus leaving a bloody imprint of his body's shape not unlike when children lay in the snow to indent an angel with wings. Adam Carter along with every private thought he ever had was gone. He came as nobody and left as nobody. He never had the chance to go beyond being not liked.

Next to him lay the valueless 12th Edition reissue of Harry Potter.

Officer Gomez found Carter's ID. She picked up the copy of Harry Potter. Standard procedure called for her to call in the Perpetrator's address so that a patrol car could be sent to the offender's residence.

"Excuse me officer can I have my book back?" asked the girl in the wheelchair who had rolled up uncomfortably close to the fallen body.

"I am sorry ma'am this is evidence," said the officer.

"But..." insisted the girl.

"Ma'am please move back – I will be over there in just a bit to take your

statement," said the officer.

The girl rolled aside Dispatcher 5133 relayed the information Officer Gomez had called in on Adam Carter's address to Patrol car 437 who was in the vicinity of Carter's neighborhood. Officer Ramirez had been resting momentarily at a Valero Gas Station, on the dash of his patrol vehicle was a thick Bible, leather bound with many sections marked in red and sticky notes throughout protruded from its side that marked passages that at one time or another seemed vital to Ramirez's survival. The call let Ramirez know he was going to the place of residence for a lone gunman. Anything could happen. Someone dangerous certainly could be there or someone dangerous could show up suddenly. One never knew the extent of crime. Ramirez did a brief reading, opening the good book randomly, before driving to the location; Isaiah Chapter 53 – The Suffering Servant:

Who has believed what we have heard? And to whom has the arm of the LORD been revealed?we esteemed him stricken, smitten by God, and afflicted. its shearers is dumb, so he opened not his mouth. in, he shall see his offspring, he shall prolong his days; the will of the LORD shall prosper in his hand;.

It was enough to calm the cop's nerves. He started the patrol car and went onto the offender's apartment. There first he checked in with the management. They reported the offender lived alone and never had guests. That was a breath of relief. He got the master key from the property manager. This guy, Adam Carter, had apparently never given any trouble to the office, except for being late on rent a few times. He always paid the late fee apparently. Ramirez moved with caution. Not many residents were visible even at the pool. At Carter's door he didn't bother knocking. He had his hand on the handle of his gun as he unlocked the door. Inside was quiet and fairly normal. There were no signs of life and the place was small so Ramirez would have noticed. He made a tour. It was a little messy, but no signs of derangement. The guy must have just flipped. It always happened every once in a while. Some guy always flips.

Ramirez noticed the computer screen was on in Carter's bedroom. There were two documents open on separate screens. The first was from some scientific text and it read:

""The first Argentine ants set foot on U.S. soils in the late 1890's, as coffee ships from Brazil unloaded their cargo in New Orleans. Being prolific breeders and constantly on the go, they moved across the southern half of the United States. A single colony may contain 10,000 female workers, and there may be hundreds of colonies around your home; the total number of ants could easily reach a million. Although they cannot sting, they can bite; however, they are only about 3 mm long and there tiny mandibles are too small to hurt humans. But, in the world of insects, these ants are truly a living terror. They are very aggressive and readily overtake other ant species, even ants that are much larger and with powerful stings.

Argentine ants are relentless and simply outnumber their adversaries until the enemy colony is destroyed. They even attack paper wasp nests under the eaves of a house, forcing the huge wasps to flee their nests in terror. Even nests of large carpenter bees are no match for these relentless ants. A "killer bee" nest probably could not withstand an invasion of Argentine ants. They also will attack bird nests, driving off the mother bird and killing the helpless young. One possible redeeming quality about these little warriors is that they may attack dry-wood (aerial) termite colonies in your home. I have observed this Lilliputian massacre in a termite infested table in the Palomar College greenhouse.

Most ant colonies are very territorial, and will fight different colonies of the same species. Since Argentine ants in the United States originated from the original colonizers in Louisiana, they are all closely related with very similar DNA. They apparently will accept ants from different colonies as members of their gigantic family. In fact, Argentine ants from different colonies will actually "team up" and attack together in vast swarms. They simply outnumber and overpower their enemy."

The second seemed to have originated from the deceased. It didn't look like a suicide note, but was likely some kind of big, parting shot. Ramirez read it:

The 1st Genetic Treaty of RACE PEACE
by Adam J. Carter

The elusive secret to American success as well as the component that threatens to tear her fabric apart is racial peace. At this time in history the balance of race is tipping in a way that is awakening the collective unconscious of a divided nation. The formula up to now of civil rights has been a profound wisdom, but certain aspects of our culture are falling out of the equation while others are getting solidified into powerful exclusive groupings often victimizing the later group. America must be careful. The memory of the extinction of the Natives Americans, a bloody war over African slavery and 3 genocidal wars against the Asian peoples in the last 70 years should show us the value of good care when it comes to cultural balance.

109

All too easily oppressed can become oppressor. Mavericks and individuals will be the first to suffer at the hands of false group bonding and political alliances. Why do you think there is so much random violence in this country? It is the lone thinkers that are being squeezed out by the trade off of the new power structures and the old elites. Being an outsider is like always eating at a cafe between rush hour, this type must listen to the waitresses gripe as they burp and collect small tips from the tables next to yours then turn around and give you slow service, but you do get to hear the jukebox or the folks in the kitchen singing... The people are infants and infants will scream... Dignity Motherfuckers, Dignity.""

It sounded intense to Ramirez. He had learned that lots of offenders liked poetry, philosophy and had problems with race. He shut off the computer.

Tito, the bartender, recognized Adam Carter's photo in the newspaper the next day. It sort of surprised him, but not really. That guy, Carter, had always seemed a little on edge. Tito had forgotten if in the feast of random discussions that happened all the time in bar life, he had told that dude, Carter, the story of Napoleon in Egypt? Napoleon had offered to covert his whole army to the Muslim faith if Egypt would hand herself over to him. It never happened though. Tito's instincts were right though. He should never have hung out with that dude outside of work.

Pearson read about Carter in the newspaper while perched in his wheelchair at the mall. It was too bad he thought. Carter was one of the interesting ones. There were not many interesting people in San Antonio. The story inspired him to go out and buy a copy of Cervantes's Don Quixote. Well, America never forgives a freak he thought.

The staff at the paper and the gazette's Carter had worked for were shocked. A lunatic had been so close. There lives were dominated by security checkpoints and printed words whose purpose was to keep the lunatics at bay, to insure the genocides happened away from the office, yet a lunatic had been so close. Well, dogs put to sleep before they could bite were the safest thought one editor and then went on with his life thinking he would never have to think of Adam Carter again.

CHAPTER 10

The House Of Flowers

Encita would celebrate a pauper's quincerneria in just two months. She thought of her how her occasion would be on the night of her brother Jesse's birthday party. She came from a loving home. Mama baked often and was a proficient seamstress. She mended garments from a radius of around eight blocks from their home. It was a small business. Papa did cement work, made enough at it, but his passion was gardening. In fact Encita's house on S. Orchard was commonly known by the neighborhood as "The Little House of Flowers." Papa had lined the yard and even the walls of the home with assorted flowers of many colors. The flowers were a drapery of scent and a living brightness enveloping a home that was generally as happy as its reflection.

Encita's coming of age party lacked in many of the visual luxuries associated with a quincerneara. It was uncommon that a family of such low status and means as the Pena's would attempt this large a quincerneara celebration for their daughter. It was often the local way to give these daughters a choice – a nice party or a car? Most choose the car. The wealthy girls got both, but Encita was not one of those. She would have the party and get the car next year or the year after. Everyone in the family thought a car was safer for perhaps an eighteen-year-old girl, but not a sixteen-year-old girl. This way too Encita could stay closer to home. She liked it that way.

As it was Mama and Papa Pena had quite the party brewing. Though other families might have had greater halls and better food, one thing not to be outdone for Encita's quincerneara were the bouquets. Some might have had more mass and volume, but none, no matter at mansion or villa, could match the excellent selection and arrangement of those flowers plucked straight from the draping of the Little House of Flowers. Governments and vast estates would be envious of the generosity of beauty and delicacy that Encita's parents created in the flower arrangement. The precision spoke of a parenting style of love and patience that surely would produce a lovely human being.

Across town it didn't take long to prep the mechanisms of Timbero's diabolical plot. It was true that this was the first time he had attempted his evil in the United States: in San Antonio. But he had fantasized for months on how every detail would play out. He was a good planner. Finding someone who had strayed from the group would be the main part left to chance. The truck was ready. So were the sneaky ingredients he would use as before. The final destination spot was arranged and prepped as well. Timbero travelled the city to find the proper disorder needed to cover the beginnings of his crime. He had discovered the monthly King William's District block party to be a fine place to seize the object he coveted. There was little lighting, a great many people and a wide area of adjoining, but separate events and booths. Beyond the ground of the street fair was an equal amount of businesses with night traffic and all this was surrounded by dark neighborhoods and even a bit of wilderness, drainage systems and running water. It was south of downtown where the people might care a little less, but the opportunity to find someone nice and plump was great.

He parked the old truck in one of the old neighborhoods not far from the street party. It seemed dusty and without life. This impression though was one of first glance. Upon proceeding to the fair he noticed a house lit with festivities, lights and love. It made him angry. Something so good should not be in such a cheap place. It was a party of sorts, with lots of young people milling about. He decided to circle around behind this house to see if there were any vulnerable openings.

Timbero cut across the main road in King Williams to get to the other side of the little house. This took him into the crowds of the street festival. There was always a chance that his timing would take him upon a suitable stray leaving the party just at that moment. He wanted to be picky for his first American conquest, but also to have enough options to make a safe first kill. The smell of good fajitas struck his nostrils as he came close to the S. Alamo Street. The street party had too much energy. It was not wise to linger there. It was not the right atmosphere for stalking. Timbero decided to cut through the nearest club to make his way to the alley that led back to the more deserted neighborhoods and the lone house party. It was a rock-n-roll club. The noise and people formed a compact organism that was part human sandwich and part radio wave blasts. Timbero could make it through this crowd though. He squeezed inside the doors of the club. He noticed almost all inside were young. It would have been a fantastic picking ground for his victim, but stalking from inside a club was against his rules. One could be remembered that way. The blasts of awful American rock music almost made him nauseous. The young Americans resonated with happiness that did not help Timbero's mood. His anger was increasing, as was his hunger. Once he reached this sort of boiling point he needed release soon and he would make sure that happened. He liked to think it was not anger that fueled him, but natural cunning and desire – yet there was anger. He had fasted too long in Mexico in anticipation of his American conquest. It was greedy habit on top of an odd need that pushed him.

Then shit! "Smile Man!" said a gleeful boy as he shoved a video camera in Timbero's face.

A fucking camera crew got him. Timbero hadn't seen them. They popped out of nowhere and they got him on video. Timbero resisted making a scene with a violent rebuke. He turned and moved to a corner and began thinking.

The camera crew seemed to be amateurs. The bastards seemed to be following the movements of a group of silly young women. It looked liked one of the asinine American reality shows, but on some small local, jackass level. Still, they got his face on video. Timbero thought how he could steal or destroy it? That was even riskier at this point. The best thing to do was move on and pray for luck that it didn't amount to anything. He moved quickly to get away from the cameras and the party entirely. He pushed his way past the final bits of the mob to the back door. He pushed hard without drawing attraction by moving like a wild bull in a China Shop though that is exactly how he felt. Once outside he moved fast to an open area in the direction of where the little house had been. There was the alley. Things could get better. He mumbled an old Aztec prayer his mother had told him and moved down the alley like a coyote in the night, quiet and stalking.

It was an awful coincidence that shy Encita Pena had chosen that moment in time to get away from her brother's party, where all the attention was on him, and go to her place of seclusion to dream about her own party that would come soon. The fifteen-year- old did not like crowds and she had been known to retreat to the alley during times of family unrest. It was her get-away – almost sacred spot and Timbero could not believe his luck when he saw the demur girl clinging to the anonymous shadows of the deserted and dark alleyway. He knew he was being blessed and was not unwilling to take advantage of the offering. Encita did not see him coming as her back was to him as she leaned against a quiet and friendly tree that had long been her compatriot in years past. It would be an event that showed how unfair life could be to anyone at any moment as Timbero crept upon his victim. The girl did not know what hit her. In fact it was a dose of chloroform applied to a red bandana that Timbero smashed against the girl's mouth and nose. He was not gentle. The girl's nose broke and she started bleeding. Timbero would take no chance that a muffled scream of her could be heard. Encita was out cold in seconds. The route to the van was simple and direct from where Timbero clutched Encita's limp body. Timbero realized he could continue down the alley with his captive and be very near to where he parked the truck. He carried Encita further away from the crowds at the street fair and the party at the Little House of Flowers. The sounds of merriment moved further in the distance as the two moved as one molded unit, Encita being folded over the shoulder of Timbero, along the crevices of the alley where the light reached the least. At the end of the alley Timbero hid Encita in a batch of brush before racing to his truck and circling back to claim his prize. He loaded Encita in the trailer as if she were no more than a sack of potatoes. His desire increased as he felt the girl in his arms. She was his in all senses of the word and concept. He would devour her in the country and life again would be delightful.

Wimberley, Texas was their destination. There he had his special place. It was a quiet place and had the right type of locals who would not notice Timbero's doings. Wimberley had many drug culture sympathizers. The Cartel supplied that town. On an unconscious level these people supported what Timbero was going to do even though they and his Cartels overlords did not know the full story of his passions. A few good people, on the payroll, who lived nearby was always good. In Wimberley many of the folks were on the "payroll" in one-way or another. Timbero relished the quiet of Wimberley even when he went there alone, always on the last leg of his journey before circling back to Mexico. He could not enjoy his meal otherwise. His technique of preserving the body alive for nearly two weeks insured the food was fresh. It was the only way to eat. Some of his ancestors had been doing it that way for centuries. He really did not understand why most of the world did not enjoy a good meal. It mattered not. He would go on with his ways. It was normal to him. He liked the taste of human flesh and needed to expand his diet. The foods and spices, the greater fats since childhood fed to American children promised a new flavor for this meal. It was a risk eating an American, but his desire was too great. He must taste what years of Big Macs and pizzas did to the meat, he must eat and he must eat soon.

There were other things he would do first to young Encita. Sexual defiling that made her more his before the final act. It was all part of the sadistic build-up. The thrill Timbero received from his twisted ritual.

When the mad man from Matamoras, Timbero the killer, the current installment of a long line of black magic practitioners had finally had his way, the life of Encita Pena would vanquish and her flesh would all disappear. She would no longer be innocent. Every sweet thing about her that is most valuable and every unique thing that is most secretive would be gone forever. It was a personal business, such murder; it happens on the most private level of intimacy and the public during and after is mere acquaintances though they try to intrude with descriptions and interviews, after the fact, they would never be on the inside of the delight...

CHAPTER 11

The Felon

Hector Rojas always had a wild spirit. Over the years private disappointments slowly made that spirit tense. Then Hector did a reckless deed. Earlier in life his free spirit had been channeled into exuberance for dancing Salsa and the Cha-Cha, running long distances and dating Marie Salazar. Marie, a genuine beauty, was gone for some time now and his lust for running and dance had dwindled. Soon the absence of worldly successes became dark and unbearable. Hector's shortcomings were all too evident in e seemed a bit atypical coming this late in life; Hector being in his mid-forties, but the response did come and it came with something of a vengeance.

It had started by overeating. Hector consumed food and then drink like there was no tomorrow. He put on nearly eighty pounds and the man who had once been a proud runner was reduced to another fat Mexican-American in the crowd. Soon after, food was not enough. Hector increased his intake of alcohol to epic proportions and then the marijuana use kicked in. Maybe it was not a gateway drug, but for Hector it did lead to cocaine next on his hit list of self-destruction. He bought cocaine whenever he had extra money. Then he began losing things like his apartment and car and job. Still whatever money he had he put into cocaine. The white powder was his God. Some people, good people, tried to help him, but Hector was hard to find. He stayed from place to place. He met more bad people. Soon they taught him things. Then they convinced him to do things. He would do anything that would get him more cocaine.

Still, Hector's arrest for burglary shocked his family. They knew he had been having troubles, but the worst of it he was hiding too well. Cousin Louisa tried to tell them Hector was really sliding into a bad place, but no one often believed Louisa on such things because of who she liked to slept with. At best the family thought if they could get Hector to church again soon things would improve for his overeating and problems with money. Then it finally happened.

Hector committed his first big crime. He was an unlucky criminal since he was immediately arrested. It was the first time for a Rojas to be put in jail as long as family history could remember – either in Mexico or on U.S. soil.

Shame descended into the family tree. Still, they loved Hector.In the case of one of their own the Rojas's would not abandon them even in the worst of times. The talk at family gatherings was of why this had happened to Hector and who could have done more? But, no one ever saw Hector they said. Hector was hard to find when he was determined to hide. Yes, it was agreed. In the past it was no one's fault, but from now on Hector would be saved. It was the family project for that year and as long as it took to redeem the soul of Hector Rojas.

Hector had held his own in jail. A few "toughs" tried to screw with Hector, but at nearly 300 pounds, even though he had a baby face, Hector pushed back any attempts to make him the cellblock's patsy. He was in jail for eleven days before his brother Pepito had found out and posted bail through AAA Amigos Bondsmen. The AAA Amigos, always being at the front of the yellow pages, were eternally glad to loan money to someone of a good family who had run into a spot of trouble. They understood. Mama Rojas rallied the family around little Hector's cause. Hector hadn't felt so loved in a while. The family had found out about Hector's full predicament by finally listening to Cousin Louisa who knew much of Hector's hidden story from a mutual acquaintance that frequented La Luna Bar on Nogalitos Street. Louisa was the only other Rojas family member with one foot in the shadows where things were experienced on the dangerous side of life. Louisa gladly informed the family on the terrible drugs Hector did, the awful people he knew and the commonness of crime in his circles. It made her look better and she relished every word. She had more face time with the matriarchs then since her confirmation. It was decided after the incident with Hector, because of Louisa's help, that the family would try to include her more as well despite the types of men she would hang out with. Uncle Travo always knew Hector had a mean seed in him, though he never told anyone in the family. As a younger man the two worked together in the loading industry. Hector, maybe not always on purpose, never quite fully moved out of the way of other men who were carrying heavy items. It was as if he somehow expected others, even those with burdens, to move for him instead of the other way around. Travo decided it was best to keep these stories and his own interpretations of them to himself. The family project was to make Hector better. It wouldn't serve to add any information that would go against that or suggest there was something inside that was wrong with Hector.

The Rojas were firmly a first and second-generation clan to the United States. Many were barely bilingual and they all dwelt on the poorer Southwest side of town. They wanted to keep a low profile, but Mama Rojas insisted they pool their money to hire a decent lawyer for Hector. Oddly Hector refused this offer. The Judge had appointed him an attorney who on pro bono day happened to be from one of the most powerful firms in San Antonio – Wayne Burke Attorneys-at-Law. Wayne Burke's face and message spread far and wide across San Antonio's billboards, local television, radio, newspaper and yellow pages. With AT&T Yellow Pages he paid $150,000 each year to have his smiling gray, mustached face on the entire back cover of the book – in full color. Burke's wry smile and Texas cowboy hat exuded an insider's confidence that he was the man you wanted on your side when in trouble with the law.

John Gonzalez from Wayne Burke's firm promised there was a way out of Hector's mess. As Hector sat in his brother Pepito's truck on the way home from jail he reflected on what Mr. Gonzalez had said back in the sanctity of the jailhouse conference room.

"So you weren't the guy who thought of doing the break in?" said Gonzalez in a manner suggesting routine.

"No Carlos kept pushing me into it," insisted Hector with fervor.

"And Carlos has quite a record," added Gonzalez.

"I didn't know that," promised Hector.

"That's fine," pause, "you have no record at all. That's good. And your immediate response to the Judge was admission and repentance – that's good too," said Gonzalez.

"I just said from my heart Mr. Gonzalez. I don't know why I got into this. It's not me. Not the real me," pleaded Hector perhaps confusing his lawyer's final opinion with that of a judge or a jury.

"I understand – I know your mother and family are in San Antonio," said Gonzalez.

"Yes my sister, mama, dos hermanos…" went Hector.

"Keep practicing your English," interrupted Gonzalez.

"Ah yes - - two brothers and several cousins, three aunts and a few nephews," finished Hector with the laundry list of family in America.

"Any businesses in the family?" asked Gonzalez.

"Yes my brother Pepito owns a garage on Culebra," answered Hector.

"A garage. That's good. You know Hector this is a serious crime you are charged with, but it is only a first offense. I think Wayne Burke himself could get the Judge to see it your way on a case like this. If we can get him interested in the case that is. If we don't you face up to at least eighteen years on this in the State Penitentiary," stated Gonzalez in a scripted, cold way.

"No. Mercy. Please you must ask Mr. Wayne Burke to help me – please, please Mr. Gonzalez," begged Hector.

"Listen Hector.I think I can make that happen. You don't necessarily have to go to prison," said Gonzalez.

"Yes anything," whispered Hector.

"Wayne Burke likes to involve himself personally in a few cases each year for charity. Cases like yours and as you know Wayne is important in San Antonio – the Judge would likely listen to his pleas for mercy in your case – you're a good person with a family who has done this bad thing only once," sold Gonzalez.

"Yes, yes, yes," blurted Hector.

"Yes... and I think Mr. Wayne Burke could even appeal for say a fine and five years probation as your punishment – with absolutely no time for you in prison," offered Gonzalez.

"Yes thank God! - make this happen Mr. Gonzalez," agreed Hector.

"Now Hector I can, I can – don't worry, but it will take a little something from your family and Pepito most important – Claro?' confirmed Gonzalez that the two's minds were getting closer to the same page.

"Yes my family will want to help – I did not want to involve them, but I can go to them," said Hector.

"Good," said Gonzalez.

Pepito's Ford Ranger, a mid-nineties model, bounced over the rocky, pock marked streets of the Southwest side as brother took brother home. The moment of silence was broken as Hector turned suddenly toward his brother.

"Listen Pepito – I need your help," he said.

"Sure Hector. I know this isn't the way you want to be," said Pepito.

"No – not at all and I'll never do this kind of thing again, but you know Wayne Burke right?" said Hector.

"Sure the big lawyer," said Pepito.

"Yeah that's him – well he and I think the Judge will offer me a way out of this – but in a way it is up to you," said Hector.

"Me. Up to me?" said Pepito.

"Yes it is. I'll only get five years probation if you do a couple of things for me and the lawyers," said Hector.

"Okay what is it?" asked Pepito.

"It's going to take some money," said Hector.

"The family is prepared. Mama does not want to see anything bad happen to you," said Pepito.

"Okay you know I would only ask if it was the only way. The family, and I know mostly this would come from you, would need to donate $40,000 to charity to make sure I do not go away to prison for a long, long time," said Hector.

"$40,000 to charity," repeated Pepito.

"Si," said Hector.

"That's a lot of money brother are you kidding?" asked Pepito.

"No no – I was given promises by the Burke firm itself that this is the way it works," assured Hector.

"Ehhhh," muttered Pepito.

"Didn't mother say," began Hector.

"Yeah... all right it can be done. You better not get into any more trouble though Hector," said Pepito.

"Never, never... Mr. Gonzalez from Mr. Burke's office has already set up addiction courses and counseling for me. He says these will help me," answered Hector.

"It's a lot of money, but – if it's the only way and you're sure it will work," answered Pepito.

"It must and it will, thank you my brother," said Hector.

"So you're going to work on your addictions," said Pepito.

"I've already started. I had two sessions in jail and Mr. Gonzalez gave me this set of books on the subject," said Hector as he patted his bag that rested between his knees.

"And a charity – what charity?" asked Pepito.

"Mr. Gonzalez will have someone contact you on that," instructed Hector.

"He will – okay," said Pepito.

"Let's go tell mama everything will be okay," said Hector.

Pepito drove a little slower, but kept the course toward mama's house. The whole family would be there. It would seem their project was within reach. The money was a bigger part of the plan than most of them would know about. All of it would come from Pepito's savings. He'd have to dip into the stash he still hid in a Mexico bank to come up with that sort of cash on hand right away. It would mean his dream of opening two more garages and branding them in a franchise sort of way would have to wait years, many more years. He'd do for mama though. He couldn't see her heart broken over Hector.

CHAPTER 12

The Set Up

Pepito was fixing the transmission on an old Chrysler when the phone rang. The engine block was hung four feet over the hood of the old car. Tools were spread about the shop. Grease painted the faces of Pepito and his workers like they were a Cheyenne war band or perhaps NAVY SEALS. That was always when the phone rang. Still, it could mean more business so Pepito stopped what he was doing and rushed to the small, cluttered office. He peeked at the pin up girl in her bikini as he said "hello" into the phone receiver snuggled between his ear and shoulder. He wiped his hands with a rag as he listened for who was on the other end.

"Mr. Rojas? Mr. Pepito Rojas?"

It was a woman's voice.

"Yes this is he," said Pepito.

"Listen I believe you were expecting a call about a charity event?" said the woman.

"Ah – yes," replied Pepito.

"Ok show up at this address tonight at 7pm..."

When 6pm rolled around Pepito went home to change into nicer clothes after a shower. He did not know what kind of building he was going to at 7pm. He did follow the directions given by phone and went to the stated address, at the stated time. The building was rather non-descript. An ivy coated wall concealed a free-standing edifice on the edge of a neighborhood that could have been anything from a dentist office to a realtor, but it was neither.

When Jose "Pepito" Rojas walked into the local Party Precinct meeting for District 13 they were glad to have him. He was greeted inside the meeting hall by smiles and handshakes from complete strangers. It was something he did not trust, but went along with it for his mother's sake. He did not think politics was charity, but knew the powers he and his brother were dealing with were assuredly greater than their own. He went along.

Politics took bodies, lots of bodies, to make it work. Everyone wanted to talk with the newcomer. They were even more pleasant when they found out that Pepito owned a small business. That was always good. Politics took power and power mostly meant money. District 13 had a tight race coming up.

"So Pepito business is good?"

"Yes very good."

"Wonderful."

"It's surprising how many shop keepers we get interested in politics on this part of town."

"It's important."

"Yes it is."

"Do you keep up with the issues?"

"Well I am just now getting more seriously involved. But I know there are some important things happening with the schools."

"That's right that's one of the big issues this round."

"Do you have a lot of family in San Antonio?"

"Yes a pretty big family."

"Wonderful."

The night went on with small talk and generalizations.

A speaker discussed issues pertaining the upcoming elections. The call was made to post for volunteers that would do door to door canvassing and placing signs. Still, no one approached Pepito especially about the trade of his help and money for the freedom of his brother. Pepito was perplexed, but he kept patient. He felt like he was in his wife's favorite movie Casablanca. The suspense of seeking the right contact, like a spy game, but it never happened. She made him watched that movie five times a year. Maybe Bogey helped him keep his cool in the situation. He waited and when the event ended he left.

When he got inside his truck outside the district office a note lay on his passenger seat. He inspected the window. He ran his fingers alongside the edge. Indeed it had been "Jimmied" open.

Pepito read the letter.

"Go back to next week's meeting.Approached S.H. Say you were impressed. Donate your first 10K."

This people played by underworld rules. He knew this was more shadowy then Hector made it sound. He may never know who was on the inside of this? He already assumed S.H had to be Sally Hernandez. He had her that night. She seemed so nice. He would have to give her the first installment of ten thousand dollars. Was Sally in on this? Or all of District 13? They seemed so normal, such

123

concerned citizens. Maybe everyone in The United States did politics this way? And they made fun of Mexico he snickered. That would be the extent of Pepito's criticism and mockery. He was determined to obediently follow through with his instructions next week. He knew he would feel funny at Mass with mama and Hector and the family this Sunday. For some reason, probably because he was the successful one in the family, the burden of seeing the totality of the nastiness of this mess and dealing with it directly fell on his shoulders. He'd pray harder this week. Maybe have a few beers and watch Casablanca with his wife or at least a Spurs game.

The week passed with routine, but the District 13 meeting was in the back of Pepito's mind. Hector seemed on track. The family was constantly with him. They made sure he made all meetings and counseling sessions. He even put in a little time at the shop to begin to pay back the loan for the bail money. Still, it seemed too easy to Pepito who had always worked so hard for what he had gotten. Even now he was carrying the biggest part of the problem. Well, it was the duty of family. He drove to the office of District 13 eager to finish a big part of this business and be done with it. He had his checkbook in his back pocket snuggling beside his wallet.

The meeting was equally well attended to the previous one. Everyone was in election mode and gearing up fast. If anything the energy was greater this week than the previous. Pepito, now not quite the newcomer, was not greeted with the same fanfare as before. Some other newbies were the ones showered with the majority of the attention. He did get a few nods and handshakes upon entering the room. Then he spotted Sally Hernandez at the snack table. He moved toward her.

"Oh Mr. Rojas good to see you. Two meetings in a row. You are committed to be involved aren't you?" said Sally.

"Yes I meant what I said," replied Pepito a little too strenuously.

"Oh sorry. It's just that sometimes local businessmen just want to network with us and end up dropping off business cards and we don't see them again," replied Sally.

"No I really want to be a community member. My kids are going to Middle School next year in the District," said Pepito.

"That's an eventful time. I can see why you want to participate. Listen Pepito we have a school initiative community – it meets on

Saturday early evening – maybe you want to sit in and hear how we see the issues?" suggested Sally.

"Ya I'd like that. Also I was thinking of contributing more directly in another way. A donation – you know in business we get to write those off, plus it's been a good year and I do want to invest in where we are living," said Pepito.

"Wonderful. I'm actually the finance chair. If you want we can set up a meeting on this," said Sally.

"How about I write you a check now," said Pepito.

"Well, sure if you want too," said Sally.

Pepito whipped out his checkbook and began writing.

"I want to give $10,000," he said.

"$10,000 that's a lot," said Sally surprised.

"Seriously business has been good. I want to help. I know Jesse Herrera has a tough fight on his hands and I don't believe in the School Rights Petition," insisted Peptito.

"Well that's great. Hmm – well only $2000 of it can go to Jesse's campaign, but I could distribute the rest toward District office needs and that would help us overall," said Sally.

"Yes do it that way. I'll make it out to the District 13 Precedent Office," said Pepito who was prepared as he researched beforehand online how such things were done.

"That'll work. Didn't expect this, but fantastic. Thank you Mr. Rojas," said Sally as she accepted the check.

"My pleasure," insisted Pepito.

"You know you're the eleventh big contributor in District 13 alone we've had from the small business community in the last year and a half. I used to think it was the other side that got all the money from business," explained Sally.

"Times are calling for all of us to give more," said Pepito trying not to do any math in his head about the scam in front of him.

"Yes. You must come to our meeting Saturday," insisted Sally. Pepito.

"Oh yes I'll try, Saturdays can be busy, but I want to make it for that," answered

"Wonderful see you there and thank you," said Sally as she scurried off with the big check to her office to put it in a safe place.

Indeed, Jesse Herrera did have a tough fight on his hands from the opponent, Oscar Mendez, since the controversial School Rights

Petition failed to pass last round. Oscar had clout. He had once been Deputy Sheriff in better times before the current Sheriff had been indicated on counts of nepotism and grand fraud. District 13 wanted school reform and remembrances of "cleaner" times. Jesse Herrera, because of close ties to the Teacher's Union, could not support the School Rights Petition, which meant some state matching dollars would be lost; but it would have added some odd and strict limitations on student and teacher freedom. He'd lose some votes that would have normally gone his way from parents that thought the funding critical, but he'd keep most of his teachers. In politics it was hard to please everyone. The only answer was to out spend his opponent and "buy" more votes through a propaganda campaign. It was the way of politics in this world. Jesse wasn't ashamed to play the game.

Sally thought of how the new money would please Jesse, like she tried to please in him in hotel rooms when they made love behind Jesse's wife's back. Jesse though was not easy to please. He was a good man, but all he could feel was his own ambition. The money would make him happy though.

Sally was continuously surprised at the generosity of local small businessmen. She had learned that they often had much more money than one might think. Over the last few years more and more of them were stepping up and making sudden donations to the Party. These donations were often more than the maximum amount an individual could contribute and the District itself was becoming more powerful in the greater San Antonio political scheme because of its access to greater funds, though a couple other districts as well had been noticing the increase from small local donors. Times were shifting. Local players were becoming state players and some state players were becoming national. The bursting piggy bank from District 13 was burgeoning results in wider and wider spheres of influence. It must have been the grace of God. The glorious phenomenon had even had made Sally begin to again attend Sunday Mass; at least 2 times a month especially during election season. Though Sally had to give credit to Judge Bustamante as well. He had come from District 13 and never forgotten it. He was respected and connected. He pushed good things Sally's way. He was the one who introduced her to Jesse Herrera. Jesse had the charisma to get things done. He had to have had charisma. No one else could have gotten

126

Sally into bed. It had been years. She was been bitter before meeting Jesse. She loved the church. Jesse could do good things. It took good work and charisma to get to Sally Hernandez. She was blessed to be associated with Judge Bustamante. He knew what was best and brought it to her world.

If she was being honest with herself, when Pepito Rojas offered Sally $10,000, the maximum contribution, toward the District 13 fund, $2000 of which under city ordinance could be allotted to Jesse Herrera's campaign it came as only a slight surprise. Sally was a believer in blessings now. She was having routine passion and orgasms. She had lots of money to manage. She was getting spoiled by it all and knew the power players and loved it. Sally was proud of her great acting skill. She pretended expertly to be as much surprised as she could muster and then waited for Pepito to write the check.

Yes, Jesse Herrera would be pleased and the good Judge Bustamante. Their political machine was stream rolling to prominence and Sally Hernandez was driving or a t least hitching a ride.

What Sally did not know was that Bustamante had promised Jesse enough money to win if he would agree to "play the game" on certain issues down the line. Jesse had said he would as he sat in the Judge's big cushioned chair of brass studs holding together red leather. At least he did not have to betray the Teacher's Union, though Jesse Herrera was becoming increasingly confused as to what organization or which individuals were the most powerful. Politics after all was about listening to people.

Jesse had limits to his interpretation of "playing the game". He didn't want to do anything unethical and certainly not something illegal. The Judge never said such things would be asked. Judge Bustamante was a great ally. He had a career Jesse could admire. His value statements were solid and he was a powerful insider. Jesse knew there were rules he needed to master, hidden games and alliances: alliances that made success in politics possible. Jesse wanted to succeed. He wanted to master. He had an agenda and it was full of good will and great plans for the people. Sally had been his main contact for the Party, but that would change if he won. There would then be more face time with Bustamante. More private conservations, more names dropped, more tricks of power revealed and more insider introductions. Jesse was excited about that part of the game as long as it didn't go too far.

Of course Judge Bustamante had different ideas on the extent of what Jesse would do for the "cabal" of insiders. He had ideas of the lines Jesse would have to cross. He also had leverage each step of the way, including now, to make sure Jesse complied.

Yes, Jesse was going to be a real Party asset. The Judge would make certain of that. "Jesse I want you to meet your latest and greatest contributor – Mr. Rojas – he

owns a garage on Concord," said Sally.

"Pleasure to meet you. I've got an old pick-up that needs some work," said Jesse.

"Please sir, bring it by. We can help – please call me Pepito," said Pepito.

"I will, it sounds like you've already helped a lot today – Pepito," said Jesse.

"I want to see happiness in this district," said Pepito.

"We strive for happiness," said Sally.

"Yes community harmony," said Jesse.

"Yes harmony that is what I want," said Pepito.

"You have kids in the District schools?" asked Jesse.

"Yes three," said Pepito.

"Great. They must be proud of their father's success," said Jesse.

"My whole family is – that's what I am known for," said Pepito.

"When they need something they come to you. My family is like that too.

Sometimes it's hard to be the leader," said Jesse.

"Yes sir," replied Pepito still unsure of who knew what and if people here all talked directly or in some kind of code.

"We will go over more of what Jesse is planning for the District in Saturday's meeting Pepito. Another reason why you must come," said Sally lightly touching Jesse's arm.

Pepito read that gesture as the too being lovers. Pepito was intuitive in that way. He wished he understood politics more though.

"Glad to hear you are going to be more involved Pepito, having more people involved in the school meetings will be important to off-set the controversy's with the Rights Petition." said Jesse.

"I will do my very best. I'm not an expert on all the issues though," said Pepitio.

"No no you don't have to be – just having your voice their speaking about what you're hearing that is what local politics is all about," said Jesse.

"I think Pepito is going to be a real assest for 13," added Sally.

"No doubt. We want you involved not just your money," said Jesse.

"But the money does help," joked Sally.

"I will do my best, listen I must go back to my shop – business never sleeps.

Thank you sir. Thank you for all your help," said Pepito backing away politely with a series of miniscule bows.

"Well, I promise to do all I can once elected. Ah don't forget to vote," said Jesse. "Good day Mr. Rojas," said Sally.

Pepito turned and walked off.

"Doesn't seem the type for politics. Acts like I've done him a favor," said Jesse. "He's one of Bustamante's leads. You know they come out of nowhere – always

in the nick of time. He really has taking an interest in your success," said Sally.

"13 is important to the Party," said Jesse.

"Yes it is. Lucky for you," said Sally with another squeeze of Jesse's arm.

The squeeze caused guilt in her lover. Sally wanted him to be her champion. That was what Constance, his wife, wanted too although without the great sex. It had started innocently enough. Jesse had never been a cheater, but the rush of working so closely with Sally and the mantel of power that already began the glow of its aura around the political contender. The aura was too much of an attraction for both of them. They had fallen into bed and now it seemed Sally loved him. Honestly, Jesse felt like he just needed the sex to relieve the stress. The demands were increasing daily. And the money people were throwing at him. It called for a responsibility to them: A responsibility to win. The pressure was on. He could not let down people like Pepito Rojas and his family. It was a matter of honor. If he admitted it though seducing Sally was a proud conquest, she was a good church girl and that had made it something to especially relish each step of the way. Since being in politics the need for strange conquests grew within Jesse. He was not sure why and did not look into it too greatly.

Jesse would at some point have to figure out a way to cool it with Sally. There was a lot on the young politician's plate to mediate. He was already doing political business full swing and not even elected yet. It was stressful.

"Sally are we going to the hotel tonight after the meeting?" asked Jesse.

"I was hoping you'd ask. I already made reservations," whispered Sally.

"Good," said Jesse.

CHAPTER 13

The Lawyer's Liar

"Geez glad we work on the right side of the law!" said Izzy to a passing attorney. "Hey those Cartels take no prisoners," replied the attorney.

"Your right about that. I guess it could be any of use next," said Izzy as she put down the local newspaper whose headline read, *SIX HEADS AT THE MALL STILL UNSOLVED.*

Izzy Cotrane was a pivotal figure at Wayne Burke Law Offices, LLC. Thirty years before she started at the firm as front desk reception and soon began a passionate affair that lasted eight years with Mr. Wayne Burke Sr. Esq. before he died and left the practice to his son Mr. Wayne Burke Jr. Esq.

Izzy was now office manager and acted as historical container, myth preserver and secret bearer for a good bit of information that made the past and present of the Burke's law practice. Her looks had faded some, but knowledge of daily business gave her clout. Rich men would no longer see her as new wife material and she had no interest in younger, poorer men. So, she focused on the daily business of the firm, Wayne Burke's offices were now a paradox of the old and new, western and popular, big firm and small firm. Athena, one of Burke's Labrador Retrievers, made residence in the crowded parking lot and minimalist backyard that was came with the purchase of the two story free standing building off the major access road intersecting at I-10 and 410 about two miles toward downtown.

Everything about the practice now was a mirror of Wayne Burke Jr. He selected the decorations, it was his decision to buy the building, the dogs outside were his and his face and voice was on all advertising. Wayne had reshaped his father's business into his own. Everybody who had been loyal to Sr. was now gone except Izzy. Wayne knew about his father's relationship with her. He kept her around as a matter of possession. He wanted to own her like his father had. She had proven wise as well. She knew when a word of wisdom, said at the right moment, counted and could be of benefit to her superiors. The rest of the time she was skillfully quiet. Wayne Jr. respected her in a way he did not respect either of his deceased parents. He never had to have Izzy in a physical sense. That she was the company emblem was enough. He felt like he owned her like some Roman might have owned their slave. Served an executive function that was useful and made him feel better than his father. Wayne had taken the firm in many directions his father never would have considered.

The artwork inside the firm was the most obvious difference. It was a combination of western pop {Indian Chiefs and shaman warriors in front of abstract flags of the United States}, Remington Series bronzes of buffalo hunts and lone cowboys, and two exquisitely framed Picasso and Monet prints thrown in for good measure. It was important for Wayne Burke to gain all people's confidence that he was a part of their culture. He didn't want to miss out on one sliver of business.

The magazine assortment in the waiting room was vast, all the guy stuff for hunting and outdoors was represented; plus magazines about Paris and world travel, Cosmo, Christian Family Values, coloring books, Ebony, La Raza, left wing, right wing, you name it. Instead of perceiving that to please all varieties would make people think Burke was a "say anything" man – Burke instead believed that the right magazine would find the right hands and all would be well. The mesh of elite and "Out West" décor of the firm betrayed a virtually schizoid split in Wayne Burke's aspirations of self-identity. It was a split Burke was proud of. He felt himself to be a man bigger than his surroundings: In a way a man of the world and a man of the people who could also converse with princes when the occasion presented itself. He did travel and hobnob with any top crowd he could work his way into. It was surprising how many friends and invitations any wealthy lawyer could get in a far away place. He always used travel and his connections to buy art from where he went. He considered himself an aficionado and had had enough reading and significant discussions with experts to know what was quality. His fascination was continuous, but contained elements of faddishness. His acquisitions were hobby as habit, a pleasant one perhaps like masturbation was for some, but not something demanding stern continued education, investment in updated second source material or deep questioning. It was just another thing for Wayne Burke to possess and pretend he knew damn well.

Izzy Cotrane was the same sort of possession – she was still trusted to degree, appreciated in context and kept around, but she did not know Wayne Burke's deepest secrets.

John Gonzalez was another matter. He walked into the Burke's Firm that day with a briefcase carrying $30,000 cash. He didn't need to be buzzed in to the big boss's office.

He was the only one allowed to perform a simple knock on Wayne Burke's door and wait for the command, *"Enter."*

Everybody knew Gonzalez was Burke's top gun. It seemed customary to have a favorite, but a favorite who brought the boss 30K large was a favorite indeed.

"Come in," said Burke this time.

Gonzalez gently went in the big office full of animal heads on the wall, some of the best art in San Antonio and a custom carved desk that was four times normal size.

"Hey boss how's it going?" asked Gonzalez.

"Well, look's like you've got something for me," replied Burke.

"Yes I do. It's the remainder of Pepito Rojas's payment. Ten thousand has already been given the Party Committee," answered Gonzalez.

"Another one bites the dust and again were on the winning side," said Burke.

"Always pick the winner," affirmed Gonzalez.

Gonzalez handed Burke the case. Burke pushed aside a Remington original painting of a lone cowboy on the trail at dusk to reveal a safe. He unlocked the combination unconcerned if Gonzalez saw the digits or not. The two had made so much money together that what was held in the safe on a daily basis would not be a temptation to the junior partner. Gonzalez was a capable point man. He arranged most of the deals and talks with the Mexicans when someone had to. He dealt with most of the local officials on the pay roll as well. He handled the "perps" who had money and persuaded them with dazzling effectiveness to join into Burke's and the Mexican Mafia's bribery system. He was perfect. He was Mexican, from a good long term San Antonio family, educated well in Texas and knew how to deal with the underworld. He was greedy and intelligent enough to know what benefitted him and not to say stupid things. He was careful and shrewd. Also, he knew the dangers of crossing anyone within this racket. It didn't hurt that he liked art, racket ball, opera, legal theory, travel and adventure of the same sort as Burke. He was also thirty years Burke's junior so he couldn't have the full wisdom of his boss.

Burke relished putting the extra cash in his safe. He thought about how soon he would be bringing over Judge Bustamante's cut over himself when they had monthly dinners in the Judge's Monte Vista residence. It was a well-oiled system.

"I heard the Mexican's wanted to send San Antonio's favorite journalist a message," said Burke who always called the Cartels, *"The Mexicans"*.

He saw this relationship as an extension of history and believed in the long run the territories won in The Mexican War would one day revert back to their original owners; The Mexicans. He wanted to form early ties with those winners. Besides, no one paid as well in Texas as the Mexican Mob.

"Yeah message sent. Pettinger's beef boys took care of it," said Gonzalez.

"Hmmm. We need a gang like Pettinger's under our wing one day I think – he's too much Bustamante's" suggested Burke.

"Someday. That Juarez guy is slippery though I wonder how deep that message really resounded?" questioned Gonzalez.

"Uncertain at this time. I think though that the bullying and the heads the other day at North Star Mall are ramping up the message on whose coming to town," said Burke.

"No doubt. I think they had that white eyelash dude fella deliver the heads," said Gonzalez.

"That dude creeps me out," said Burke. "Me too, but it's force that's gonna take this place," said Gonzalez. "Yup it's just like Old West, things never really change and the toughest muscles rule the roost. You know Bustamante is the favorite with the Mexicans and between you and me I think they are going to support some moves on his behalf," said Burke.

"Any details?" asked Gonzalez.

"Best not to worry about the details looks like all they want us to do is turn the clients and run the money so we have to stick to that for the time being," replied Burke.

"Got it. You know Bustamante has some kinks," put forth Gonzalez.

"I heard something about that through the grapevine. We better increase the file on him – who knows how high up he'll go?" said Burke.

"Should I use Renolds?" asked Gonzalez.

"He's the best – yeah use Renolds," said Burke.

"You know Chin wants a raise," said Gonzalez.

"The Chink?" said Burke.

"He does good work," said Gonzalez.

"Yes he does, but I always felt he was a little bit of a Trojan Horse, the Chinese always are – bring one in and they've got plans for dozens more to follow," said Burke.

"The Chinese will never have any leverage in this town," said Gonzalez. "Maybe not, still maybe next year we might want to bend the city counsel's ear to

consider a new Medical Examiner, maybe get Chin a job in Houston or something – make it look like an unavoidable promotion and then bring someone in from the East Coast who'd play ball and be happy as a soloist," said Burke.

"I'll start some motions," said Gonzalez.

"Good. Freaky what happened to that city inspector McKinley," asked Burke.

"Yeah that was the Del Rio Mexicans. They're small fry in San Antonio," said Gonzalez.

"Still," said Burke.

"But it's good. More violence gets the city ready for political change then we can help the Juarez Mexicans move their people in," suggested Gonzalez.

"Maybe," said Burke.

"Any plans for tonight?" inquired Gonzalez.

"My daughter wants me to go to Club Rio – they're filming some Reality TV show there she's all excited about, but I might just take Izzy for some drinks at Chacho's then go home and call it an early night," said Burke. "Pretty good haul today, makes it easier to sleep well," said Gonzalez briefly pointing to the safe.

"Yeah nice job. You happy with the status quo?" inquired Burke.

"I'm happy," said Gonzalez.

"There's no limit to this ride my friend – believe me no limit, America is for sale and drug money is gonna buy this bitch, soon everyone will be on the take and the early adopters like us will be pulling most of the strings," said Burke.

"Do you think the Mexicans will ever move up here?" asked Gonzalez referring to the Cartel leadership.

"Unlikely – they'll always need proxies – think about it – what's the life expectancy of a drug dealer in America?" said Burke.

"Good point," agreed Gonzalez.

"The strength of a democracy is in direct proportion to how good it can hide the true enemies of the state from the people. And the American people are dumbass's that don't got a shit licking clue on how deep drug money owns them," said Burke.

"And what a democracy we got - can't go wrong siding with the winners," said Gonzalez.

"What are you doing this weekend?" asked Burke.

"Not much," answered Gonzalez.

"Can you make a run out to Wimberley – take the wife and kids – I need something dropped off to Catfish," asked Burke.

"Sure sounds fun – business and pleasure," said Gonzalez.

"Business and pleasure," confirmed Burke.

Burke hands Gonzalez an envelope.

"Okay Boss see ya Monday," said Gonzalez as he exited the big lawyer's office.

Gonzalez made his way past the several of the busy law firm employees. They all deferred to him in the halls with a nod. He was at the boss's right hand and they knew it, if not fully knowing why. He'd make one pit stop before heading out to the parking lot. He was anxious to get to his car. He had to make an important call, but nature was calling too strongly. There was one thing he didn't like about the restroom at Burke Law.

"Hey Governor," greeted Laslo in a bad Cockney accent as Gonzalez entered the nicely constructed and paneled restroom.

Gonzalez was not sure why Burke kept Laslo around? It looked kinda classy to have a restroom attendant, but Laslo was so odd it seemed to offset any advantage. He thought at one point Laslo might be an illegitimate child of Burke's, but thought twice since the apple could not fall that far from the tree.

"How's it hanging Laslo," retorted Gonzalez.

"Darn fine, sir, darn fine," said Laslo.

"Cool," said Gonzalez.

Laslo's eyes seemed red – he was probably stoned thought the lawyer.

"You know I invested in an IPO - actually I helped start it up, working on getting the word out on it – marketing the prospectus actually – it's paying 25% on a hundred bucks. A gentlemen like you might be interested in accommodating such a proposal?" said Laslo.

"Sorry Laslo got money all tied up right now – sounds interesting though," replied Gonzalez trying to hurry and finish his urination.

"It most certainly is. It's something a real top hat type would like – you know a guy who likes to carry around thousand dollar bills in his pocket not just Benjamins," said Laslo.

"Beyond the Benjamins huh?" snickered Gonzalez subtly.

"Most definitely – it involves rap music and farming," stated Laslo now entering the really bizarre.

"Wow never heard of that kind of thing before," said Gonzalez.

"No one has yet – but it will be huge, cologne sir?" asked Laslo.

"No thanks," said Gonzalez.

"Well maybe sometime we can go to lunch together and I'll fill you in on the lay of the land," suggested Laslo.

"Burke's got me hustling, but maybe in a couple months we could find the time so I could learn more," responded Gonzalez.

"Gotta always learn more, gotta do it, in the meantime sir if you know anyone who wants to get in on a poker game – a big time one with some nasty stakes – I'm your man – I know the place and the time – {Laslo begins singing} "everyday I'm hustling, everyday I'm hustling"," voiced Laslo.

"Poker – I'll keep that in mind too," said Gonzalez.

"Always running like a train, but not into each other – just going forward," said Laslo peculiarly.

"Alright – see ya Laslo," said Gonzalez.

"Good day sir, Good day good sir... oh and you know there still are those days where you sitting quietly with your family over lunch and right before your eyes you see the benefits of your destiny as the dominos of your enemies careen to the pits of Hades" said Laslo.

Gonzalez resisted peering into Laslo's eyes.

The lawyer zipped up and washed his hands while Laslo stood by as to attend to any possible need. When Gonzalez left the room it was relief that at this for one full day he would leave behind any times of conversing with the odd and creepy Laslo. There must be some secret as to why Laslo was kept around. Well, Gonzalez didn't have the time to investigate all secrets. He made his way to the parking lot. The old dog avoided him as usual. Gonzalez threw him a treat he had snatched from the front desk jar to try to get the thing on his side. Appearances and superstitions were important when one was both a lawyer and a criminal. He wanted it to look like even the dog liked him.

In the car he made an urgent call. It was to the Medical Examiner of The City of San Antonio: a man of Chinese descent that he had known for many years.

"Hey Chin – it's Gonzalez. The old man said no to the raise. Yeah I know. Listen we need to meet and discuss things. Yeah Susie's is fine. Yeah that's a good time. See you there," said Gonzalez.

Gonzalez hung up his phone and started thinking.

CHAPTER 14

Judge Not

He was not always this way. Judge Bustamante Carlos Pena, {with absolutely no direct relation to Encita Pena}, had begun as an honest person. He had always pleased his mother with little gifts and that habit translated well into pleasing his teachers and eventually the professors at law school. He excelled at St. Mary's University. It's campus on the southwest side of San Antonio was a pride of the city and symbolized Hispanics who rose from difficulty to prominence through higher education. It's had an adequate law program. Many of the professors where priests who after long careers ended up in the graveyard for clergy in the center of campus; an open patch of land studded by crosses and overseen by a jagged-edged, modernistic sculpture of St. Francis. Bustamante Pena's habit of pleasing people continued into his professional career where he had great facility, but not total enjoyment of practice. Likely, Bustamante Pena would have been happier as a musician, but that would not have pleased his mother - so early on he learned to abandon his dream of jamming on the saxophone with a jazz band. Slowly, Bustamante Pena substituted women for music. He carried a series of mistresses until he met Anna Santos Rose. It was then that he reached the top leagues. After meeting Anna he only required one woman on the side. She had a way of making a man feel special. It was an exact formula that rocked Judge Pena's boat.

Anna Santos Rose was not cheap, far from it. She coldly demanded her high price be it in furs, diamonds, cash or property. Bustamante Pena was deep down, by nature, a people pleaser. The fact of Bustamante's ingrained need to make others happy made Anna Rose's web all that more enticing. Bustamante Pena also spent much time pleasing his friends in the Party. He was a champion fund-raiser for local elections. After all he owed his comrades a great deal, they had gotten him elected, over and over, as Judge on the influential 13th District. Bustamante was not one to forget his friends. Nor did he let an opportunity for greater power slip by without an attempt to grab and exploit it. Bustamante set his own webs. He knew how to take his time. His eyes were on bigger fish and using big fish to get rid of other big fish so that he could swim into a greater ocean of luxury and elitism. Namely, Bustamante had his eyes on the mayoral ship and his friends in the Cartels did not think that such a bad idea. They had not taken over San Antonio completely and still many fought them. Having one of their men in the mayor's office was a step in the right direction.

Bustamante had a lot of his mind. Anna Rose was pestering him about her latest "needs". He was busy distracting himself with a severe case of lust directed at the Trinity University professor who was his neighbor down the street and conjuring schemes of how to seduce the woman. He would like to have her at least one time. His wife wanted to do $30,000 in home improvements. That meant he had to put down ten grand the ten grand Burke would be bringing over on a bank loan for the remainder. Anna Rose's latest manifestation of "proof of affection" was a romantic trip to Aruba, which was of course impossible since his wife or the city itself might find out. She was pushing him to prove something or destroy himself. He knew this, but could not help his continued desire for the lovely courtesan. He knew, under no circumstances, could he be photographed in Aruba with another woman. He realized that much. She was having the expectations of a wife and it was not a good sign. He might pay to send Anna Rose to Aruba, but then she might have sex with another man there just for spite. He didn't like that idea. It was risk all around.

That night was a night of fateful meetings, of pairs of people who would influence the bigger future of the local scene. That night Wayne Burke, the "scum" lawyer according to a few in town, came to his old friend's house, Bustamante Pena, with a satchel full of cash in his hand and in his vest pocket, for personal kicks, he kept a Mini- DV tape of a secret recording of Bustamante in a hotel room screwing a woman while the two wore fuzzy animal costumes of a wolf and sheep. There was some specific name for this fetish that Gonzalez had told him, but Burke forgot it quickly and simply referred to the deviant practice as, "Bunny suit fucking." What Gonzalez didn't know was that Burke had his own allies in the Cartel's: Ones that saw great benefit in a long-term famous lawyer who managed things and people instead of a weirdo Judge that could possibly be elected out of power by the whim of the people. Burke was just waiting. He was waiting on the take down of the Judge.

Burke parked a couple houses up from Bustamante's place. There were a few cars juxtaposed between where he parked and Bustamante's house, but more than enough room for him to have parked closer. He could have made it easier on himself by parking much closer. Instead he parked in the least crowded spot, a little bit away from his destination. Years of hanging out with gangsters had added careful and strange habits to the lawyer's repertoire. It was best never to be where they thought you might be or when they thought you would be there. Even a couple houses distance gave instinct the chance at warning if it were a set up. The neighborhood was quiet even though the Spurs were playing that night.

San Antonio was not the kind of big city where the hometown ball team's winning or losing could be discerned by shouts coming from windows during a stroll down a street where storefronts and apartment homes mingled. Windows with neighbors yelling out and the TV blaring the play by play was not part of the San Antonio scene. For all its corruption San Antonio had a safe, conservative front and this was why people like Burke, Bustamante and the Cartels could do so well here under the radar. As a rule commercial and residential areas were segregated in San Antonio. The Monte Vista neighborhood adjacent to Trinity University was not overrun with Spurs fanatics anyway.

Overall, in San Antonio, the days of massive Spurs flags fastened to trucks tailgating down the road with drunks hanging out the window as they bragged, "they were the champs". As if they were the champions of anything thought Burke. The last championship had been won in 2005. The green muck of the river walk was the real soul of San Antonio. It seemed to remain that color year round from the day when the city put green-dye in the river so that on St. Paddy's Day the tourist walking downtown could be charmed. Green muck. That was Burke's soul since he had given up the idealism of his youth that had brought him to law as a vocation. He would have corrupted any place he inhabited. He was like Mark Cuban, the owner of the Dallas Mavericks. They were the Spurs rivals. Or like the old Ozzie Osborne who had once peed on the side of the Alamo. Or like "Cloak and Dagger" - the silly spy movie that was filmed in San Antonio where a young boy discovered a plot in between not so dazzling footage down of the river walk and downtown. That was the soul of Burke and the Cartels he worked for, but it was not the soul of San Antonio.

One could blame the shoddy work of San Antonio's only feature film, however cheesy, to gain even a modicum of acclaim on bad camera angles and poor direction, but it was no excuse. There was something about San Antonio that resisted imitation. It had it's own gravity and like a primitive tribe did not want it's soul taken prisoner by photographs. It was a place of absorption. It defied trends and change. It was a cash town that recessions barely touched. It wasn't impressed by culture or learning. It knew itself. It was as if it had it's own manifest destiny, and like the wishes of some new age scientist or Christian theorist was a universe that knew how it was supposed to grow with its own mysterious intelligent design and DNA fabrics forcing it to imperceptible, yet definite conclusions. As tiny, yet critical factors, always invisible, were adding to its journey strange mirrors reflecting great heavenly entities that beamed down into the nano-seed, quantum expansion of this place. New things arrived in the city like the Joint Military Cyber Command and the NSA's micro-tech division headquarters: Secret agents of all persuasions abounded trying, building hidden forts and observation towers, trying to discern the direction, scope and trigger points of this city.

San Antonio had always though been a place of spies. The Yellow Rose of Texas had gotten info from Santa Anna when she prostituted herself to him before the battle of the Alamo – and more importantly delayed the conflict thus letting the forces to the north to better organize and train for the eventual victory. In the bed of that San Antonio hotel the gallant Mexican general had given in to his inner generalissimo of lust. And there had been more than one massacre by Santa Anna in Texas. The locals say "Remember Goliad!" as well. The call Texans use and was never just "Remember the Alamo". Now the only open wars in San Antonio were fought when drunks hurled peanuts at Howl at the Moon, the piano bar on the river walk – though many say, not far away, one can feel the ghosts of the dead soldiers along the crusty walls of the Alamo where so much of the killing took place in that terrific battle. Perhaps now some of those souls gain freedom by floating with morning light into the body's of one of the hundreds of Mexican "Ilegals" who daily stand in globs on downtown street corners waiting to get picked up for work.

142

Yes, San Antonio is an ancient being of great power: a nexus of spiritual truth and a congregation of the future. San Antonio is a holy pie filled with meat of songbirds. It had been founded on the exact lay line directly north of Mexico City as to be the new capital of the northern frontier and one day it would be. It is the once and future Capital, anointed by the divine and plagued by earthly devils vying to be the marionette masters of its strings.

The haunting of old sea ballad of the conflicts between Mexico and the Untied States is still rings out along the coasts:

Have you heard the latest news?
Sailing out of Liverpool
When I leave this ship I'll settle down

Burke fiddled with the "Bunny suit fucking" tape in his pocket as he approached Bustamante's door and the thoughts of San Antonio's history subsided to be replaced by recent accounts of the inner conflicts between the Cartel leadership as to whom to trust in San Antonio as they expanded their infiltration. Juarez was the most powerful group and Burke had the ear of the first son of their godfather. That was the main move he was waiting for, but others were possible. He connected other families who did some business in San Antonio and circumstances or strokes of luck could always interfere with the timeline. Bustamante had brought him in. He was the oldest living link in the chain, but did not do the biggest workload. He was important in rulings, but already three junior judges were in positions to take that away. They had councilmen too now and another likely on the way. Bustamante was a fat relic who fucked too much and sat on his ass expecting money. He moved mere pawns. Burke moved the Bishops, Rooks and Queens.

In a way Burke could nearly initiate the take down of the Fat Judge at any time. The local players were mostly under his control. Everybody knew Burke had the brains. He was the one who did the hard work. Still, he felt like he needed a spark. It would happen if he were patient. That's something his father might have said.

Burke smirked for before he rang the doorbell:

On the tape Bustamante could be heard saying, "I'm a furry little sheep who caught the big bad wolf, take it wolf, take it."

Knowing something like this about one's rival gave power.

143

This tape might be one of the many possible deathblows that Burke would unload on Bustamante someday. Burke took the sick pleasure of having it in his pocket on the night of merriment and frivolity with his old friend and his family.

Across the entire city it was a night of secret meetings and nefarious back dealings. It must have been something in the positioning of the stars and suns and galaxies. On another side of town, Burke's right hand man, Gonzalez, met with Chin the Medical Examiner for the City of San Antonio. Chin was an expert in making murders look like suicides and reporting them thus. He had been on Burke's and the Cartel's payroll for over a decade. Gonzalez had a message for him and that night was when they would meet about it. Also that night Dr. Julia Brown went to the Havana Club, instead of taking Professor Hatkin's advice and trying the Coco Club. There, at the Havana Club, Jack Pearson had pulled up in his vintage, handicap adapted, 1975 Buick wide ride. He had guided his wheelchair to one of his favorite tables and ordered a 7 and 7. It was a corner spot, but adjacent to main congregation of bar patrons. His favorite seat, like Pearson's position in society, was at once inside and outside and was a natural spot for the professor, fresh to the nightlife scene, to gravitate toward. Pearson thought he was waiting on Adam Carter who, due to the shooting at the Good Will, would never show up. Pearson though had learned to take whoever came. He was in a feisty mood. There wasn't enough gossip stirring in his veins to keep him entertained. He needed to create something. Rumors, secrets and the news had replaced the physicality he lost in the accident. He sucked his drink and thought of what nourishment some good inside information would afford him.

Also on that night of fateful turnings, Spurs starting forward, Demetrius Azul, ran his car into Mario Rodriguez's garage, killing Butch the dog. The garage happened to be in the district where Jesse Herrera would oversee if he won he upcoming election bid for City Council.

The cell phone dialed. The home phone rang. The maid picked it up. "Sir it's for you," said the maid. Bustamante put the receiver to his ear.

"Hi Sir, I'm totally wasted and wrecked my car," said the basketball player.

"Where are you?" asked the Judge.

"I don't know – in San Antonio I think," said Azul.

"Look at your GPS!" instructed the Judge.

Azul complied. He read the address back to Bustamante.

"Listen just wait there. I will send someone," said Bustamante.

"Thank you sir," said Azul.

The Judge dialed another number quickly. "Hello," said Renolds.

"It's Bustamante. I got a gig for you," said the Judge.

"Okay. What is it?" replied Renolds.

"I need you to pick up and clean up Azul Demetrius. He's been in a single car wreck on the Southside," said the Judge as he then recited the address to Renolds.

"No problem sir, I'll be there in 10 minutes," answered Renolds.

"Good," said Bustamante. Both men hung up their phones, but while Bustamante went back to thinking about the night's merriment, Remolds made another call as he started his drive to Rodriguez's garage.

"Hey it's Renolds," said the hired man.

"What's up?" asked Burke.

"Bustamante wants me to pick up Azul. He wrecked his car," said Renolds.

"Ok. Call me tomorrow and let me know how it turns out," said Burke.

"Yes sir," said Renolds.

The pair hung up. It was San Antonio diplomacy at bargain rate. Bustamante opened his door with a wide smile and welcomed Burke, who had just closed his cell phone, with open arms, "Old friend we don't see you enough," said the jolly and fat Judge.

"Maybe my little gifts will make the absence less painful," said Burke as he handed Bustamante the cash and a bottle of good wine.

"I appreciate it come in, come in," offered Bustamante. The families embraced and all sat at the finely decorated dining table to be served. The maid brought in the first courses and drink. It was well done. The conversation picked up.

"You know Burke, I will be mayor one day – maybe sooner or later. And you know what that means – mayor's get paid more than Judges..." the joke seemed funny to the families, but on a level of private business it was a demand to Burke that his side of the contacts in the Cartel's, the ones that pulled some of the big strings, began to appreciate him more. As always he wanted more money.

That could be the straw that breaks this camel's back thought Burke, but let the fool reveal more. With enough rope this bunny lover would hang himself thought Burke bemused.

"You'll make a fine mayor – mayor," added Burke to the humor.

"Your still have your comedy Wayne," said Bustamante' wife.

"It's a funny business in a funny town in a funny life," continued Burke playing the light hearted one that made this crowd most comfortable.

"You know I have some new fish on the line for some business ideas, when we retire from dinner I will explain," said Bustamante.

"Your ideas are always good Judge. I like what you are doing with the house Sarita," said Burke.

"Yes Buste's business ideas better be good – I need more money to finish the job," said Sarita Bustamante.

"We don't have to recreate the fucking Taj Majal in San Antonio do we!" snapped Bustamante. "Darling," said Sarita.

"Sorry. It's election season," apologized the Judge.

At the Havana Club when Dr. Julia Brown walked in the room Pearson noticed her right away. Professor Brown was a fine looking woman. Pearson could tell right away she was lonely. With the right come on this woman was primed for being seduced. Having money gave Pearson confidence despite his setbacks. He loved to womanize even though with the success the accident brought him – it also provided limits to how he could play in bed. Dr. Brown was the cautious type. She circled the perimeter of the establishment while peering across its dwellers. As she came near Pearson's spot he boldly began conversation as she stood near his table surveying the patrons.

"How do you do?" said the wheel-chaired man.

"Oh I'm fine and you?" the professor could not help, but be nice.

"Doing great, listen I can tell you are new in town why don't you join me for a drink? I know the city really well maybe I could give you some tips," said Pearson reading exactly, which button to push on the curious professor.

"I suppose. Sounds nice," Dr. Brown was somewhat relieved. She did not know how to mingle well in such places and the fake Cuban setting replete with photos of Castro, the hull of a cargo plane and gaudy cigar boxes everywhere did not inspire her. She would not feel like a complete outcast if she sat with this disabled

man for a while. The professor's major flaw was that she did not know how to be unpopular no matter the setting. Besides, she was after information after all and this fellow had a sly, knowing look about him. He said he'd fill her in.

"You know I know the owners of this place," bragged Pearson.

"That's cool," said Julia.

This fellow seemed odd, he had money, but it did not appear he had much upbringing. He knew people and that meant he probably did have knowledge about the town. Again, that was what she was after. Maybe he had gotten a settlement for some accident – she guessed to herself correctly.

"I am fairly new to San Antonio," she said.

"You do have that look. I know San Antonio like the back of my hand. I'm 7th generation. It's an okay place," said Pearson.

The waiter stops by their table.

"Yeah another 7 and 7 and a martini, did I guess right?" added Pearson.

"A martini will do. Thanks," said Julia.

"Make it with Stoli, dirty and an extra olive," added Pearson.

Julia nodded that that was fine.

"San Antonio seems to be full of all kinds of adventures," suggested Julia.

"It is – it's calm on the surface, but just underneath a lot is going on. It's a city of insiders and the masses really. Lots of low-level networking – that's important to the Hispanic community, solid ties that translate how business is run. People like to say a few socialite families, the ones that came out of the to the old Catholic Canary Islanders or the powerful Presbyterian guilds of the 1800's, run the whole place, but that is just surface stuff," said Pearson trying to build excitement.

"Oh really what really runs the town?" asked Julia.

"Corruption of course and crooked cops, crooked law people, crooked drug runners," said Pearson.

"Is it that bad?" asked Julia.

"Worse than anywhere in the country, but you wouldn't know it for how calm it is on the surface. That the nastiest way the evil ones buy their power, they give the people peace and protection and the people in turn let them do anything," said Pearson.

At that moment, across town, was when the star forward of The

San Antonio Spurs Demetrius Azul, high on cocaine and brandy, lost control if his 2011 Porsche Carrera. He had been texting the wife of a fellow player about a midnight rendezvous. The Porsche veered sharply off the road and violently struck the fence and part of the side walling of RODRIGUEZ'S GARAGE. Old Butch, the faithful garage yard mutt was instantly killed and the new Porsche was totaled. Azul lay unconscious in the driver's seat until a person from the neighborhood named Mario arrived. Mario, a loyal Spur's fan, recognized Azul and the fact that he was terribly intoxicated. He couldn't turn the star forward of the home team in to the cops. He applied what first aide he knew, getting Azul to a conscious, yet groggy state and called first his neighbor Jesse Herrera, the local activist and connected man, instead of the police. Jesse Herrera was also a Spur's loyalist. If there were a better way to resolve this situation that held the fate of such a local celebrity, a demigod in fact, at stake, then the wise Herrera would know of it; a way that included some profit perhaps or at least season tickets for Mario. Herrera came quickly. He was a big Spurs fan, but was not sure how he could fully help in this situation. He was conjuring ideas all the way to RODRIGUEZ'S GARAGE. When he arrived Herrera found the situation normalizing. The car was a lost cause, but Azul was now sitting off to the side outside of the vehicle with an ice pack on his head. He had already called Bustamante and Renolds was well on his way. Mario's wife had shown up and was attending to Azul in a proper fashion. She was an LVN. Herrera was surprised to learn that no one had called the police, an ambulance or Rodriguez the owner of the damaged property. Azul told him that Bustamante's fixer was on the way. Jesse Herrera began to surmise what kind of situation he was in the middle of.

Herrera searched inside the husk of the lifeless Porsche. He found a bag with traces of cocaine and two marijuana roaches in the ashtray. Then Herrera found something he did not expect. It was something almost beyond his comprehension, but since his niece worked for the military he had an idea of what is was. It was a folder with classified information {and copies from Fed Ex/Kinko's} about U.S. Army Cyber Command and it was sitting in wide-open view on the passenger seat of the famous Spur's Basketball player wrecked car. It made no sense, but Herrera knew it was trouble. He took a breath and sat down next to Azul. Out of the corner of his eye he noticed a SUV pulling up. It was Renolds – Bustamante's man – his fixer. Herrera had met him only twice before. He decided to stick around instead of running off. This way he could try to control how they used his name in this situation – a situation that wasn't at all good.

At that time on another part of town... Susie's was a place for men to relax. It was a Korean song bar where old and forgotten men paid $15 a drink to have a pretty girl sit next to them. It was hidden off the beaten path, behind ill-fated Austin-Highway, at a location few ever saw. That was good for Susie since it was the type of place, because of the odd sense of false intimacy it created and it's "foreignness", that wives would protest against even more than strip joints. It was one of a kind as far as San Antonio and mainly attracted a specific type of Korean and Viet Nam War vet as its regulars. It brought in the odd balls who believed in conspiracies they never talked about, wore shaded glasses, drank only the classic drinks on the rocks, listened to Sinatra or Bing and paid for quiet comforts. These were men who could not easily socialize in other venues, their shock from violent wars, never shared – never healed, were worn as strange badges that formed halos of difference and low sonic field that emitted the command, "Stay away – I've seen the worst – things you know nothing about..."

Few liked these men and fewer had a clue as to what they were ever thinking. They rarely talked, even to each other, and their primary function at Susie's was to slowly sip away at liquor. The atmosphere there was something else. It was also good cover for Chin and Gonzalez when they had to meet in person and in secret.

The two sat at a dark, corner table without girls. The only outside company the two had were the mixed drinks. Still, Gonzalez spoke in hushed tones.

"Burke wants you out," said Gonzalez.

"It's too early to remove him, can you stall on that?" suggested Chin.

"He's suspicious of you," said Gonzalez.

"Well, rightly so. Many of my people are here. We already own things. We already have connections," said Chin.

"How about laying low in Houston for while until we make the big transition," suggested Gonzalez.

"It's an idea. How much time do I have?" asked Chin.

"I'd say three or four weeks. It's really on his docket to get rid of you. He doesn't trust Chinese. A few things are priority ahead of you, but I don't see him forgetting about it," said Gonzalez.

Gonzalez had met Chin in the Army: in Korea. Chin got him in with the Chinese Triads organizing an opium smuggling operation from Afghanistan through Seoul to Houston. Gonzalez had an Army doctor under his influence. It was amazing what an Army doctor working with an Army lawyer could get away with. Houston was a great, untapped market for opiates.

Burke's suspicions of Chin were well founded, but he had no idea of the extent of the Chinese man's ambitions or network with the deadly Triads. The Triads had some footing in Houston where there was an Asian community and a "China Town", but San Antonio was for the Mexicans. The Triads inroads in the Alamo City were slim. Still, Chin and some others had infiltrated. Making Gonzalez the number one man in town would go a long way in gaining power for the Chinese in Central Texas. Gonzalez had gotten Burke to place Chin as the inside man at the city morgue. It had worked at the time. Chin had the skills and was corrupt. The Morgue was actually hard to penetrate. A Chinese guy was not suspect in San Antonio so the move was approved. All murders could not look like murders. They needed a man in the Morgue to make some of them look like suicides or accidental deaths.

As Chin and Gonzalez conspired Burke was passing the ham to Bustamante.

At the same time, at the Havana Club, Professor Brown sipped her Martini.

"What do you do?" asked Pearson.

"Me. I'm a blogger. Oh sorry my name is Denise Richards," said Julia.

"Like the actress?" commented Pearson.

"Whose that?" said Julia.

"You must not blog entertainment," said Pearson.

"Oh no politics," said Julia.

"Interesting what's your site –," asked Pearson.

"The Random Thinker," said Julia.

"Cool," said Pearson.

"And what do you do?" asked Julia.

"I'm into a lot of things. Independently wealthy. Like to keep my *eyes and ears open you know," said Pearson.*

"A man who knows the city," said Julia.

"Oh yeah and this city is on fire," said Pearson.

"Fire – really – you were saying that corruption runs the city right. Do you think there are deep ties to the Cartels from Juarez?" asked Julia.

"You can't quote me in your blog or ever mention in fact," said Pearson.

"No problem," said Julia.

"Yeah I'd say there are deep ties. Don't you think those six heads at North Star Mall betrayed deep ties," said Pearson.

"That was quite the message," said Julia.

"You bet. They are moving in force here. That's because they have the foothold.

It's a game of intimidation that they play. Texas will be like Mexico in twenty years. All the profit comes through Texas and California – why wouldn't they use the same techniques of power here once they are strong enough?" said Pearson.

"We might send in the Army if it gets bad," said Julia.

"Where to Mexico? These people are experts in having the authorities, of any nation, kill off their enemies while they get stronger. That is why corruption of so powerful. You can never get to the root and once you cut one half off another half gets stronger. It's not like normal power," said Pearson.

"Hmm. Bleak. You know what I am really thinking about is writing about the disappearing women of Juarez. Do you think the Cartels or anyone in San Antonio knows or is involved in that?" asked Julia.

Pearson knew to be careful. This lady was a liar. He had figured that out. He'd check her website later for certain, if she even was a blogger at all and had a website? Still, he liked to tell a good story and this chick was definitely a MILF. Pearson would pour it on for the slight chance of at some point getting some sex from this lady. He wanted to continue impressing her with his local wisdom and lore.

"Do you know the tale of the 47 Ponchos?" queried Pearson quixotically.

"The 47 Ponchos?" replied Julia attempting to hide her amusement.

"Yes, it's famous down here and to understand San Antonio – you must understand the 47 Ponchos," insisted Pearson.

"I might have heard something like it somewhere, but please tell me it," said Julia of course thinking of the Tale of the 47 Ronin from Japan.

"You can't have heard anything like it, but I will tell you this tale so you know of this place," continued Pearson, "It was in the time of Zapata and Villa. There was a great and revered warlord who insulted one of the greater men of his region; a Baron with many houses, women, much land, cattle and connections to Mexico City. The warlord was summoned to the Baron's property. He was told he must apologize publicly to the Baron in front of all his wives and mistresses. The warlord would not do this. Hence he faced death and was killed. His men, 47 bandit gauchos, swore a pack to be true to their lord, but they had no hope of real revenge against the powerful Baron. Their vow could only be acted out in one final, desperate act. They blindly charged the Baron's main bank. A bank with three Gatling Guns armed on the roof. The 47 Ponchos were cut down by a hail of bullets in the rain and mud – all dead, but they remained true to their vow and their lord," Pearson paused for dramatic effect, "If you can understand this you understand San Antonio.

"It sounds strangely familiar, but I am sure that is only because it is so universal," demurred Dr. Julia Brown.

"Exactly. That is the power of San Antonio," finished Pearson triumphantly.

The night, seeking a song, but only composing the music and not the lyrics, ended with plans and few answers. Burke relished the small talk of home remodeling as he looked into the Bustamante's faces conjuring images of their future great and tragic suffering. They had brought him up the ranks from early on, but Burke could never shake the feeling of having been a second-class citizen to their first. It was Burke now who the

Cartels needed most and he'd call that chip in soon enough. Chin decided to announce his retirement in two weeks instead of getting murdered in Burke's Purge. He could rally the Triads from underground and when the time came they could strike taking over vital points in the San Antonio/Houston I-10 illegal traffic corridor. The Cartels would not be the only top players Texas someday. Gonzalez would continue to feign allegiance to Burke. His paycheck *would increase greatly at some point. The Chinese paid him well. They were his old teachers. He was loyal in that way.*

Renolds dismissed Mario and his wife. He gave them $300 to keep quiet and Azul got their address. He promised to send tickets.

Renolds gathered the documents.

"You and the politician are coming with me," he said to Azul and Herrera.

Both men knew if they wanted to stay on the good side of Bustamante they'd have to comply. Azul rode with Renolds and Herrera followed. They ended up in a Cartel safe house in a neighborhood not far away. Renolds had taken care of the drugs and the car. He had brought in one of the Cartel controlled tow trucks. The clean up was swift and just in time, a SAPD patrol car cruised just as the tow truck with Azul's Porsche made a turn away down the block. The cop called in the mystery of a broken fence, a damage garage building and a dead dog. Insurance would compensate Rodriguez for everything, but the dog.

Dr. Julia Brown did learn a few things from Pearson, the part-time private detective, odd man around town. She learned San Antonio liked its myth and it's mythmakers. She learned that Pearson seemed to know who was corrupt in the local government and that there was a few differing sorts involved in that. She learned too that the Cartels had to go through people here to get things done, that they didn't rule directly – at least in Central Texas. She also learned that weird handicapped guys in expensive wheel chairs still wouldn't mind having a screw with a clever middle-aged professor – though she certainly decided not to act on that option.

Chapter 15

Discovery

Barry Juarez kicked back at his desk. He was active man who constantly had to be moving, had to be getting things done. For a second, that second, he breathed. Then he thought. The idea came to him to check his personal email. He hadn't done that in a couple days.

He opened the inbox.

It looked like the usual junk mail. An email from his sister he did not feel like opening, a memo his editor had sent to him and then another email sitting there that caught his attention. It was from Samantha Burke – entitled – *Reality TV*.

Barry opened it.

There was a video attachment.

He pressed play. It was some trash at a downtown festival: Girls going wild or not so wild in San Antonio. Man, Barry hated the social elites in this town. They loved to promote themselves in the media. They had access to everything and even published their own magazines. All they seemed to do is flaunt their wealth and power. Wayne Burke's daughter probably thought Barry Juarez should write a feature piece about her being on TV. How little he cared, she probably sent out this video to hundreds of people in town thinking that the pictures were worth one thousand words, when in "reality" they were worth less than ten – two in fact – *"this sucks"*. Barry was hoping he was being asked to be on some show, but that was not the case with Samantha's email. Still, he'd finish watching it. This was the new media. He had to stay informed.

The video link went to a website for Coyote Productions: A local shop wanting to be the next big Hollywood thing. They never needed writers and if they did would only pay a pittance. On the right hand the website were four demo videos. One caught Barry's eye. He clicked it.

A muscle bound guy was talking with an interviewer. "Yes Fitness is the key to happiness. My personal training system is a revolution in..."

It was that bastard! It was he: The fuck that fucked with Barry Juarez was right there on the video. The voice was unmistakable. The tone of conceit the same. The build and look made sense. That was the asshole that Barry Juarez vowed to find and now *Providence* had delivered.

Barry could track this guy now. The plan of revenge and then justice came quick to Barry's mind. He knew whom to call and he knew what to do. What a quick blessing had fallen into his lap. He didn't even have to pay anybody. The egomaniac thought of himself as a promoter, an inventor and worse a teacher of health – this Tom Pettinger. Barry Juarez would have his revenge soon.

CHAPTER 16

Breakaway

The safe house was nothing special. In fact it was a modest and inconspicuous house in a lower middle class, working neighborhood. Perhaps fifteen or twenty Cartel and affiliates had keys to the place. It was for doing simple and quick business. It was in a neighborhood where people kept to themselves and only put their heads outside if they went to work, if they worked at all.

Renolds was there to get the complete story and give orders. Already he knew he was dealing with the unusual. He wasn't an educated man, but he was a clever criminal. He knew some scam was going on with the top-secret documents he had in his car. He needed to find out what that was and who knew about it.

Azul and Herrera sat on the couch. Renolds pulled up a chair in the middle of the living room near them.

"Okay the scene is clean. That means your not going to get busted because you're a dumb ass who drinks, gets high and wrecks their $100,000 car into other people's property," said Renolds.

"Thank God," spouted Azul with a great sigh.

"Herrera, your job is to check up on that Mario and his wife every once in a while. Make sure their needs are met and that this oaf gets them those tickets to games, got it?" said Renolds.

"Sure, no problem," said Herrera realizing his favors to Bustamante were starting even before the election.

"No one try to contact or go near Rodriguez's Garage – no need for any of that," stated Renolds.

The two nodded. Renolds stood up.

"Now! What the hell are those papers!" demanded Renolds.

The two men were quiet. Herrera did glance at Azul.

"Your gonna tell me," said Renolds in a threatening whisper.

"Your boss knows," said Azul.

"Oh yeah he told me to double check your story – so do that for me, tell me the whole thing" said Renolds. There was little doubt that Renolds had at least one gun and likely a knife on him in locations one could not see easily, there were no big bulges in the former Frenchman's clothes, though whatever he was armed with one could be certain he had expert facilities with that weapon be it a .357 or a stick.

"They are the NSA papers Bustamante wanted from my wife," said Azul.

The pressure of the interrogation-like atmosphere, being in an unknown place with an armed villain and the high stakes of treason made Herrera pop.

"What the fuck are you doing stealing those!" said Herrera.

"You don't understand my wife is Syrian – they are insane!" pleaded Azul.

"You mean she did for Syria or for money!" screamed Herrera.

"Calm down! Calm down!" yelled Renolds.

Herrera stood up. Renolds took a step back and began to reach inside his jacket. Azul freaked. His long arm swiped across the room in a great arch as he stepped up from the coach.

The blow from the giant man, who was much closer to seven feet then six, crashed across Renolds face sending him across the room destroying the cheap bookshelf and knocking the gunman, the local fixer, out cold.

"We're fucked now," said Herrera.

Azul sprinted out of the house. Herrera checked to see if Renolds was alive. He was. Herrera rearranged Renolds body to be more comfortable. He stood and left the house as well. Renolds awoke around twelve minutes later. He felt his head and scanned the room. He had the feeling he was alone. Renolds sat up and gathered himself before dialing a number on his cell phone.

It rang twice.

"Hello."

"It's Renolds."

"Yeah."

"The car situation with the ball player is clean, but something unusual happened," said Renolds.

"What's that?" asked Burke now driving home from Bustamante's get together. "Well, I had to ditch some coke and liquor, but I also found some government papers, spook stuff in Azul's car," said Renolds.

"What?!" said Burke.

"It looks like Bustamante and Azul's psycho Syrian wife, from what I gather who possibly works at Spook Hall, pulled Azul into something where either for love of country or love of money or love of pussy or all three - they were going deal in these papers to some other side," said Renolds.

"Listen go somewhere safe with this. Wait till I have Gonzalez contact you," said Burke.

"Got it. Hey Bustamante's man, Herrera, and Azul ran off a little spooked after they gave me the story," said Renolds.

"You got the papers right," asked Burke.

"Yeah," said Renolds.

"Don't worry then – I'll handle the rest," said Burke who hung up abruptly.

Back at his Monet Vista home Bustamante sipped a cognac while waiting for a mid-night delivery that never came. Azul was supposed to bring those secret files by. There was huge money in them. He had to stretch his contacts and powers of persuasion to make this one happen. That crazy Syrian wife of Azul thought it would hurt the heathen capitalist pig Americans who she worked for at the NSA and help out her beloved Middle East, but it was the Israelis who were waiting to pay a goodly sum for the top secret data. Bustamante had been ingenious in seeing the strands of the one-off, highly creative plan come to fruition and now Azul was late. In fact he'd never come. This had been a free spirit move on Bustamante's part. It wasn't Cartel business at all. Azul and Bustamante both did for the extra money to cover gambling and women and the plan seemed to materialize before Bustamante's eyes like a holy and assured vision. Now, it was all going to hell.

Burke was reveling. This would be the straw that broke the camel's back. There was no way the Cartels would sanction such a screwed up notion as using a basketball player and his Syrian wife to steal from the NSA. They did not need that kind of heat of them. They already won public opinion, tacitly, of the American people who were all addicted to drugs, pills, booze, cigarettes – how could they hate the provider, but to dip into national secrets was a sacred cow that could would only mean bad press and far worse for the image of the drug dealers. It was the tipping point to act on Bustamante. Burke knew it.

Any resistance to Burke taking over proxy operations in San Antonio would be negligible if Juarez found out about "Bunny Suit Man's" espionage bender.

Burke buzzed his com. "Yes sir," answered Izzy Contrane.

"Have Laslo sent up," said Burke.

"Yes sir," said Izzy.

Izzy walked to men's room and knocked on the door.

Laslo peeked his head out. "The big boss wants you," said Izzy.
"Right away," replied Laslo.

Laslo who rushed up stairs. Laslo knocked on Burke's door.

"Come in," said Burke.

Laslo entered with a smile.

"I've got an assignment for you Laslo," said Burke.

"Be glad to get out of the office for a while sir – hope it's a mobile mission," said Laslo.

"Sure is son," said Burke reaching into his desk drawer.

"Whatever you need – you know I got lots of talents and skills on file sir, you've seen the resume and rolled the dice," said Laslo oddly.

Burke pulled out a large, taped envelope.

"This is one of those fun jobs we like to do real quiet like with the usual bonus," said Burke.

"Black ops - the best kind, Laslo's the man – high score every time," said Laslo churlishly.

"Awesome. Listen take this package to this address listed and sneak it in the mailbox – the way no one sees you and you never talk about it," said Burke.

"No problemo sir," said Laslo.

"Go to it," said Burke as he handed over the package.

CHAPTER 17

Angle of Attack

Sam Caine knew immediately after laying eyes on Tom Pettinger that Barry Juarez had chosen the wrong angle of attack to corner his prey. Sweet Veins was one sexy bitch, but a vain pretender like Pettinger would not go out of his way to get a piece from a thin, long straight-haired woman with witchy eyes who obviously did not come from a job or family of note. Still, Juarez had hired the badass street duo to lure Pettinger to room #107 of The Roosevelt off Broadway. So they had a job to do. Herm would improvise. It was his specialty. Sam Caine could read that Pettinger was braggart and a man with a need to know. Someone who wanted to be an expert, but likely a little bit cautious too – not exactly a fool. He'd still have to send in Sweet Veins alone for the approach, but sex could not be the bait. In a moment of lightning thought, as the heroine peaked in his system the night before the take down, Sam Caine came up with a double move gambit that was precious.

"Whisky and sour, top shelf," spouted Sweet Veins as she sat next to her Tom Pettinger at the Bombay Bicycle Club.

The order was meant to impress. It got a glance.

"Here you go sweetheart," offered the bartender as he delivered the drink.

"Keep the change," said Sweet Veins as she handed over a ten spot.

"Big spender," said Tom Pettinger.

Something about her style got response.

"I like to pay for a good drink," she said.

"Wise philosophy," said Pettinger.

"All good things cost," she said.

She got another glance.

"You look like a man of experience," said Sweet Veins.

"All kinds," said Pettinger.

"I appreciate that in a man," she said swinging to the side and showing the skirt that opened far up her thigh.

Nothing there.

"This place has got all kinds of planes on the ceiling," said Sweet Veins noticing the many cargo plane parts, models and trading company themes that decorated the bar.

"It's an homage to the East India Company. You know big international trading system and cargo," said Pettinger.

"I like to fly, yes indeed boy I like to fly," said Sweet Veins playing high.

Pettinger glanced again.

"You know my man does business with planes, yes sir – planes, trains, automobiles and boats too," said Sweet Veins.

"That's interesting," said Pettinger.

"You look like a man who likes interesting things don't you," said Sweet Veins uncrossing and slightly opening her legs.

Pettinger peeked then looked away.

"You know all good things are for sale – my man's away and I got a little place around the corner," said Sweet Veins.

"No thanks mama," said Pettinger.

"You sure – you could play with some of my man's toys – he's got books of all kinds of photos too - of planes if you like planes maybe ones from Bombay – but for sure from Colombia and Cuba and Venezula," said Sweet Veins.

The places caught Pettinger's attention. This hooker's pimp sounded like he was a player of some sort.

"Come on baby we got about two hours before the Chinaman comes to collect," said Sweet Veins.

Pettinger looked at her. She seemed wasted, but honest and wanting to deal.

"You like China things – that's near India right – listen sugar your fine looking – I'll even let you stick your nose in the pile of white powder – you like to party right – I can tell," said Sweet Veins.

"And you'll show me the planes from far away places huh," said Pettinger.

"You got it honey – planes full of white powder – lovely souvenirs those pictures, that's what my man says," said Sweet Veins.

"Is it far?" asked Pettinger.

"Not far at all," she said.

"Ok let's do it," said Pettinger.

161

"Oh we gonna do it all right," said Sweet Veins brushing her hand across

Pettinger upper thigh, she pretended to like doing it like a hooker pretends she likes all sex and he pretended it was what he wanted from her.

They walked out of The Bombay Bicycle Club together.

Pettinger let Sweet Veins get in the passenger seat of his car. She noticed his bumper sticker.

"You like Austin?" she asked.

"I liked it," he replied.

The sticker read, "Keep Austin Weird."

The two did not talk much more on the way to the hotel room as Sweet Veins pointed directions with her fingers.

Pettinger thought about Austin on the way to the hotel and his unconscious mind as well formed thoughts of the truth of Austin – each brand and stream of contrary thoughts overlapping, unsure and unclear who was the master voice and because so neither getting a clear message across to the man who made his own decisions. Keep Austin Weird. The bumper sticker could be seen periodically in San Antonio. It was the first thing Sweet Veins noticed about Tom Pettinger's car. He liked going up to Austin to score co-eds. It was easy with an ample supply of cocaine. He wasn't talented at reading the sub-conscious: – the sticker might as well read "Keep Austin White" for finding the deeper meaning of its message. Weird white culture was Austin; outlaw country music, alternative world stage music, Republican state representatives, downtown condos, the bat bridge, small scale boating on centrally located Travis lake, biking, off-beat food, eastern medicines shops, Inde film scene, the technology corridor and Sandra Bullock with Jesse James. Austin was white and weird in all it's leaning despite all its laudations and self-proclaimed aspirations as the liberal Mecca of Texas. It wasn't San Antonio, and as well Austin wasn't as deeply penetrated by Cartel corruption. It was a place for Tom Pettinger, the slave of drug kingpins, to get away from his masters. Going to Austin was his sub-conscious rebellion. It was the place where the person he was supposed to be could come out and play. He should have been an educated, good middle class boy striving for the upper tiers, running a business – at one point he was on that path, then life deviated. Austin was where his delusions found oasis. Where he admitted he

162

did not know who he was, but realized to how to pretend. His own sub-conscious mind knew all these things, but they never fully formed to make his identity grow. He was an arrested adolescent. The boy whose family had long ago colonized South Carolina and staked Barnum Bailey circuses, the old southern top class, he represented a lineage now degraded to drug lord lackey and pretentious street thug. Thus go all empires. The hotel parking lot was formidably abandoned, yet the manager's sole car that was near the office kept Pettinger from getting completely spooked. Sweet Veins pointed him to a spot in the middle section. It was an open area and made him feel more secure. He parked.

"Baby we are gonna party and relax and have us a good old fashioned time," said Sweet Veins as she went to the room door and opened it with a key.

"Yeah right," said Pettinger following her somewhat cautiously.

Inside the room he could see a few items of interest – maps on the walls with place routes, indeed some toys and trinkets from far away places and a pile of something large in the back corner covered with a tarp. Maybe someone was scoring big deals of coke from the Latin trade ways and dealing them to the Chinese in Texas? This would be a real feather in his cap with the Cartels when he told them. They tended to eliminate such competition at the ground level. He walked in the room fully.

Zap.... zap, zap. It took a few charges from the Tazer to put Pettinger down.

When he awoke he was blindfolded and sitting tied to a chair with what he guessed was the same tarp covering his body. He took that to mean he would be executed right there and then.

"Whatever you want," he said in a voice that was not a yell, but more than a whisper.

The extent of Barry Juarez's torture, of what he would to the tied man for the first five minutes, was to remain completely silent. It was excruciating for Pettinger. The steroid boy did not know what or at any moment when something would happen. He could have a finger cut off suddenly or he could have gotten Pettinger hooked on heroin, but instead Juarez just let time pass in silence. After three minutes Pettinger was sobbing. It seemed like whoever had him planned on handed down a death sentence, but making him suffer first.

Then Juarez asked his questions. He used a voice box for disguise.

"Who do you work for?"

"Just odd jobs for The Cartels."

"Who is it that you report to?"

"This guy called The Teacher. He works out of a house on the northwest side in that new Maribela sub-division. You can't miss his house. It's got a corner lot with an old brown mustang always parked out front," said Pettinger.

Barry tried to contain his excitement.

"What are the next big plans?"

"I don't know the plan I just do the jobs. Supposedly we are going to start shaking down bigger fish in town – like council people and such. That might be part of the plan."

"What other players do you know?"

"The guy who delivered the heads to the mall. He's still in town. He'll head out to Wimberley. That's a base of theirs sort of. He's a real weirdo. Rumor is he does strange things – I wouldn't be surprised if that kidnapped girl from King William wasn't his doing. If you follow me."

The buzzer on Barry Juarez's cell phone ignited. He walked outside the hotel room.

He turned off the voice box. "Barry Juarez here... Your kidding." Barry Juarez had about as much information as he anticipated from Pettinger and now even more. He took his pound of revenge too. Going to Wimberley would now be priority in order to investigate this Cartel headhunter and if he was real lucky save Encita Pena, thus making him a double hero for exposing corruption and saving a child. It couldn't get any better than that. Yes, he had gotten his revenge on Pettinger. Barry's guess was that the young man would leave town forever after what he was just put through. Juarez was tempted to have Sam Caine juice up Pettinger with a massive dose of heroin. That would give the steroid junkie something to remember him by, but no, Juarez was not a criminal after all – he was a reporter. He'd have Caine do what was done to him, give the loser a knife and tell him to free himself in five minutes. Instead of the ritzy hotel though Pettinger would be loose in the Roosevelt – a place he more belonged.

Pettinger though had been careful. He had not giving up any local names. He had learned that from his father. Give them good information, but save the great. They would believe the good so much that they would forget about asking the great. For now Bustamante and Burke were safe.

CHAPTER 18

The Bishop's Due

Buck "Walt" Whitman cut his chops in the 1970's in Saigon. He was with the Agency. Those were hairy times. The Agency was still his place of employment. Things were still hairy in his line of work, but in a different way. Big bombs, nukes, terrorists, evil chemicals, traitors that could burn a nation with smuggled contents in a flash-drive – these were the bitches of today. In Saigon Buck had learned to torture and how to kill, but more importantly he had learned trickery. Good trickery still paid dividends in the current climate. Actually few operatives of any service have a natural gift for trickery. In all ages of all nations deception was something that from an early age parents and schools beat out of children. Buck was one of the few rebels who surpassed this childhood conditioning. The real trick of tricks was to train your own instincts to not betray yourself. Even an expert fights the urge to tell the truth in the face of nearly anyone asking. Even Buck, a near sociopath by textbook definitions, fought "being good", but lying – bold-faced and turning the tables viciously were his true first and second natures. He was a sinister man working for the good guys and had gained a reputation as a man who should be allowed to run his own gambits. Now in his 60's he was cagey as all hell. If his "namesake" the American poet of wild nature, Walt Whitman, happened to have a gift for nation saving black ops, instead of writing verse, then he'd be damn proud of his namesake Buck "Walt" Whitman. Buck's life and deeds for one long, eloquent and inverted "Leaves of Grass" – full of black beauty and stunning, poetic endings of men's lives.

Buck did have entire passages of "Leaves of Grass" committed to memory, but the days of seducing young men were behind him. If he wanted sex these days, which occurred infrequently, he'd hire anonymous rent boys and pay cash from a hotel room registered in a fictitious name. He'd go so far as to keep the lights dim as his face would not be easily made. Another of his nifty deceptions that he'd pull on such nights was to give a neighboring guest $300 at the last minute to switch rooms. He tell them the pretense that he simply didn't want to bother with going downstairs to the front desk as to amend arrangements. This way if anyone had his first room wired or by chance the rent boy tried to track him by room assignment later then he was covered. As far as he knew no Agency had him on tape screwing anyone. He checked the files at his clearance level, and two above, yearly. Either way he was beyond caring at this point. The Agency had made peace with the few fags still remaining. The value of homosexuals, and their limits, were known and appreciated. Besides, the job was Buck's priority. There were a few rouge groups he still wanted to hobble. A few vendettas left to settle as well.

He knew the Southwest well. His Spanish was excellent. His cover went back decades. He had friends in most countries south of the U.S. border and got along with Texans, despite being gay, a trait Texans seemed to forgive if one could be passionate about some of the ordinary things of life first and foremost. Buck was nuts for Willie Nelson, big trucks, sawed off shotguns and enchiladas. That was good Texas cover.

Buck had a permanent condo in San Antonio as part of his alias in which he was the owner of a trading company specializing in Latin American Art – a subject he did know in depth. The cover fit well with long periods of travel, odd hours, weird associates and a quirky overall attitude. Buck shared the condo with other operatives passing through the region, but all the décor was personally bought and owned by him. The furniture was of quality and was purchased back to the 1980's. There was a good representation of modern and classic art and folk-art from Columbia, Mexico, Peru and Argentina. The CD collection was substantial and currently updated with popular and offbeat artists. The place had a security system, which was terrific, and enough hidden spy gear, ease dropping devices and weapons to equip the special forces of Papa New Guinea. Buck liked these toys and knew how to use them.

Most of Buck's enemies in Mexico were long dead. In truth he hadn't worked Mexico in fifteen years. That was why his face was chosen out of the blue for this "big pop" operation. Buck was excited. This was a real thrill kill deal. The target was Cartel and from the years of reading reports on all aspects of their activity Buck was certain they were a group that needed humbling ASAP. They were on his Christmas wish list to be taken down a few pegs and now they were his assignment. Some of their scope and power in Latin American and even in the American southwest was rivaling

Agency and F.B.I assets combined. This wouldn't do for an "old schooler" like Buck. Buck's generation matured, whether gay or not, with the expectation that America to be "Numero Uno" on all counts. Everything from his generation's feeling of family, of history, of the news, from their education and their concepts of freedom, religion and prosperity demanded and expected winning.

It was a question of national security. The Cartels had to have a leg broken. It was in a way personal to him and a matter of national pride. These Cartels activated some deep Teutonic instinct that called for all evil to be eradicated no matter the cost. Buck relished when his supervisors authorized a strike. In his opinion it didn't happen enough. So, in turn, when it did – he made sure each one counted hard.

The confluence of factors in San Antonio opened some green lights for Buck to act. The six heads at North Star Mall even turned the CIA Director's stomach. Buck was advanced $200,000 under the front of Art of the Latin Nations Inc. The money was for him to take steps on behalf of the United States of America to create instability in the leadership of the Mexican Drug Cartels and so said NSA/CIA Top Secret Memorandum 102.1116678m.

Bishop Gerato Humberto was a dirty bastard and most citizens wouldn't have wished anything better on him than what Buck "Walt" Whitman planned for this errant representative of the Vatican. Little boys were on the Bishop's "to do" list and that rubbed Buck the wrong way. He never fucked with a minor and hated people who did. Beyond that, Bishop Humberto had his hands in numerous nasty businesses. His Swiss accounts had more than 3 million dollars in them from his efforts to please, provide, inform, harass, and set-up for jail or murder any number of people from many walks of decent and indecent life. The Bishop was a real pearl of religion. He suited Buck Whitman's plans for one particular reason. He was the only man alive and in the region of northern Mexico that the heads of all the different major Cartels all had some respect and relationship with. Catholicism ran deep when one was south of the border, even in the Mexican Mafia. When information or treaties or Papal requests were passed on to Cartels, it was Humberto, the fella who baptized their children and wed their sons and daughters, who delivered them. He was a messenger for governments, Popes and killers and he always got paid for his services.

Buck went into Mexico modestly, on a bus tour, cheap rate fare: The Del Rio Line. The smell of the man in the sit next to him did not faze the veteran of many foreign lands. He tried not to notice the spit drooling down the man's mouth, but all in all it was a good preparation for Mexico. Mexico was raw, natural and real. It was kind and harsh – extreme, but full of silence and humility if that was what you brought inside yourself or violence and mayhem if your spirit happened to carry that sort of luggage. Buck thought of himself as a man who could choose his atmosphere. This mission he would contain the fury he intended in the meekness of a saint as not to be noticed. Grace would protect him. He read a copy of the Bible all the way through the border checkpoints and as expected his passport easily gained him access to the neighboring country. He was inside Mexico. One could feel the difference instantaneous. People in Mexico walked across the street differently than in the States. It was a charged, but subtle atmosphere where people's eyes still darted around as if constantly searching the savanna for predators. The feeling of money and transaction was different in Mexico. Successful shops reached out to consumers with a low level magnetism, an aura of gentle safely and welcome verses pulled you in with a hyperactive, advertising energy. The acceptance of one's station was evident in the vibe of people. Generally they were more contained and less exuberant proof themselves equal to their betters. It was the counter-revolution. Except for the small children at the border who sold gum, knock offs they called "Chicklets", with the fierceness of an Indian beggar or the pickpocket ready to dart suddenly out of the shadows towards a plump tourist – Mexicans were passive citizens.

Buck surveyed the crowd on the bus. Travel as related to class distinction had gotten all screwy with the recession as train prices approached bus process and plane prices approached train prices. Those traveling on the Del Rio Line were of mixed breed. There were Mexican labor bums sleeping off binges as they returned home and slightly bourgeoisies Americanos who were afraid to fly and believed that Jihadists wouldn't bother to blow up the Del Rio Line. Buck surveyed them all, taking in who they were, or who they might be as related to greed, corruption, violence and treachery and did so

169

all without attracting attention to himself. That was the C.I.A. way. It was what agents did. When the bus arrived in Cuidad Acuna Buck exited without one person on it having any clear idea of what he looked like or who he was.

Buck went by taxi to the Hotel Duran for his stay. It was a fourteen room Inn run by an older couple that didn't pry. According to plan Buck would only be there for one night. He knew exactly where Bishop Humberto would be in three hours time. Agent Sasha had done a good job. Buck had recruited her fifteen years prior in Key West. Sasha was hot and just Humberto's type. She came to Mexico four times a year on her "lover tour". Buck had created it for her. She seduced several powerful men and liaison with them alternately on pseudo business trips to Mexico. Humberto was marked for information, but also for death. Buck had been waiting to call his number. He thought of these things as he perched in the closet of room #315 at the Hotel Mariposa.

The door to the room opens inconspicuously, no foreshadowing of the murder to come.

"Long time baby. I imagine you got quite a gift for me," said Sasha giggling as she reached for Humberto's penis.

"Bitch how many lovers do you have?" replied the Bishop as he turned her around.

"A girl never tells," she whispered.

Buck would have to listen to the fucking and worse so the talking while fucking. It didn't last too long. Humberto's "gift" had been so long waiting it seemed that delivery time was expedited.

Buck never opened the closet door until the Bishop was well on his way to death. The micro-dart he used from his blowgun served two functions. One, Humberto would not feel it during passion of love making as Buck expertly placed his shot near Sasha's scratching paws. And two, no medical personnel in Mexico could discern it's effects from a heart attack. In the end Bishop Humberto lay dead after having his final organism. Buck gave Sasha a kiss on the cheek. They both left and the landlady hysterically reported to the police and the press finding the Bishop dead in one her rooms after having met with a prostitute.

It was a good kill, but what Buck was really after would occur one week later. Changing hotels twice then on the third day when any suspicions of the Bishop's death had fully subsided Buck travelled, again by bus, to Nueva Laredo. The Bishop's death was not investigated as anything beyond a tawdry affair. Overall, except for local rumor, that part of it was kept hush-hush. Buck opened the paper while sitting on The Border Trials Line and happily reading in Spanish that the funeral of the honorable Bishop Humberto would be well attended at Our Lady of Inception three days hence. Buck knew the lay of those church grounds well. Nueva Laredo was the perfect location for his plans. It was an easier exodus back to the States than Ciudad Juarez, especially if the heat was on. Except for the excessive farting of the passenger in the seat in front of him, the travel to Laredo was cordial.

Buck stayed at The Hotel Grande, which was anything but, the sixteen room extended hut rested off a mini-plaza about one mile from Our Lady of Inception. It was a CIA recommended location. He had never been there before. He entered wearing his white; sweat stained jacket, no tie, light shirt, short sleeve, and loafers – just like a spy or tourist from the 1950's should have looked. Consciously to be slightly conspicuous was Buck's game plan, besides he couldn't compromise on style while in Mexico. The romance of it called. The front desk of The Grande also served as its bar. He paid for two nights in advance, cash, and ordered a Tecate.

"Are you having fun in Mexico sir," asked the matron of The Grande.

"I love Mexico. Been many times," answered Buck.

"And Mexico's loves you too sir – it does – extra lime?" offered the matron. "Please," accepted Buck.

"Are you here for the funeral of the Bishop?" asked the woman.

"What Bishop?" replied Buck.

"Oh, a renowned Bishop is being buried here soon. They say he was a great man," said the woman.

"Oh, that's nice," said Buck.

"Of course some say he was not so nice," said the woman.

"Only human I suppose," said Buck – this was how it was done when one stumbled on a conversation about the mission with a stranger. One pretended not to know about the situation, the Bishop's death, but in an off-handed manner. Then one followed a natural course of disinterested dialogue about the matter, the Bishop's funeral, while not encouraging great talk about it nor being

171

the first to change the subject. This way in the memory of the other person, the stranger, you are not suspicious later on.

"Yes only human. Do you like great Mexican food sir?" asked the woman.

"Oh of course – that's half the reason I come to Mexico," said Buck.

"And the other half?" asked the woman.

"The beautiful people," said Buck.

"Your charmed sir, charmed – well then don't eat next door tonight – go down the block to Juanita's – it's simple, but delicious food, if you like real Mexican enchiladas you will be happy – I bet you do like real Mexican enchiladas, not that stuff they serve in Tejas!" exclaimed the woman.

"Oh yes the more mole sauce the better!" concurred Buck.

"He likes mole! Wonderful. Listen I am going up to double check on your room. Do you need help with your bag or another Tecate now sir?" asked the woman.

"No I am fine senora, thank you for the hospitality," said Buck, though almost slipping, he wanted to say "hospitaliano" to be cute, but an agent never wants to use unique phrases in the field that will cause someone's memory to connect you to something out of the ordinary. Besides that was an Italian phrase. Hmm, he was slipping, charmed by the old matron, he still had "mother" needs perhaps, getting old, that's okay he thought, this would likely be one of the last jobs of this form of daring the company let him do. Maybe he'd go independent. He liked these sorts of jobs. He swished his Tecate and gulped down the remainder before exploring the center court patio of The Grande. Maybe he would read up on his Freud when he got back to the States – just in to toughen up a little.

When Buck went out into the center patio there was a lone man standing with his back to him at the far end. This was never good in the spy game. Soon though the man moved on and appeared to be no more than a vendor taking a respite. The patio area was calm. Buck put his bag down. He breathed. It might be his last carefree breathe in a while. He was trying to pull something big off. Something certainly dangerous. He did love Mexico. He loved Mexicans. They were always inviting and willing to meet good cheer with good cheer. Most Gringos had it wrong about them, including a lot of specialist who analyzed "culture" back at Langley. Gringos mistake was that Mexicans always wanted something. They believed them unskilled and needing an edge or angle at all times. That there was no real freedom to the culture and they mistook the Latin way of relaxing, of taking the middle moment for peace, siesta, etc. as an innate need in the Latin to be told what to do: All that "telling Latins what to do" kept Buck in business, but was disaster for overall personal or long-term relations between the neighboring nations. No one at Langley listened to Buck about such matters of scale and policy. He'd have to settle for his little gigs of death and mayhem. He did enjoy those and the folks on the other end of them, Latin or not, always deserved what they got. Buck knew. He had read the files and seen the bodies.

Buck spent the two days waiting for the funeral developing his cover and implementing the device. He talked with local artists about who was good in town. He bought a couple pieces from a teen artist who had talent: Jose Toticaliun. Jose was a street artist who painted local pottery in fabulous ways. Scenes of old Aztec and Mayan rituals adored handcrafted pots and vases. It was superb work. It didn't try to pass itself off as antique, yet it had an old feel and was not at all glossy kitsch art – it was true, modern folk art. Buck would feature one in the San Antonio apartment and at his online shop. He always arranged for shipping of the work from Nueva Laredo to his San Antonio holding point. His trip all seemed so harmless except for the plastic explosives he fashioned to look like church walls.

A CIA courier/mule had stashed the components in a safe house from which Buck retrieved them before assembling them in his hotel room and then making a late night visit to the church. When Buck returned that night in his room there was a faint hint of the scent of woman. He reached for his revolver, not very quickly, but before he drew it out the lights came on and there was Agent Sasha standing in a nightgown. She looked ready for bed.

"I took a nap," she said.

"No problem baby. Glad to see you," said Buck.

"Tomorrow's the big day," she said.

"Yeah everything's ready," assured Buck.

"Thought I'd stay here tonight – less paper trail," said Sasha.

"Good idea. I'll take the couch," said Buck.

"We can share the bed," said Sasha.

"Oh honey your sweet," said Buck.

"Just thought I'd offer," said Sasha.

"Hey don't wear a red dress tomorrow," said Buck facetiously.

"I never wear red to funerals," said Sasha.

"Light out," said Buck.

Sasha turned off the lights. She crawled back into bed and Buck fell on the coach exhausted. He'd gladly take the three hours rest before the job began in the morning. Neither agent snored, which was a comfort and both set their company cell phone alarm clock to the right time though likely each would wake up five minutes before it went off. Trained agents usually did that. They usually woke up five minutes before alarms rang.

Five minutes before it was time for the alarm both Buck and Sasha were up yawning.

"You know in mammals those who yawn alongside you show an innate nature of kindness," said Buck.

"Of course – how else could I make love to evil men who you are about to murder," retorted Sasha.

"Touché," grinned Buck.

The two got up and changed clothes. Bashfulness was not part of an agent's demeanor. These two had striped naked before in the same room many times. Sasha when ready left ahead of Buck. She only nodded a good-bye. The rest of the mission would be conducted by signals and silence. Buck was dressed in casual wear intending to pass himself off as a bystander who by happenstance was visiting Our Lady of Inception on the day of the Bishop's funeral. Sasha had disguised herself. Hair in a bun, glasses and formal, black work suit and a small faux badge on her lapel as to give an appearance of perhaps being a member of the media. She'd move closer to the main group of mourners as Buck administered the operation from the periphery.

The funeral was well attended though travels to the church were not slowed by any obstructions. It wasn't a sea of black, but there were the required regional heads of the Catholic Church, some faithful parishioners of some means that knew the Bishop better than most, a couple members of the media, some local hanger-ons and best of all nearly a who's who of Mexican Drug Cartel leaders from the border cities.

There were Captains, sub-captains, lieutenants and even two heads of major families all at the same location to honor the death of the man who had married so many of them, baptized and married their children, buried their dear parents and most loyal associates, no matter how violent the death and negotiated countless treaties and deals with the Americans, officials in Mexico City and not the least between the Cartels themselves that ultimately staved off violently civil wars. Also the many Papal dispensations, blessings and forgiveness's Bishop Humberto had given in confessional or last rites to the mafia didn't hurt attendance from this quarter either. Here gathered on the grounds of Our Lady of Inception's for the burial of Bishop Humberto were the gangster masters and sub-masters of Matamoros, Reynosa, Roma-Los Saenz, Piedras Negras, Ciudad Acuna, Ciudad Juarez, Palomas and even Agua Prieta, Naco and Nogales not to mention the rep from Mexico City.

Boy, this bombing could have been a PR cluster fuck. If done wrong it would wipe out an assortment of innocents. Yet, Buck knew two important factors about bad boys at social events and this place in particular. Otherwise he might have killed some Mexican officials, a couple reporters, children and some "Average Joe" Churchgoers right on the U.S. border and that would not have been acceptable even by CIA standards. Even taking into account the 6 heads these bastards placed in the Easter Charity display at North Star Mall. The PR math would not have added up. Still there was no other time or place for these men to have gathered and it was up to Buck's ingenuity not to squander that opportunity.

The American public wanted blood. Ever since the heads were dropped off there had been an uproar of media commentary and citizen vocalization whose sub-text basically read, "What the Fuck – are these greasy Mexican gangsters, these half ass Al Capone's doing coming into our turf and showing blatant defiance with something out of a God damn cheap ass, B-rated Godfather flick on one of our most sacred institutions – a first tier Mall - and oh yeah by the way that was a mother fucking Easter display for kids for friggin sake – gosh darn it, exclamation point, PTA, Girl Scouts of America, Apple Pie, etc – fix this you fuckers in government and by God draw a little old fashioned blood in revenge ASAP – Afghanistan and Iraq style if need be – P.S. don't let these fuckers get away with it like you did the Russian army in Georgia or friggin

North Korea shelling islands and blowing up submarines – understand me dudes in government??? – or your ass is grass..."

Buck knew why he was there. He was there to give an answer for the American people about the invasion of their soil. He was prepared. The courier had dropped a Smith & Wesson, 6-shooter, snub nose revolver, paint, paper mache and just the right amount of plastic explosive for the job. Of course putting the bomb in the coffin would have been the most dramatic. Yet, that would violate the guidelines of the casualty plan. Buck knew there was never any sense in killing innocents. He shuffled his feet near the back corner of the main church pretending to be engaged in some personal meditations. He smirked when the main services inside the church ended and the group moved to the hole in the ground reserved for Bishop Humberto. Like clockwork the burial ritual of the bad boys at church played out as it had every other time Buck had been at Our Lady of Inception or any other gangster event be it in the movies, on TV or as in Buck's experience – in reality. He saw Sasha move safely with the pack to the hole in the ground. She lingered toward the rear as to keep Buck in her line of sight. No one seemed to know her as the whore who had last shared the Bishop's bed though even if they had had room service the waiter would not have easily recognized her from mid- range.

Like clockwork, the men of the Mexican Cartels, stressed from the idea of death and being at an institution, a church no less, when their whole lives had been rebellion away from institutions, running from angry teachers at school, avoiding the police, the jail, the prison, the asylum – the one thing they needed to do when at such a place, setting differences aside for the moment, was to take a smoke break. It might as well have been the boy's restroom in middle school. The spot at Our Lady of Inception was the same as before – the middle, supporting column on the east side of the church building. It was an easy place to peel off from the main group after leaving the service inside and provided a natural shelter from the pack seeing what tricks the bad boys were up to. All the big men of each of the Cartels and most of their gunmen waddled over as innocently as they could to the column and began lighting up cigarettes; the universal public stress reliever. One tough had a cigar. Grimaces and smirks were their sign language as the group shared a ritual together older than the days of their rivalries and civil wars.

This went back to grade school. Buck could not have been more pleased for that column was the exact spot where he had hidden his plastic explosives under a paper mache replication of the stone that comprised the south wall of Our Lady of Inception.

Buck was about to detonate the device: Then a boy, a teen, emerged from within the pack of hoodlums. Darn. Buck didn't feel like killing a teenager. Quickly he knew what to do. Sasha, already on the same page, reacted to his signal. She separated herself from the main congregation, shuffled her hair down from the bun and pulled up the tight dress suit just so then walked sexily as possible, considering it was a funeral on church ground, in a direct line where the gangsters on their smoking break could naturally ogle her. The men noticed. Some grinned. Some formulated a plan. Others counted their cash on hand, but none moved for her except the teenager. Again some knowledge of culture and region had allowed Buck to know what would happen like clockwork. It was an old adage of the men of the Southwest – "A bull and a young bull go atop a hill and see down in the valley a bunch of sexy cows. The young bull says hey let's run down there and fuck one of them. The old bull says – why don't we just walk down and fuck them all." None of the macho men would leave the group and look desperate enough to chase some tail in front of everyone. It just wasn't done. The teenager of course did, a good solution. BOOM! Buck exploded the device. Fourteen of the Cartel men were killed instantly and a few others would never be the same again. One moment they were leaning against a church wall inhaling smoke and the next... dead or crippled for life.

The violence of the moment was ugly. Mourners dressed in nice black clothes had to see people, some were loved ones, shredded by a sneaky device designed to "impersonate" a church wall. Men who had been thinking about screwing the lovely Sasha one moment then the next were killed or gravely wounded. Some mourners and officials came to help clean or hold down the ugly mess and then some ambulances. By then Buck and Sasha were long gone. This was the way with the CIA. They did not clean up messes. They started them. They did it in advance, or like today did it for revenge. Speculation would range from the killing being a hit by rival gangs, or a member from inside who wanted to move up and take out a lot of the competition fast. Maybe it was the Mexican government who

177

did it? The war there had been full on in the streets for some time. Maybe they had decided to take it to the next level? Or of course it could have been the Americans. The dirty, rotten Americans who can come in and kill so easily in another's country and not feel bad about it in the newspapers the next day.

CHAPTER 19

Flight

Jesse Herrera ran for his life, but after running far and getting as far as he could he stopped. There really was nowhere to run. He sat at 24-hour donut shop drinking coffee and eating donuts to think it through. By first light he had a plan and was determined to act on it.

Obviously Bustamante would know what happened. Jesse figured with goons and secrets of this scale the retribution would be swift and great. It was the end before the beginning. Then again what had he really done – that is in the eyes of the law, nothing really if he could get a good lawyer. He was at the car crash, but was sort of coerced into going along and he was going to the authorities right away so that might not count for anything in the big picture. He had to think like his enemies. Someone had to be the scapegoat. Coming clean was the best course.

There was one person to call.

"Barry Juarez here," answered the reporter.

"Mr. Juarez. I have some vital evidence to tell you," said Herrera.

"Your kidding," said Barry, "Who is this?"

"It's Jesse Herrera – I'm running for the council seat in 13," said Herrera.

"Yes Mr. Herrera how can I help you," said Barry smelling a good lead.

"A lot. I have some pretty damning information," said Herrera.

"Do you want to meet?" said Barry.

"Let me just tell you," said Herrera.

"Okay go ahead," said Barry raising his mini-recorder that he quickly retrieved from his breast pocket and pressing play.

"Well some funny things have been happening in the 13 office and Bustamante kept asking me to do more funny stuff to sort of keep up with it and," began Herrera.

"Judge Bustamante Pena?" asked Barry.

"That's right, well first of all he keeps sending in all these no name small business owners with lots of cash to donate out of no where – it just seems odd then he sort of suggests that there are trade offs to be considered," said Herrera.

"You mean in exchange for this money going into campaigns like yours," said Barry.

"Yeah like that – nothing specific, but really the money is bigger than that – these guys keep dropping the top limit on 13 – 10 grand and so a bunch gets spread out over the party as a whole as well – you know it's not illegal, but just weird," said Herrera.

"And then he asked you to do something specific – Bustamante that is," said Barry.

"Well yeah just last night I got a call from him," said Herrera.

"And," said Bustamante.

"That's where it got weirder. He sent me to a business in my district –

Rodriguez's Garage and there was Demetrius Azul who had wrecked his car," said Herrera.

"The basketball player?" said Barry.

"That's correct. So I begin to look after Azul and see how he is doing – assuming we are waiting on an ambulance then all of a sudden Jack Renolds show up," says Herrera.

"He's associated with Bustamate," said Barry.

"Yeah he is and I don't know if you know this, but he sort of a tough character – so I realize something strange is happening, but am not sure what to do. Next thing you know Renolds says that Azul and I are supposed to go with him – I guess to see Bustamante – I wasn't sure," said Herrera.

"Ok and then what happened," asked Barry.

"We all ended up at this house and Renolds pulls out this NSA secret document that he says he found in Azul's car, and Azul's pretty drunk I think and Azul says something about the his crazy Syrian wife stealing these government secrets for Bustamante and then Azul goes nuts and knocks out Renolds so I ran for it – I'm going to the police, but I wanted to get my story to you first," said Jesse.

"Smart move. Listen Jesse your covered. Yes calling me first was the right move and going to the police is too. A couple things – your sure these NSA files were the real deal?" said Barry realizing he had struck journalism gold Watergate and Deep Throat style – he was already envisioning himself sitting as his computer typing the first draft of the story. As the two men spoke Juarez used his cell phone to email his editor that he had a huge scoop.

Herrera continued, "They looked real and from everybody's reaction it seemed so, but I don't know much about all this stuff – I was sort of dragged into it just going along with what my political sponsor asked of me."

"And no one blames you Jesse. Ok can you also give me the names of all those fund donors Bustamante sent to 13?" asked Barry.

"Gosh – I don't know – I can get that – the last guy was Pepito – yeah Pepito Rojas – he owned a repair shop on Culebra I think," said Herrera.

"Good – do what you can on sending me all those names when you get them – and when you go to the police bring your lawyer and ask for Captain Stark – he's a trustworthy guy – you got a pen?" said Barry.

"Yeah sure," said Herrera.

"Here's my email I want you to use: Pulitizer_to_B@salight.com - I always thought there might be something funny about Bustamante," said Barry almost to himself as he gave the would-be politician his special email address he reserved for the big ones.

"Believe me I was as shocked as anybody about all this," said Herrera.

"You did a good job. I'd like to meet with you in person later in the week. From what you're telling me you got sucked into this and informed, which is good, I don't think you'll be in any trouble," said Juarez.

"I hope not," replied Herrera.

"You did the right thing," affirmed Juarez. "Sure – this in my cell I called you on," said Jesse.

"Alright got it plugged in - thanks and good luck," said Barry.

"Thanks," replied Herrera.

"Good-bye," said Barry.

"Bye," said Herrera.

It was too good to be true, but it was obviously true. Barry Juarez would run to the office and file the initial reporting of this story into the editor's log. This was breaking. He glanced at the door of the Roosevelt hotel room. He did not have to go back in there. He walked over to where Sam Caine was parked with Sweet Veins doing look out.

"You got what you need boss?" said Sam.

"Yeah I got it," said Juarez.

"What do you want us to do?" asked Sam.

"Give him this penknife, tell him to free himself in five minutes, any shorter and he'll get stuck – let him go," said Juarez.

"You got it boss," replied Sam.

This was freaking media goldmine, big bonanza time, adding up all the new information about Pettinger, The Teacher and the possible abduction tie in and maybe a confrontation with or even capture of the man who terrorized San Antonio with "the 6 heads", as they were now being called nationwide, and now a corrupt and powerful Judge in the mix, a real political mover and shaker, this was huge and it was all Barry Juarez's. He looked up Pepito Rojas on Google from cell. He'd get his side of this on tape then go to Wimberley and call Bustamante on the way for an interview.

Barry drove to Pepito's shop in ecstasy. This was the big bitch. A glorious cross section of forces were aligning to deliver into Barry Juarez's hands the story of the decade or two or maybe since Kennedy was shot in Dallas, at least as fare as Texas was concerned. The top tier of journalism was in sight. It was Geraldo time. The whole thing was hitting him with the intensity of great tax deduction for a miser. It would be the journalistic equivalent of going from bouncer in a rave party to head of Homeland security.

Manically Barry Juarez retrieved the appropriate "books on CD" from the case in the glove box. He forwarded to the track to the one he always played when a good story was about to break – the voice of Patrick Stewart, though not a fan of Star Trek: The Next Generation, always raised Barry Juarez's spirits, it was the tone of goodly authority and conscience – the tone of an individual winner against the great forces of fate and having Patrick read the most moving passages of all time for winners, winners who went through a spell of turbulence and conflict, was Barry Juarez's triumphant and consistent ritual every time a big story broke:

"The hatch, removed from the top of the works, now afforded a wide hearth in front of them. Standing on this were the Tartarean shapes of the pagan harpooneers, always the whale-ship's stokers. With huge pronged poles they pitched hissing masses of blubber into the scalding pots, or stirred up the fires beneath, till the snaky flames darted, curling, out of the doors to catch them by the feet. The smoke rolled away in sullen heaps. To every pitch of the ship there was a pitch of the boiling oil, which seemed all eagerness to leap into their faces. Opposite the mouth of the works, on the further side of the wide wooden hearth, was the windlass. This served for a sea-sofa. Here lounged the watch, when not otherwise employed, looking into the red heat of the fire, till their eyes felt scorched in their heads. Their tawny features, now all begrimed with smoke and sweat, their matted beards, and the contrasting barbaric brilliancy of their teeth, all these were strangely revealed in the capricious emblazonings of the works. As they narrated to each other their unholy adventures, their tales of terror told in words of mirth; as their uncivilized laughter forked upwards out of them, like the flames from the furnace; as to and fro, in their front, the harpooneers wildly gesticulated with their huge pronged forks and dippers; as the wind howled on, and the sea leaped, and the ship groaned and dived, and yet steadfastly shot her red hell further and further into the blackness of the sea and the night, and scornfully champed the white bone in her mouth, and viciously spat round her on all sides; then the rushing Pequod, freighted with savages, and laden with fire, and burning a corpse, and plunging into that blackness of darkness, seemed the material counterpart of her monomaniac commander's soul..."

Barry Juarez breathed the air of victory as the words inspired him and he cut his engine to his car, which now parked in front of Pepito's shop. He walked into the shop's office with pen and paper in hand, but his tape recorder was also on and hidden in his side, jacket pocket.

"Pepito Rojas?" asked the reporter.

"Yes – who are you?" asked Pepito who was alone behind his desk.

"Barry Juarez of The San Antonio Light," stated the reporter.

"How can I help you?" asked Pepito.

"I just spoke with Jesse Herrera," said Barry.

"Oh – yes I support his position on education in 13," answered Pepito.

"Yes right," said Barry who was taking his time, building the atmosphere of a big confession like a cop who spooks people.

"That's why you're here right – about the election," said Pepito.

"In a way. How well do you know Judge Bustamante?" asked Barry.

"Judge Bustamante?" said Pepito.

"Yes didn't he oversee your brother Hector's case?" asked Barry.

"Perhaps – yes it was Judge Bustamante," answered Pepito.

"Listen Pepito I know what the Judge did for you and your brother in return for the money, Jesse Herrera told me everything.

"Jesus Christus! Jesus Christus!" cried Pepito putting his bowing his head into his

hands.

"Listen Pepito – it's not too late to be the good guy in this – I know the Judge must have pressured you hard to go along with this plan," said Bustamante.

"We never talked to the Judge, only to that lawyer Gonzalez who said Wayne Burke knew this was how the Judge would make things easy for Hector.

"Wayne Burke," said Barry not believing how juicy this was getting.

"Yes Gonzalez said that was the way it was done and Burke knew Bustamante cared about the District so if I helped there would be a consideration for my brother – no time in prison," confessed Pepito.

"I see. I just have a few questions more questions," said Barry.

"What are you going to do to me?" asked Pepito.

"I am not going to do anything to you Mr. Rojas. I am just telling the story," said Barry.

"Should I go to the police," asked Pepito.

"That's a good idea and bring another lawyer, not from Burke's Firm," suggested Barry.

"Yes," said Pepito head bowed again.

Raul popped his head into the office.

"Hector we're getting backed up in the lines today," he said.

"Raul you guys are going to have to handle today by yourselves – I've got business outside the shop all day," said Pepito.

"Yes sir," responded Raul, his head popping out of sight as rapidly as it came.

Judge Bustamante Pena believed it would be just another day. Another day on his steady climb to magnificence. A climb to a place he could please many women, any woman. He did a brief texas two step dance move as he lazily retrieved the mail and brought it to his desk, not particularly noticing the slightly oversized and differently shaped envelope that was in the batch.

He had a drink and began staring at the television in his study. There was more local news about that poor girl Encita Pena, from

184

what the press was calling The Little House of Flowers. What a kind and humble family she came from. Life was not fair reflected Bustamante. It was heartbreaking. There were killers on the loose that Pena know about.

Then there was more news on the "6 heads in a bag" – the local stations loved to pile tragedy on tragedy – they scared ordinary citizens in way, with such great effect, that they made Pena's world of allowing the bad guys to have more power much easier. If was as if they kept implying connections within connections, impossible things to know, but things that would always keep the public doubting and on edge. Maybe they were more right then they knew? Manuel, Bustamante's best insider from Juarez, had intimated that Timbero was involved or used to procure young women, for those atrocities to the female gender that occurred all too regularly in Juarez. It was believable. Having been a judge of decades, Bustamante had never seen someone with such a cold stare as Timbero. Maybe he was starting to murder women freely here in the States? The wheels in Bustamante's head were spinning more than they had since finals in law school at St. Mary's. Bustamante Pena thumbed his mail.

Then breaking news came across the television:

"In Mexico twelve high ranking members of various Mexican Drug Cartels were killed and several others were injured during an explosion at St. Mary of the Immaculate Conception Church. The various Cartel members who are rarely all together at one time had been attending the funeral mass of Bishop HumbertoLocal speculation about the cause of the explosion at this time are ranging from a faulty air conditioning unit to revenge by C.I.A. for the delivery of twelve heads in San Antonio's North Star Mall by suspected Cartel members."

The news elated and shocked Bustamante. More room to have influence, though perhaps one of his friends had died, and then it meant someone was cracking down hard. The Judge didn't like all these games with heads and bombs.

He thumbed the envelope again.

One piece seemed solid. Something different was in it. He had some random thought that made him laugh, but then gave him a chill. He then thought how he would have liked Burke if he could trust him. Burke though was invaluable, but lesser ones had to be kept in their place.

He opened the one piece of odd mail. It was a DVD. On it said the word, "Your Busted."

He played it.

He was aghast. He lost his breathe. Others knew about his bunny suit. A note inside read,

"America never forgives its freaks – all will soon know about you."

His first reaction was to put a gun to his head.

Then the thought came that Burke was behind this one. The epiphany he should have seen all along. The plot to take his spot was right in front of him all the time. It had to make sense. His mind was sharper than ever before. Renolds could not be trusted. He had had a weird tone of late. Why hadn't this perception come earlier? The final knowledge was that it was all too late. The bunny sex was on its way to all the wrong people. His wife alone would murder him. The press would crucify him. He could be disbarred and certainly would be removed from the bench. Maybe they wanted money, but no this was going to be a public lynching with no bones about it.

The phone rang. "Judge Pena?" said the voice.

"Yes," the Judge squeaked barely audible.

"It's Barry Juarez from The Light.I wanted to come by and talk with you," said the reporter.

"I don't wear those clothes," said Bustamante.

"Sir, I just wanted to get your comments about the NSA papers you had Azul's wife take before anyone misinterprets this," said Barry.

Bustamante hung up the phone. The celestial landscape was committing treason on his soul. Had he heard what he had just heard? They knew of everything at once? Who were these people? It was over. Instead of putting his gun to his head – the Judge grabbed his car keys and ran outside with his gun in hand. He had to make it to Mexico. They needed new leaders now that so many Cartel heads had been executed. He was the man for the job. They had often talked of him retiring in Mexico in luxury when his tenure was over. Now they would welcome his wisdom and command at headquarters. They would need him in Mexico and he could have as many new women as he wanted. He was saying good-bye to his wife and America – he elated in a zany way, out of himself with crazed eyes, but happy in an insane way nonetheless. He pictured the rode to freedom as he got inside his car and another pretty thing caught his eye.

CHAPTER 20

Never So Much Time

Wayne Burke had been trying to reach his daughter for days. She was caught too much in the fast lane and he needed to sit her down. She'd been bugging him about funding this or that project. She thought she was Paris Hilton sometimes. He wished they were that powerful, but they weren't. He needed to bring her down to reality. Likely some of her pitches were in his email box. Maybe that would tell him where she was.

He searched through his *SPAM* files – where the excess video files often went, sure enough there was a file from his daughter. Burke pulled it up, darn, it was one of those where the video begins playing automatically. It was that San Antonio Realty TV show she was always going on about. He looked at it for minute, what the fuck, the white eyelash was unmistakable, it was that killer Timbero, he walked right by his daughter in the video, - Burke's mind raced – he speed dialed her again, still no answer, maybe Bustamante had already set up retribution or someone in the Cartel had it out for him?

He dialed Renolds.

"Yeah."

"Meet me at 35 North and 1604 in fifteen minutes, were going to Wimberley," said Burke.

He raced to his car, on the way telling Izzy to keep calling his daughter and to call him right away if she reached her.

Dr. Julia woke up with a weird feeling. She never paid too much attention to feelings, but lately her experiences and thoughts seemed to be widening her perceptions. San Antonio was proving to be quite the riddle box to figure out. There were a lot of layers and almost a low-level feeling of constant conspiracy to the culture. It was as if the city was aware of being involved in something bigger than itself, but like the best of children's game it keep it quiet from the adults.

Julia made some coffee. She glanced at the paper. Her son had been gracious enough to put the San Antonio Light on the table before he left for his karate class. He was growing up. That meant she was getting old. That was okay. There was plenty of intellectual work for the mind of an elder to handle over the years. Maybe she'd give up men, focus on finishing her career with strength and perhaps wait for the grandchildren to arrive.

Her thoughts soon turned back to the women of Juarez. Maybe blogging some would put a new spin on her investigation. Likely most of the key people were online at this time of day – no matter where in the world they were. With some of them – their insights were so keen it did make sense to form more of a professional relationship with them instead of her just being the content provider to their role as online information consumer. She thought she probably wouldn't say that if she were not unmarried now and living in a new part of the world where things happened she did not know how to control. It sounded desperate making colleagues or even friends online. Still, she was after all a single mom and that did something to a woman. She had to admit she needed people. She needed help. Those people – Tomorrow, Red Herring, Fem Nazis and even Will Rise expressed themselves consistently as caring and thoughtful people. Still, they were online a lot. Maybe they were young or perhaps very old? Maybe they were unemployed or disabled? Still. Then again she was none of those things and she was online a lot. But hey, she was a content provider. Didn't that make a difference? Didn't it mean she was less needy? It was unclear. She wasn't making money or even furthering her name by the anonymous blog she did under the pen name: Legion. It did help her solve problems though. That was key. She was all about solving problems – ever since being a young girl and those puzzles she played with her father. Pleasing the admired man was what she had lived for. Now she had the urge to rebel against that conditioning, but she lived with compromise. She had too. She held a real position in society. She had a name. Except on her blog.

She logged in.

Legion:
Went out. There are a lot of odd ducks in this town.

Tomorrow:
Oh what town is that?

Legion:

No fair asking. Suffice it to say a local revised the Tale of the 47 Ronin to fit local culture and lore and then claimed it for this region.

FemNazi:
What's the 47 Ronin?

Will Rise:
A bit of Japanese history.

Red Herring:
Exactly. The story tells of a group of samurai who were left leaderless (becoming ronin) after their daimyo (feudal lord) was forced to commit seppuku (ritual suicide) for assaulting a court official named Kira Yoshinaka, whose title was Kōzuke no suke. The ronin avenged their master's honor after patiently waiting and planning for over a year to kill Kira. In turn, the ronin were themselves forced to commit seppuku for committing the crime of murder. With much embellishment, this true story was popularized in Japanese culture as emblematic of the loyalty, sacrifice, persistence, and honor that all good people should preserve in their daily lives. The popularity of the almost mythical tale was only enhanced by rapid modernization during the Meiji era of Japanese history, when it is suggested many people in Japan longed for a return to their cultural roots.

Legion:
Except in the local slant here - the 47 – realize there is no chance of revenge so they go on a suicide mission at a bank that uses Gatling guns for protection.

FemNazi:
Sounds like a fatalistic bunch.

Will Rise:
No fun in that.

Legion: Flash news. We've had a local girl go missing.

Tomorrow:

190

You know I've figured out your location. Maybe we should all open up on things.

FemNazi:
Yeah you're getting into some serious ground. We could help with more specifics.

Legion:
Well... maybe just mine. Though all the fun of the anonymity of my location will be gone.

Tomorrow: San Antonio.

Legion:
Your too smart.

Will Rise:
Isn't that where some psycho deposited 6 human heads at the local mall?

Legion:
The Easter donation and photography booth to be precise - right near the guy in the bunny suit.

FemNazi:
Creepy.

Red Herring: San Antonio, that explains a lot.

Legion:
Yeah the six heads are already becoming local lore. My son says at school the kids joke about it already. This place is sort of on the frontier of the American Mainland Empire – the mecca close to the border region with Mexico and a gateway into the real United States.

Will Rise:
The Alamo!

Legion:
Yeah they have that here. It's smaller than you'd think.

Tomorrow: Do you think someone is funneling girls from San Antonio to Mexico?

Legion:
It's possible.

Red Herring:
Maybe, but the case of the missing girl in San Antonio, Encita Pena of what they are calling The Little House of Flowers, might not be related to Juarez at all?

Will Rise:
I'm looking it up online now too. Geez heartbreaking.

Legion:
It's sad and does not seem the normal predator or family abduction in a way. She's a little older and comes from a very close family.

FemNazi:
The bastard.

Legion:
I know.

Tomorrow:
You guys got a lot of weird things out of that town lately. The city worker who was knifed to death after he stumbled on a drug deal. They say he put up quite a fight. The article nicknames him "Big Red".

Will Rise:
I have red hair.

Red Herring: You guys are becoming another Phoenix with your drugs and drug lords, but the problem with San Antonio is that the war is fighting for the hearts and minds of the citizens not just revenge kidnapping within various drug groups.

Tomorrow:
Do you think the killing of those Cartel heads at the funeral is related?

Red Herring:
Likely a company operation.

Will Rise:
The C.I.A. - damn.

FemNazi:
Why can't they direct some of their fucking energy to saving these women of Juarez and poor Encita.

Legion:
That's true. Our blog has more focus on the issue in Juarez than all of the American press combined. This stuff is happening right next store – of course it's going to bleed over.

Will Rise:
Your neighbor's dog food is your dog's food.

Tomorrow:
What?

Wise Rise:
It's a southern phrase.

Red Herring:
It is another way of saying your neighbor's problems are your problems. You know I can do a little digging on who might really be looking into the borders and running covert operations there. If there are activities of one kind sometimes they gather information on other doings.

FemNazi:

Like they might have data on the women of Juarez. You have access?

Red Herring:
Let's say I've done some government work.

Tomorrow:
Your not American. Your somewhere in the Middle East.

Red Herring:
Don't be too wise for your age – young one.

Legion:
Okay gang. I like the energy we are creating. I think we can make a difference and I do feel compelled. Any research that seems relevant forward to the inbox. I'll do the groundwork from here.

FemNazi:
Sounds awesome.

Wise Rise:
Yes let's make a difference.

Tomorrow:
I'm gonna surf the net and brainstorm too.

Legion:
Excellent. Until we meet again.

Will Rise:
Same Bat cave, same bat channel.

Tomorrow:
What's that mean?

Will Rise:
you are young.

Red Herring:

Adios.

FemNazi:
Yes adios amigos and amigas as the cases maybe.

Tomorrow:
I have a theory on that too.

Red Herring:
Not now.

Legion:
All right. Bye.

Julia's Internet counterparts were proving as valuable as she might have hoped. Her determination was kicking in to unprecedented levels. It was as if she was summoning allegiance for a great battle, but allies from outside the normal spheres to take on something different and greater than she had ever taken on before. It was a big task, with unclear pathways and edges.

She needed some fresh air. It would be hot outside, but the hope of a breeze or just inhaling something that was not filtered by air conditioning would be great. The intensity of the trying to go deeper, trying to look for answers, the filtering of the new information about San Antonio from her big night out on the town and her encounter with the cripple Pearson. The new way that the seriousness that her blog and her fellow participants were trying to do something about these horrible killings – it was becoming consuming. She liked this state, but knew when to take a breathe in the deep middle of it.

The outside was nice: cool and fresh because of a breeze just like she needed. Out of the corner of her eye she noticed something stirring up the block – like one does when they are one of only two entities moving on a block that is of course, at all times, full of the potential for much more movement. She ignored the stirring. It was of course just a neighbor stirring at the same speed, relative mood, motivations and socio-economic group as her. Her mind relaxed and wandered further into thoughts of a happier past. Back when her and her husband shared passion together. The kids were small. They were like adorable ornaments that love could be gushed over and as well returned unlimited love. That was before San Antonio. San Antonio was her new reality. It was the challenge. It had an undercurrent of harshness that most here ignored. How did they do that?

"Hey Professor!" shouted a voice.

A car had moved up from down the block and stopped in front of her house. She had at once noticed and not noticed that happening.

"Come here – come here please," said her neighbor Judge Bustamante.

Dr. Julia Brown walked over to the Judge's car. He pointed a gun at her: a smallish revolver.

"Get the fuck in," said the Judge.

"What?" said Dr. Brown incredulously, but somehow registering the gun was certainly real.

"You heard me cunt, get in the car," said the Judge.

He pointed the gun closer to her stomach. She knew this was truth. Dr. Julia Brown got in the car.

"Put your fuckin' seat belt on," ordered the Judge. She complied. He peeled off burning some rubber off the tires as he exited the neighborhood in as much of a hurry a suburban car could manage.

"What are you doing Judge Bustamante?" asked Julia Brown as sweetly as she could muster.

"We're taking a little trip honey and your going to be my new bitch. I've wanted you for some time you know," said the Judge.

"I don't understand," replied Julia as the shock deepened into a set reality.

"My god damn life is ruined – is that enough of an answer for you!" yelled what was becoming the former "Judge" Bustamante, unraveling right before Julia Brown's eyes.

"Maybe you just need to relax and center," offered Julia.

"Don't give me that Buddha-shit," demanded Mr. Bustamante.

"What about your wife?" cried Julia as she glanced again at the gun loosely pointed at her waist and wondering what kind of fate she was entangled in with this unstable man who suddenly appeared to be abducting her.

"Fuck my wife, fuck the mayor, fuck my mistress, fuck Burke, and I'll likely fuck you when I put you in a cage somewhere deep in Mexico," retorted Bustamante.

"Mexico," mumbled Julia as she noticed Bustamante headed north on I-35.

The idea of being held as a sex slave by Judge Bustamante south of the border, after her current investigations, still seemed hugely surreal. Yet, on some level it made sense. As if some vibe that had been telepathically sending out this exact message had been circulated in her neighborhood for months. She remembered the coarse way the Judge put his wife in the passenger seat of their car on trips, the lecherous stares, the strange energies coming from the parties at his house, a woman once stopping by – yes she had looked like a whore – when no else, but the Judge seemed to be home. It was funny how much the unconscious minds picks up, but doesn't bother to warn you with until the bad event is happening.

"Maybe we can think this through, talk to the Burke or the Mayor?" Julia tried to reason.

"Burke is the one who set me up with the cops and tried to betray me as pigeon to the Cartels. But I still have bosses on my side baby, oh yeah big bosses..." Bustamante went on sounding cracked, like the Joker from Batman.

Cartels. A corrupt Judge. Another lawyer who was in on it. Julia's mind was working and putting the facts together silently as to formulate an approach that would help.

"I like Bunny Suits? Do you like Bunny Suits?" asked Bustamante having seemed to retreat into some fantasy aspect of what was happening, yet still holding the gun tight enough to do damage.

"Yeah, I like Bunny Suits," answered Julia trying to lull and play along.

"Goody," whispered Bustamante as he drove on. They drove out of town, in a mood good enough for the type of truce that would not encourage the gun suddenly going off. It seemed vocalizing the words "Bunny Suit" in the car created the vibe. Julia went with it. There was no use in trying to flag help down. Bustamante was a man ready for anything. He was ready to kill if need be. Julia saw that much.

"Beans," said Bustamante twenty miles north out of town.

"What," said Julia using any opportunity to engage the mad man.

"My wife was going to cook beans tonight," said Bustamante.

"Beans are good," suggested Julia.

"Hey to insult the bean is to insult the Mexican!" shouted Bustamante.

She didn't know how to answer.

"Are you involved in the Cartels sir?" she decided to try a direct tack and get inside the situation.

"Maybe I'm Homicidally Depressed," announced Bustamante.

You mean Suicidally Depressed," offered Julia.

"Won't you hope," jibed Bustamante showing his mind was still fully present with his sarcasm and wit.

"You've killed people Judge?" asked Julia sincerely.

"Of course I haven't killed anyone. Not yet. But we are going to meet a man who kills, a very great and scary killer indeed. He will guide us into Mexico where we will start our new life – did I tell you I've always fancied you Dr. Brown," stated Bustamante.

"Thank you sir," said Julia now curious to more information. Bustamante rubs her leg with the cold nose of his revolver.

"Yes I like you a lot," said Bustamante.

"This killer will help us get to Mexico?" asked Julia.

"Yes he is a great guide. He works for my supervisors. They say he has strange predilections, but he is valuable. He delivered the six heads. He is the one who will take us from Wimberley down into Mexico – to our new home," said Bustamante.

Julia was really piecing things together now: An odd killer for the Cartels who liked strange things: A Judge on the take and on the run who also liked strange things.

They sent a message of the six heads. This was the center of it. She had been on the outside with her blog and her flirtations with odd people at bars who seemed like insiders, but now her tracking of killers in Mexico had her in a car with someone, somehow in the loop of all this. The New Agers in California would say she made her reality. How strange, then the unpredictable happened within the unexpected. Bustamante had not been paying attention to the road and he suddenly realized he was in the other lane, he pulled the steering wheel back to adjust, but did this too sharply – his vehicle spun, clipped another car and then both began a terrible roll.

It was almost one of those moments that showed how life is fundamentally gentle. Mostly after car accidents strangers slowly leave their vehicles and meet together calmly on the side of the highway as if gathering for picnic by what can be a raging river of traffic going in excess of 70 miles per hour. There they casually greet and share information. It is as if one can see a hint into the true character and movements of the universe immediately following the Big Bang.

Even with the metal rod of the broken highway sign sticking through Bustamante's neck creating his gurgling death as blood flowed, this moment too had its peace as traditional highway accidents often begin with. That moment when time freezes and one realizes what one is about to go into. Professor Julia Brown looked at Bustamante in the eyes, just for this moment of his and then carefully exited the car, she only peeked back once, slightly aghast at the dying Judge whose eyes pleaded for some mercy. She then fully turned and left the car behind as the other driver, unhurt, came toward her slowly and considerately. Those in his car, like her were unharmed, but this transaction deviated from the kind pattern of many car wrecks, the picnic greeting on the side of the highway would not happen as Julia Brown bypassed the driver of the other car and walked ever more briskly toward any distance and freedom far away from the demented Judge's vehicle that so traumatized her such a short span. She, not being one to turn to salt, never looked back after that.

"Dr. Brown?"

"Dr. Brown?"

Someone out here on this highway far from home knew her name. It registered. Dr. Brown. A man ran in front of her. He held her arms. Dr. Brown. She recognized his face. She had spoken with him before.

"It's me Barry Juarez from The Light," said the reporter.

"What the hell are you doing here?" said the Julia Brown.

"I'm headed out to Wimberley for a story. Then I saw you wandering on the side of the road," said Juarez.

"Judge Bustamante kidnapped me," said Julia.

"What, that's Judge Bustamante in there?" said Barry.

"Yes he went crazy and started talking about the Cartels in Mexico and some murderer in Wimberley – we were headed to Wimberley," said Julia.

"The Judge is dead isn't he?" asked Barry.

"Oh yeah," said Julia.

"Listen wait here for the police. Your not crazy I am actually casing a story involving Bustamante, the Cartels and a missing girl," said Barry.

"Encita Pena. You know where Encita Pena is?" demanded Julia.

"Not exactly, but she may have been taken by that Cartel thug the Judge seems to have mentioned to you. Wimberley is apparently some sort of base," said Juarez.

"Ok – ok I'm going with you," insisted Julia.

"You can't do that," said Barry.

"I said I am going with you," repeated Julia.

"Ok, let's go," agreed Juarez.

The two rushed to his car and sped up the road to Wimberley.

CHAPTER 21

Lost Consequences

Gary "Catfish" Pigg was waiting for Gonzalez from Burke's Law Office on that day.

Wimberley, Texas: Founded by Gary "Catfish" Pigg or rather created by him after he won the war for its soul in a pitched PR & Development battle against Reb Hellard of Baptist Inc. Reb was a fundamentalist preacher who wanted Wimberley to be a right wing religious haven, if not paradise. His father owned the First Independent Baptist Church of Wimberley and passed it on to Reb at age 25 when the elder suddenly died of cardiac arrest while walking on a country lane. Reb was no match for radical liberal "Catfish" Pigg though. Catfish had been a bigwig Austin lawyer and had friends in high places. He used cash and clout to convert Wimberley into a mini-liberal, consumer and pot-smoking heaven in Central Texas – where stone walkways led buyers through a series of over-chic ice cream shops, custom salsa stores, and city slicker western wear vendors named things like "Wall Street Western Wear" subtitled: "A Rock Star Western Boutique" where one could purchase b.b.simon, Marrika Nakk, Tutus and Brazil Roxx. The restaurants were not just restaurants in Wimberley, Texas. There was the Cypress Creek Café & Club where "Texas –Style Cookin' and Legendary Live Music Come Together" and a few jazzy, yet provincial Tex-Mex dining haunts.

The main newssheet in town was the "Doobie Times". It was a psychedelic rag permanently displayed everywhere including in the middle of the finest places downtown Wimberley, population 345, had to offer. This unique, Baby Boomer town preached pot use in all forms. It was the dirty little secret bragged about in the open, as if commonplace in the nation overall – as if this town was a suburb of wild, hash-bashed Amsterdam. These rich old hippies didn't care. They enjoyed fine wines, the best houses and clothes as well as a good toke when they liked in the privacy of their own dwellings. There was not open pot smoking in the streets. The "Doobie Times" complete with marijuana leaf cover art blessed the benefits and pleasures of a good joint in 60 pages of articles and photos alongside ads for bongs and other paraphernalia. Pot was a natural relaxer, a medicinal and a spur to creativity – every one who had a B.A. in one of the seven liberal arts knew that. If the "Successful Classes" wished to partake then Catfish Pig was going to make sure the local law didn't interfere. Texas Highway Patrol was none too welcome in Wimberley. This town was about business and retreat and anything ex-Austinites wished itself to be in regards to open marijuana culture. Wimberley had enough friends in high places in Austin and with the Texas Visitor's and Convention Bureau to make sure heat was not fixed on the small, if illegal, pleasures of Wimberley, Texas, just 30 miles away.

Catfish himself smoked daily. He controlled the local distribution routes. He was friends with the Cartels and Burke and Bustamante and met with Timbero, Tom Pettinger, Gonzalez and other representatives frequently. These packs were with simple devils who could be managed and whose return was much greater than the trade off price. Business was nothing too difficult and none too many strings attached. Why, Tom Pettinger presented himself like a businessman. He always wore a tie, had some college, was healthy as an Ox and besides his dad had done prestigious things for the military of The United States of America. The town and Pigg himself had done no spiritual grieving for how they came about the prodigious quantities of marijuana they consumed. Besides it was tax-free.

Pigg though had several levels of connections to evil powers. He had to in order to support his fantasy kingdom of pot and tofu. "Paying too close attention to the morality of the weather was for the godless," – that's what Pigg's father used to say. When Pigg met every three months with Don Wilcox to pick up pounds of marijuana he knew that Wilcox was one in a chain that went through to Bill Jimenez in Eagle Pass who in turn was connected to the Juarez Cartel in Piedras Negras that in the trade of gold for pot went all the way into the heart of northern Mexico, to some small town with nearby fields that nobody had every heard of, to harvest.

In fact Wimberley, Texas had a spiritual doppelganger town in Mexico that supplied the marijuana that was smoked by many people. The marijuana that was distributed for Catfish Pigg by Ed Haskells, Paul Thompson, Derek Peters, Manny Jones, Freddie

Roach and Dilbert Cummings. Of the many, many users of marijuana in the Wimberley area there was Bob Brocken – a farmer who liked to smoke on Sundays when relaxing away from work usually watching a sports contest on TV, but occasionally listening to the music of Sting, The Grateful Dead or Bob Dylan, then there was Pam and Don Banks – they lived in town and worked modest jobs in sales – but liked to take a toke before lovemaking in their King sized bed usually on Tuesday or Thursday evenings and Saturdays, there was Warren Mayfield who liked to smoke all the time, but he was a craftsman who worked from home shaping iron into artwork that sold well in town – he never once harmed himself with his tools while under the influence as he was an expert artisan, then there was Julie Rose, she could be considered an addict as she smoked nearly seven days a week and drank as well – both strong compulsions – though she was harmless in her role as bartender of the Green Shed Tavern. She walked to work and slept with an average of nineteen new men a year so none complained about her excesses. There were others as well such as Barbara Olsen the 7th grade English teacher, Bill Murphy the gas attendant at Louie's, Sue and Max Brenner who did it for fun a few times each month, Wally Koontz a reverend's son who scored his weed third party from Bill Murphy and smoked when partying with his fellow high schoolers on Friday and Saturday nights. Along with these there was a host of others in Wimberley who partook of the ganja in varieties degrees and dosages.

Now, Wimberley, Texas's sister city, the supplier at the head of this river to Wimberley's mouth was El Ebano, Mexico off Mex 85 and 6. El Ebano was not a large place, in fact in comparison it was near the size of Wimberley. It was somewhat isolated off the main road and not much noticed. Driving time to Wimberley was around 6 to 7 hours moving at a fairly fast speed. In the configurations of the cosmos the karmic tie between Wimberley, Texas and El Ebano, Mexico was as tight as a harpist's string. One half mile east of El Ebano were the marijuana fields that supplied Wimberley with its copious stock.

In El Ebano there were corresponding spirits to each of the grand partakers of pot in Wimberley that benefitted from their Mexican counterparts labors and each of these spirits supplied in equal measure, these labor for pleasure, to satiate the Texans desires of consumption and for each gratification there was a corresponding consequence. In the fields of El Ebano there was fourteen-year-old Petras Milangras who harvested and processed enough weed each month to keep Bob Brocken's habit in full bloom. Petras walked to the fields daily, seven days a week, and had a cruel father who enjoyed beating her and on occasion had her steal amounts of pot to bring back to him, which he used or sold. Before her thirteenth birthday Petras was caught in a small theft of product. Her Cartel overseer made a bargain with her. He raped her instead of telling on her.

Then there was Gabriel Munoz, a twenty year old, who had worked the Cartel fields since he was eight. He never gained education though he could write poetry that rivaled Antonio Machado. The thought never crossed his mind that anyone would care to notice his writing. The thought of school was impossible. Every peso he had ever earned went to taking care of his ill father and grandmother. He only knew work in the fields. His output had carried Don and Pam Bank's marijuana habit for quite a few years.

Then there was Ramon Penzula. He was twenty-eight. He suffered injury in a factory job in Monterrey and came home to El Ebano only to find work in the marijuana fields as his only possibility of employment. Due to his injury he could not work as fast as the other, but still he tried. His Cartel overseer had chosen Ramon as the example to be occasionally made. When he feared a general sloth amongst the workers, perhaps on the ninth hour of a day that had reached 120 degrees in heat, he'd whip the slower Ramon a few times in front of everybody. This always picked up the pace for the remaining hour or two of the day. Even with his disability Ramon cultivated enough pot to keep Warren Mayfield in bliss and his works of craft-art unique in their drug-manifested originality.

Then there was Rocio Menendez. She had commuted and worked the fields for twelve years and was presently 76 years of age. Her husband and his two brothers had been murdered right before Rocio started her tenure working for the Cartels years ago. The brothers had complained too much about the work conditions in the fields. It had been a time when, briefly, the enthusiasm of reform took wind around Mexico. Rocio's two-year-old daughter was taken from her after the murders. The Cartels said the baby girl was safe, far in the west, and being raised as one of the family of an important man. Rocio never saw her daughter again, but she still gave her Cartel foreman 40% of her pay each month on the promise that it went directly to her child for those little extras that made life more pleasant. Even at 76 years old Rocio's output in the fields was great enough to cover all of Julie Rose's innocent marijuana addiction.

There was also the sad story of Juan Ortiz who despite his heart condition toiled in the fields daily, chewing on baby aspirins intermittently as to stave off any sudden attack. His work fed Barbara Olsen's cravings. The equally sad stories of Roberto Feliz, Maria Vasquez and Manny Ramirez – all coerced in some fashion into mandatory labor out of merely being guilty of some passion or necessity. Hence they all transmuted the seeds of a stinky weed into the smoke-able substance that traveled the Mexico 85 corridor to the hungry lungs of the Americans in Wimberley, Texas: Bill Murphy, Sue and Max Brenner, Wally Koontz and others…

Timbero cooked the recipe on open flame in the wild of the Hill Country Texas. It was his mother's recipe. He always fed it to his girls before the final act. He had purchased this land from one of Catfish's men: Dilbert Cummings. It was a modest track with a cabin and smallish barn. It was away from things and the local men knew to leave him and his place alone. None within Wimberley's jurisdiction would bother Timbero, a Cartel emissary. Wimberley was where Timbero traded his vehicle for the return trip to Mexico. Dibert always met him on old man Johnson's abandoned property to take care of that. If there vital messages or items of business that had to be done in person with Catfish Pigg or sometimes Gonzalez then they would all meet at Johnson's old place. It was a clever, circuitous route that took him first northeast of San Antonio then encircled back and bypassed the major cities altogether so he could cross the border at any number tiny towns over a 1000 miles expanse that would take the hired killer back into Mexico.

Encita was not hungry, but Timbero forced her to eat. He had already taken one precious thing from her, her virginity. Now he was going to take the most precious item and do something even more unthinkable. It was a culmination of the grandest, personal stresses that had been eating away at Timbero for weeks, months and even years as far partaking in the ancient feast with American flesh. It was his greatest taboo and desire for some time and the heavy workload his Cartel bosses had been placing on him let him know now was the time to indulge. Killing the Americans, taking their heads and dropping them off at fucking North Star Mall was not simple. It took an emotional toll that made Timbero's need to act out the old blood rites of black magic his mother's lineage had passed down even more immense. He needed it greatly. More so he deserved it. It was his birthright. The ritual was part of his family history. He could not and did not conceive of going against it and though it did not prick his conscience, he knew, in a sense what others thought of such, minority deeds.

They pair walked to the barn. The air was quiet. Burke glanced at Renolds. He was glad the man was with him. Renolds, gun drawn, had steely eyes. Anything could be around the corner. Burke knew that. He imagined seeing his daughter in some terrible way. She had to be alive though. The men crept forward. Renolds was the first to peer around the corner of the barn.

He gasped. Burke jumped forward to look inside. He too gasped. The girl was tied by both arms and legs, suspended in the air from a rafter beam, as she hung naked. A bit of dried blood ran down her leg. Her hair was cut off and marks were painted on her upper body and face: Ancient, awful symbols that had no meaning to the modern eye other than fear. There was a bloodied bandage in the girls' left hand and in front of the strung up girl lay the finger in some sort of cooking pot as yet unheated.

Burke's cell phone rang.

He quickly answered it.

"Why the hell have you been calling me all day - I've been at the salon," said his daughter.

Burke hung the phone up and began running, he ran for his life and out of terror and in the hope of getting to a populated place where people would see him and keep him safe.

Renolds instead moved forward to release the girl.

Timbero had heard the cell phone from the rear of the barn as he was returning. He pulled his knife. He circled to the front of the barn. Peering inside the barn he saw the man, with his back turned, cutting the ropes from the girl's right hand. The man had left his gun on the ground next to the ritual bowl. Timbero charged stealthily. When he got within three feet, the man, Renolds, instinctively wheeled around. Timbero's knife struck home as Renolds elbow crashed into the side of the Mexican killer's temple.

"Argghh," cried Renolds.

Timbero fell to a knee. Renolds attempted to slash downwards with his own knife to cut the murderer's neck. Before the blade got halfway to its goal Timbero launched his arm upward and drove his own knife into Renold leg, exactly at the critical point in the upper thigh where the major artery rested like an underground river. Timbero's thrust exposed the river to air and daylight and Renolds gasped, fell backward and Timbero crawled on top of him, putting his hand over the Renold's mouth as Burke's man bleed out quickly to his death. Timbero stood up like a crazed coyote from the kill. He twisted his head about.

Encita, the girl, was still fastened securely. No one else was coming right at him. He ran outside the barn. Off to the left about one hundred and fifty yards into the fields he saw a man running. Timbero gave chase.

The run took the men across three fields before the younger, more agile Timbero caught up to the flabbier Burke, whose sweat had drenched his clothes, his hand still gripping with insane strength his cell phone, his thoughts alternating between himself and his family – as Timbero reached him, his feet fleet with the movements of a hunter, still it took three fields to gain on his opponent, they were all opponents deep down to the hunter, the killer, but the old man had wanted to live so he had run fast.

The knife blade entered the kidney sending a rush of blood inside the old lawyer's system that at once came out his anus and gurgled up into his throat, Shakespeare's line, "First, We Kill All the Lawyers," flashed through the old attorney's mind, then he fell.

"Daddy why is that man chasing that other man?" asked Gonzalez's child.

Gonzalez looked up from *Rebecca's Porch*, a chic Wimberley dining haunt where patrons ate on the back porch in a farm like setting outside of town.

"Sure enough," whispered Gonzalez as he watched Burke get stabbed and fall.

"Oh my God that's Wayne!" said his wife.

Gonzalez knew who had gotten Burke, but his wife didn't. It was like watching the safari channel from the comfort of one's home:

Two wild beasts running across the field. It was just like that weird restroom attendant at the law firm, Laslo, predicted. That thought came to him. The weird kid in the restroom who spoke in odd ways had said something about one day destiny suddenly happening while you were watching comfortably from your seats – your enemy would fall... well Chin wouldn't have to leave town now thought Gonzalez as he summoned the conviction to begin acting even more surprised than he was.

Timbero after executing Burke, calmly turned and began jogging back to his farm. The wildness in his eyes slightly dimmed. He knew on some level he had to flee, but he was still going to finish his personal business in a manner methodical enough to insure the pleasure he had waited for. Meanwhile Burke's blood fertilized the field as he died. He spoke no last words. His final thoughts blurred, he exited.

Thoughts of all he stood to inherit danced in Gonzalez's head. In the least he'd move up in importance. In the short run he could control many things. In the long run there was a chance of him taking completely over. He plans for the Chinese in the least would remain on track and more likely gain important ground in the coming months.

"Honey take the kids outside to the car and drive into town okay," said Gonzalez to his wife.

"Yeah sure," she said as she scooted the kids out front.

He dialed his phone.

"I don't think you need to transfer to Houston now. I'll tell you more about it later," he said.

"Thanks, sounds great," said Chin.

Gonzalez jumped the fence, dialed 911 and went out into the field to make the appearance of caring. The workers from Rebecca's Porch congregated and witnessed as Gonzalez went to the man, checked his pulse and shook his head. It was like watching a television show for them and they knew what it meant. The man was dead.

Barry Juarez and Dr. Julia Brown were making a pit stop right before they were about to enter Wimberley to begin their search and investigation. They weren't sure what to look for, but had keen eyes for anything suspicious. Of course Encita Pena would be the best thing they could find. Likely someone would let them know were

Timbero might be staying, still they knew some in this town must be working directly with the Cartel's – in a way it was the perfect job for an investigative reporter and a college professor – both were used to getting information from hostile and reluctant sources. They both knew how to ask around. Someone would tell them about the deranged looking man, people with links to the Cartels, rumors – whatever they could kick up by beating the brush, a bird would fly, they hoped.

The child smiled as she saw the woman.

She was holding her mother's hand and said, "We just saw a man kill Uncle Wayne Burke with a knife!"

"Hush Cynthia. There's been an accident," said the mom.

"Wayne Burke the lawyer?" said Dr. Brown.

"Excuse me ma'am I'm Barry Juarez with the San Antonio Light – your saying someone just killed Wayne Burke here and now?" he asked.

"Out in the field, some lunatic chased him down and stabbed him – out of nowhere. We were just eating and all of sudden... Jesus... I gotta get the kids out of here," said Mrs. Gonzalez.

"Where did he go?" said Dr. Brown.

"Who?" said Mrs. Gonzalez.

"The lunatic," said Dr. Brown.

"Here went back that way across the field," said the child.

"Get in the car girls," said Mrs. Gonzalez as she pushed the children in the car. Brown & Juarez jumped back in the car and raced in the direction the little girl pointed toward. Circling around the field they found the small road that led back toward the farm area. They raced down this path, speeding up to the barn where through the open door they could see some a portion of a crumpled body, its legs protruding out of the barn door. Julian Brown held her breath for a moment then opened the door of the car before it was stopped. Barry slammed the breaks and stopped fast, the car spinning slightly to the left and Brown & Juarez hopped out of the vehicle as if two actors playing cops on a one hour primetime drama. They ran toward inside the barn and fully saw the dead body of Renolds and then Encita Pena, her eyes driving to wildness and nearly out of her mind, tied by rope and suspended naked. They were at the center of the crazed man's violence and fetish and they didn't know how much time they had.

209

Barry peeked at Renolds' body while Julia found a saw beside the barn door and cut loose the ropes that held Encita. She unbound her mouth.

"The man will come back," said the girl.

"Don't worry honey we'll get you home," promised Julia.

She felt for a moment the pride of having accomplished her noble goal then a scream, a horrid war cry, it was Timbero staring at the three of them from the near side of the barn, they had released his trophy, all his tension of wanting to complete this act, for months and years, now interrupted and facing with fury the liberators of his prey.

A boldness, a giant courage, not unlike what the men who landed on the beaches of D-Day or what the ancient gladiators of Rome must have felt, surged through Barry Juarez as he took a large step straight told Timbero and spoke.

"Are you the one of those whose been fucking with Barry Juarez?" queried the reporter condemningly.

And like a cat Timbero did not respond in words, he moved quickly and lunged in a stabbing motion at Barry Juarez. Juarez moved slightly, though it was not enough as he got punctured on his side, near the wound of Christ on the Cross, though for him blood came out.

"You stabbed Barry!?" said the reported incredulously, but then motivated as the attacker began another motion.

Barry, aware of his surroundings, took two shuffle steps backward. Timbero, operating on all instincts as if it were he that was the cornered animal, stepped forward several paces toward Juarez. Barry Juarez eyes had already honed in on the item that would grace his revenge. In a swift motion Barry pulled the bale lever, hundreds of pounds of hay, bundled and wired tightly in sets of 50 lbs., crashed on the two men from the loft above and each was crushed to death.

It all happened so fast. It was as if fate had intervened. The two men were dead right in front of Encita Pena and Dr. Julia Brown. As a consequence they were free from danger. Julia held the girl and walked he back to the car. They got in and raced away from Wimberley, Texas and the dead bodies. They raced straight to San Marcos in record time and straight the safety of the populated Tanger Outlet Mall. The police were called and then the F.B.I. Julia was a living hero and Barry Juarez a dead one. The villain Timbero was dead too. Some of the players fled away, others were rounded up, many things were investigated and there was enough media splash created for two years on the national stage and twenty in San Antonio. Red McCoombs, a fat cat San Antonio car dealer and tycoon, that once owned the Minnesota Vikings, donated three hundred thousand dollars to the Mayo Clinic for the best surgeons to reconstruct Encita Pena's missing finger. The Little House of Flowers became a tourist's place to drive by while El Ebano still produced copious amounts of marijuana.

Yes, after the inquiries, rounds ups and arrests there were still plenty in place of the Cartel system. Dr. Brown's blog rose in prominence though and the academic as well as the social philanthropic communities took a greater interest in her specialized research. Independent funds were established to research the women of Juarez and Red Herring, her blog friend – the ex-Israeli Defense Forces operative, had discovered gained copies of certain CIA files on the crimes against women in Juarez. He brought those with him by airplane when he landed in San Antonio and was greeted by Julia a few months after the rescue of Encita Pena. The two had tickets to fly into Juarez, Mexico in two days time. The hunt for liberation would continue...

The End